Death

at

Hill Hall

(Book 4 in the series)

by

G J Bellamy

Sarah & Tom series - Coming soon

COPYRIGHT

PREFACE

Dear Reader,

Here is a very brief note because I have no wish to keep you from your story.

This book might be set in a mythical and highly fictionalized US state - let's call it Transatlantica - where, and I humbly apologize for this, stories are recorded with British spellings. Can you believe it?

So, you'll find grey instead of gray, flavour instead of flavor, and I have little to offer in defense/defence for this international outrage.

Why do this? - you might ask if you're a US reader. The answer is simple. The US is a dynamic place and is the only venue where certain elements of the story could be played out (and this goes for the rest of the series, too.) However, from my mother's knee I have learnt British English and it's the way I speak and write.

I could never pass myself off as a US national, lacking the intimate knowledge which comes from having grown up in or having travelled extensively through the US. Even if I had attempted to use US spelling and phrasing, you'd undoubtedly smell a rat and the story itself would be diminished. Neither of us would be happy with that.

Therefore, please look upon the following work of fiction as a story set in the USA but narrated and recorded by someone with a British accent.

Enough from me, I think, except to say, I hope you enjoy the story.

G J Bellamy

PS. Transatlantica is about 150 miles due East of Nantucket.

Death
at
Hill Hall

Chapter 1

Hill Hall, Thursday, December 4, 7:45 p.m.

$\mathcal{T}$he butler opened the double doors to the smaller of
two dining rooms at Hill Hall. He entered and stepped aside
in a very dignified way, allowing ingress to the waiter who
carried a magnum bottle of champagne in a solid silver ice
bucket on a solid silver tray.

The party of ten elegantly dressed people grouped
around the long, ancient table had been talking quietly,
neighbour to neighbour. With the stately advent of the
champagne, the group visibly brightened, becoming more
animated.

The waiter attended to his task. A cork was popped, the
bottle was wrapped in a napkin, and the wine was efficiently
poured into one-hundred-year-old glasses. Two hostesses,
hired for the evening from an agency, served the people

seated at the table. These people constituted the Brewster family which was having a minor celebration. Dressed formally and seated in the dark oak-panelled room, they presented the perfect picture of a wealthy, well-connected family enjoying itself. A full glass was set at each diner's hand. The overhead lights were dimmed causing the white linen table cloth to appear ivory in the candlelight from large candelabra. A log fire burned in the huge grate.

"Good health, long life… Welcome home, Mother!" said Franklin Brewster.

A babble of unified voices uttered similar sentiments. There came the chinking of glasses followed by the movement of chairs - the family came up by ones and twos to the top of the table where sat the head of the family - the Brewster matriarch. They each hugged or kissed the old lady. The others present that evening consisted of two Brewster brothers and two Brewster sisters, two spouses, a girlfriend, a companion and a friend of the family.

The companion, Marjorie Bellingham, came forward second to last and she shook her employer's hand.

"I'm sure it will be no time at all before you are walking about just as you used to."

"Well, thank you, Marjorie. I sincerely hope you're right," said Evelyn Brewster. "I've had enough of this wheelchair."

"Mother!" called Jimmy Brewster, her youngest son, from his seat mid-way down the table. "More Champagne?" Smiling, he held up another bottle that had appeared in order to supplement the now-exhausted magnum. He handed the bottle to one of the waiters and asked her to refill Evelyn's glass.

"I shouldn't, you know." Evelyn looked vivacious, girlish, her animation belying her eighty-four years, "but, yes, half a glass won't kill me."

"You really shouldn't. You're on medication and the Doctor said..."

"Nonsense, Franklin. You worry too much. It's you who should not have a second glass."

After this remark, there came a slight lull in the conversation around the table but it was soon dismissed as though it had never occurred and the conversation flowed on.

The last to approach the smiling grande dame whose silvery dress was adorned with a rope of pearls   and from whose hand sparkled a brilliant diamond ring, was Lloyd de Sainte-Croix, an old friend and one-time admirer of Evelyn. He, a year older than Evelyn, was very upright, possessing a full head of white hair and a ruddy face. The dark suit he wore fitted him well.

"It is so good to see you up and about again." He tenderly kissed her hand.

"Lovely of you to come, Lloyd, lovely." She squeezed his hand in return. "Although, it's so unnecessary to make such a fuss over me. Hip replacement is a commonplace surgery these days."

Dining table chatter resumed. The glasses were cleared away. Dinner was about to be served.

After dinner, the Brewsters of earlier times would have divided into separate parties: ladies in the French-style drawing-room; gentlemen remaining at table with the port or adjourning to the fabulous library for something stronger. That tradition had long since passed. A spacious and comfortable lounge now accommodated the entire family for their after-dinner conversation.

Three men stood in a small group near the drinks cabinet.

"How's the electronics biz?" asked Steve Aimes, the husband of Laura, the youngest Brewster daughter.

"It's doing fine, thank you," replied Franklin curtly. He disliked discussing business with anyone and in particular with Steve Aimes, his brother-in-law. He would prefer it if Steve Aimes did not exist.

"I was thinking, you should branch out into consumer electronics. You know, high-end audio and TVs."

"As I've explained before, Sadler-Creme dominates a niche market in navigation technology."

"Yeah, I know, I know, but you're missing an opportunity - a big one. You could leverage the company's reputation and make a killing. Loads of companies are doing something similar."

"A family celebration is no place to discuss business matters," said Franklin decidedly. He helped himself to a second large glass of whiskey and half drained it.

"That's it. Play it safe." Jimmy Brewster glared at his brother, Franklin. "I could come in and operate a new division just like Steve's suggesting."

This was an old, problematic issue between the two brothers that arose from time to time. Franklin ran the family's company and would not allow any other family member to interfere with the way he ran it.

"Jimmy, you know very well that it isn't possible. My hands are tied by the terms of the trust. I get no thanks from anyone for the hard work I put in."

"You always do that, don't you? You're no martyr. You get paid for your work. Why not hire family members and spread some of the wealth around a bit. It's your choice not to do so. It's entirely your decision to keep the rest of us out. Even when *Laura* asked for a job you turned her down."

"You fail to understand that I'm preserving the company for all of us under the terms of the trust."

"Preserving it for yourself, you mean," sneered Jimmy.

"Boys!" They both turned towards Evelyn, their mother. "I will not have this behaviour in my house. You have differences of opinion and that's all there is to it. Learn to live with it." They could hear her rings tap-tap-tapping slowly on the arm of her wheelchair as she stared them down into a civilized silence.

"Sorry," said Jimmy. "I know I started it. But it's just that…"

"Not… another… word." She waited a few seconds then turned back to her eldest daughter to ask,

"Now, Sophia, you say Aurelia is finishing her Master's this year. Is she finding it difficult?"

Franklin refilled his whiskey glass after the other two men had drifted away from him.

"He's thick-headed and stupid. Will not listen to anyone," whispered Steve Aimes as he shot Franklin a vicious look.

"Franklin's always been difficult," answered Laura Aimes. "Although, as I've told you before, he was very nice to me when we were little."

"That was a long time ago, Laura. He's no brother to you now. Jimmy's right. He's waiting for your mother to die and the trust to be wound up. Then he gets the company and he doesn't want anyone else involved. It's all about him."

"Oh don't, Steve. He's my brother and I'm sure he means well."

"Means well? Him? I don't think so."

Jimmy was agitated. Talking to his partner in a corner of the lounge quietly, he said,

"We have to get money from somewhere." He shook his head. "That note is coming due and I can't find an investor for the sports stores."

"Honey, ask Evelyn. She has money." Merrell Fortier, Jimmy's current girlfriend, was not of the Brewster class. Merrell was too flashy, too showy, and had a different accent.

"I *have* asked her. She wanted to see financial statements. I had to show them to her. Mother had her financial adviser with her to look over the figures. They both said the business hasn't a hope. I asked for a personal loan. I almost pleaded with her but she was adamant and said that it would all amount to the same thing of propping up a failing business."

"Then, let it go. There are plenty of other things we can do." She caressed his cheek and then turned his face to hers. They stared at one another. "We can do something so don't worry."

"Like what?" He took a sip of his drink.

"I have a couple of ideas. But we'll need to act quickly."

"Yet another pleasant family get together!" Sophia Halliday, eldest Brewster daughter, had a sour look on her otherwise pleasant face. She was talking privately to her husband and they stood apart from the main group.

"Why does it always have to be like this?" responded Mike Halliday.

"Why? It's Franklin, of course. How I hate him."

"Come on, Soph. It was a long time ago."

"It isn't just that. Though he's never paid for it, one day he will. It's all his grovelling before mother out of pure self-interest. I know she sees through him. She knows it's all about money and control with Franklin but she lets him get away with it and go on with the charade. What he wants is everything. The company - he's got that. All of Mother's money - he's after that. And this house. Do you know he made another offer to buy me out when Mother dies? He's not getting it. He's *not* getting it." Sophia almost spat out the last words.

"Don't let this hatred eat you up." Mike put his arm around her shoulder. She suffered his affection for a second then shrugged off his arm.

"Don't be nice to me now. I'm not in a nice kind of mood. I could kill him."

Superficial grace and manners gradually returned and, on the surface, the gathering appeared to be a success. Evelyn enjoyed herself - enjoyed the careful attention of all her loved ones. In the attentiveness league, Franklin Brewster reigned supreme.

"Are you warm enough, Mother?" he asked Evelyn.

"Of course, I am," said Evelyn, "but thank you for asking. You're a kind boy."

"Oh, it's nothing. You are looking very well," said Franklin. "Are you feeling any discomfort from the surgery?"

"Very little… You needn't fuss over me." Her smile seemed to contradict her words. She enjoyed his filial devotion even though she found it excessive and irritating at times.

The evening drew to a close. Evelyn retired early, claiming fatigue from the excitement of the lovely party as her reason for leaving them so soon. Her departure meant Marjorie Bellingham, her personal assistant, went with her.

Lloyd did a round of the remaining group, chatting a while with everyone. He had a long, private talk with Franklin before going upstairs to the room that was always his on such occasions and that was always kept ready for him. Jimmy and Merrell slipped out from the lounge inconspicuously at the earliest opportunity.

Franklin made a few attempts at desultory conversation with several people but quite pointedly gave Steve Aimes a wide berth. In a stilted way, he spoke or enquired about a few mundane subjects. As though realizing he was not particularly entertaining or even welcome, he soon bid a general and perfunctory goodnight to all present and began to walk unsteadily from the room. Franklin looked gloomy.

Before he reached the door, Laura intercepted him.

"Please don't go away in a bad mood," she said. "Let's sit and talk for a while. It's ages since we've seen each other."

"Why, Laura? Why would I want to talk to a useless little mouse like you?" He glowered at her with bloodshot eyes.

"Franklin, be nice. You've had too much to drink..."

"Mind your own business. Go back to that fatuous moron you call husband and never speak to me again." He lurched from the room.

Laura, flushed with anger, stared after him and found herself to be shaking. It took her a few moments before she recollected she was just standing there alone, staring into the space from which her brother had so rancorously absented himself. She left the room to find a coat. Laura wanted to walk outside in the cold night air and think things over.

When she returned to the lounge a short while later, no one remarked upon her absence or return. No one noticed the determined set of her jaw or that to re-engage her in conversation she had to be startled out of her distraction of deep thought. Once startled, she quickly recovered her poise.

Only the Aimes and Hallidays were left in the lounge now. The conversation was pleasant, revolving around their respective broods of children. The Halliday children were a little too old to be termed as such by Sophia and Mike. Robert, 28, was a top salesman at the car dealership at which he worked. He had the ideal temperament for such work and enjoyed it. Aurelia, 23, was an intellectual struggling with a master's degree. Chloe, 18, was quite different and wanted to become an actor.

The Aimes children, Karen, 16, and Brad, 14, were at school and having normal teenage problems with which to worry or exasperate their parents. For Karen, it was boys while Brad had become morose to a point equivalent to that of a religious vow of silence.

All five 'children' were arriving the following afternoon and staying for the weekend.

Sleeping Hill Hall was in darkness except for a hall light on the ground floor. Outside, a sliver of moon revealed the building as one long block of shadow among leafless trees, relieved only by its central triangular pediment. The interior hall light was too feeble to do more than pick out the edges of two of the four massive columns that fronted the portico.

The air was chill, damp. The soft wind threatened a cold rain and a cloud-mass in the east would fulfil that threat. The quiet, cheerless noises of a wet December night would urge any roving traveller to find admittance to warmth, light, rest and peace; all of these desired qualities he would find inside, beyond the imposing entrance.

The traveller, entering through the massive double doors, would come to stand under the monumental, unlit chandelier - only a pair of dimmed wall lights permitting sight in the long, wide hall. A single, broad, sweeping staircase could be seen in the centre at the back. An upstairs gallery ran around the space aloft and, above that, large, classically painted figures on the high ceiling might be vaguely distinguished in the imperfect light. The traveller would note that the few pieces of furniture situated on the tiled floor were old and exquisite - undoubtedly the finest examples that money could buy.

At 4:30 a.m., the traveller, standing in the hall, would have time to remove a wet overcoat and shake off the drops but, without footman or butler on hand, would stand nonplussed as to where to put the garment. Waiting a moment, the traveller would then hesitantly step forward to stand upon the massive, hand-knotted rug to look about, wondering what to do next - wondering whether to call out or not.

At that moment, there comes a terrible clamour from an upstairs passage - roaring and shrieking by turns. Faintly at first, the bestial sounds rise and fall and come nearer, definitely nearer and louder. Something crashes to the floor and shatters. There are thumps on walls, banging on doors and, all the while, the incoherent animal sounds come closer, echoing along the corridor and into the big hall, filling the house with the atmosphere of torment, fear, and agony.

A dim figure in extreme distress - arms thrashing, doubled over - appears in the gallery. He grips the handrail of the banister for support at the topmost step of the long flight of marble stairs and comes to a halt, quivering in the gloom. The seconds lengthen. Doors open further back in the corridors as a result of the noise. The figure hesitates and is still. He then pitches himself head first down the hard staircase.

The traveller, transfixed in horror while the scene unfolds, would witness that dreadful descent, would see the spread-eagled body sprawled across the last few steps of the staircase, would find it difficult to recognize the features of Franklin Brewster in the contorted face and, immediately, would flee the mansion, never to return.

Within the house, frightened faces inquired fruitlessly of one another and peered anxiously this way and that until the discovery was made. From that moment on, the inhabitants had something definite to worry about. A strange and hideous death had occurred in the family. Absurd in its incongruous night attire and stunned almost to disbelief, the Brewster family gave way to horror, terror, tears, and the exhausting strain of the unchecked rumination always evoked by death and more so by this particularly ugly death on the stairs. Morning had come early to Hill Hall.

Chapter 2

Hill Hall, Tuesday, December 9, 9:45 a.m.

$\mathcal{A}$ policeman guarded the large iron gate, the main entrance to the grounds of Hill Hall, his primary function being to keep the small knot of reporters out. One had already been threatened with charges. The media picketed Hill Hall in hopes of being first with the story of an arrest. The sixty-acre property lay on the extreme edge of Newhampton's jurisdiction in one of the last remaining areas that could lay claim to anything like a rural atmosphere.

The gate opened and the reporters did not pay much attention to the old, blue Jeep as it was being admitted. The man inside, though undoubtedly very personable, looked to be of no consequence for their purposes, and certainly not police. The arrival was dismissed as probably being a tradesman by the onlookers. It began raining again.

The battered vehicle shot past the gatekeeper's house and wound its way up the long, sweeping gravel drive. The policeman could hear the noisy gear changes the vehicle made as it climbed the ascent. He turned to look and saw the vehicle going well above whatever sensible speed limit was deemed reasonable for the driveway.

The vehicle swerved, pulling up sharply on the level half-acre of lawn-surrounded gravel in front of the massive house. The tires sent out a spray of stones. The driver had left small skid-marks behind him. Other cars, mostly police vehicles, were parked to one side. He had parked in front of the doors.

Brent Umber, private investigator, got out and slammed the door shut because it had to be slammed to have a chance of actually shutting. A fraction over six feet and with light brown hair, he looked to be a little younger than his age of thirty-two. When very serious he seemed to age a good ten years. When excited and exuberant he looked like an overgrown teenager. Brent had one of those faces that looked different in every photograph but it was an open and friendly face from no matter which angle it was viewed.

Brent noticed the damage he had caused to the driveway so he picked up his old, student-style backpack, slung it over his shoulder, and walked to the back of his Jeep to fill in the gravel with the toe of his black training-shoe. He was well dressed but in a very casual way. His attire neither suited the surroundings nor his attendance at the scene of a murder.

He knocked loudly on the door. While waiting, he counted security cameras and took note of their positions - some nestling among the leafless vine that clung to the wall. He turned back, saw a bell and rang it several times. The door opened some moments later to reveal the tall, stately form of the butler.

"Hello." Brent smiled, speaking before the butler said anything. "My name's Umber. I'm here to see Lieutenant Darrow. May I come in?"

"Lieutenant Darrow is expecting you, sir. Please step this way."

"Thank you." Brent entered and stopped. "My goodness, what a fabulous place." He looked from medallion-patterned rug to painted ceiling, from furniture and vases to paintings, and to the marble staircase with its stone balustrade. He scanned the passageways on either side of the stairs and looked in admiration at the gleaming ten-foot-high wooden doors which were all closed. He turned to the butler standing patiently beside him. "My name's Brent. What's yours?"

"Jackson, sir."

"Well, Mr Jackson, would it be any trouble if we were to light up the chandelier?"

The butler hesitated but then complied without answering. A discreet switch operated the lights. Even though it was daytime the chandelier glowed gloriously and became a cascading fountain of warm light. Brent looked up in wonder.

"It's magnificent. When was it made? Baccarat, isn't it?"

"Yes, sir. Baccarat 1923. I have never ceased to marvel at its beauty."

"I bet you haven't. Thank you. I must apologize for making such a request under the family's current circumstances but sometimes... I'm seized by a beautiful thing. Let's chat later. Please point me in Lieutenant Darrow's direction."

Towards the back of the mansion, the butler opened the door to a small room which had been temporarily converted to a command post. Inside the room, a uniformed officer was typing on a laptop. Two detectives, standing nearby, were deep in discussion. They both looked up when Brent came in.

"I'm not disturbing you, am I?" said the investigator, smiling.

"Brent. Good to see you," exclaimed Greg Darrow. "This is Detective Sergeant Alice Bates, and Officer Tom Fletcher is keeping us organized." They all said hello and shook hands with one another.

"So, what have you got for me?" asked Brent.

"A lot. It's one big mess. I'll bring the files and we'll go next door where we've room to lay it all out." Greg gathered up a sheaf of file folders.

They entered a cheerful morning room painted in yellow with glossy white trim. It was a long room with windows at the side overlooking the garden. Its proportions produced the effect of cozy spaciousness - intimate yet with a feeling of airy lightness. A mahogany table occupied the centre. The prosaic buff-coloured files were spread out across the table's dark and richly polished surface.

"Sorry to haul you in when you were on vacation," said Greg.

"Can't be helped. I wish I'd brought some nice weather with me. Oh, by the way, I have those two pairs of huaraches you wanted for Carrie and Maggie. They're in my car."

"Thanks for remembering. I'd forgotten about those," said Greg. "What do I owe you?"

"Nothing - they're a souvenir of Mexico from me."

"That's good of you… Very nice. I know Maggie loved her old pair so much they fell to pieces."

"Great… What have we got here, then?"

"Before we get to the murder itself, the first item to take note of is the trust." Greg slid the thick folder marked 'Brewster Family Trust' across the table towards Brent.

"I have to read all that?" said Brent as he opened the file and saw the numerous legal documents it contained. "Can you give me the bare bones, please?"

"There's a recap in there somewhere but it's like this. The trust has a current value of well over 1.2 billion. The major asset is a company called Sadler-Creme which has a value of about eight hundred million. From what I've been told, it would probably be worth a lot more if it was taken public. A hundred per cent of the company shares are inside the trust.

Next, there is an investment fund that has a market value of nearly three hundred million. There's another fifty million in bonds. Then there are the properties... eleven in all, including this place. Cash accounts are about twenty million."

"All tied up and no one can get at it." Brent was leafing through pages of legal text as Greg spoke.

"Yes. The trust was set up fifteen years ago by George Brewster who died shortly afterwards. Evelyn Brewster, his wife, has her own money... about eighty million. She derives no income from the trust but she has this house to live in until she dies, at such time the trust will be wound up and the assets distributed."

"And then... who gets what?"

"Sophia Halliday, 55, eldest Brewster daughter, gets the house. She also gets a 5% share in the company and a quarter of the trust's residual amount. Laura Aimes, 48, youngest daughter, and Jimmy Brewster, 49, youngest son, both get the same distribution and an expensive property each. Five grandchildren will each receive ten million and 2% of the company. The deceased, Franklin Orville Brewster, was to receive the balance of the company shares and the residue was to be split equally between the four siblings. No one else is named as beneficiary."

"So it strikes me that if the Brewster clan had produced a surfeit of grandchildren, Franklin could have lost controlling interest of one valuable company. If my calculation is correct, he currently has seventy-five per cent."

"That's correct. You should understand that this arrangement is likely to be the primary motivating factor in Franklin Brewster's murder. If there are other motives we haven't seen them yet."

"That makes sense. Sadler-Creme... It's funny, I have heard of the company from time to time but I've only a vague idea of what they do. In my mind, they're synonymous with technical excellence in navigational equipment."

"That's about right."

"Okay. A strange way to set up a trust, isn't it?"

"It gets stranger. Income was paid out of the trust to Evelyn alone. Another investment account held outside of the trust pays fifty thousand a year to each of the children and ten thousand to each grandchild. All other profits and income were ploughed back into investments. That account's worth another seven million."

"Oh dear, the income amounts seem disproportionately low to what the occupants of such a lavish house would expect. I suppose that means more than one person has run short of funds."

"None of the beneficiaries are short of money in the overall scheme of things although, it's true, that none of them could be said to be independently wealthy, either. Except for the deceased, that is, who, as of last week, was earning eight hundred and fifty thousand a year as the manager of Sadler-Creme."

"And a company car and a benefits package, too, no doubt," added Brent.

"Exactly. It seems to have been a source of annoyance to several people."

"I'm sure it was. Now that the deceased has been removed from the picture what happens? Hold on… I have it here." Brent skimmed through several passages, muttering the words aloud. "Does Franklin have any heirs?" he asked.

"No. Married twice, no issue."

"You make it sound like a sports result. So, we have a far more equitable distribution of the wealth among the three other children but it is the trust managers' responsibility to find a new executive for Sadler-Creme. Who are the trustees?"

"An accountant called Adolf Shickleman…"

"You can't be serious…" The two men stared at each other. "You are serious. Excuse my interruption."

"A lawyer named Andrew Galbraith and, the last name is of much interest to us, Lloyd de Sainte Croix. He was staying in the house on the night of the murder."

"Would he put himself forward as Sadler-Creme's new manager?"

"I doubt it. Let me see." Greg opened the de Sainte Croix file. "He's… eighty-six… and look at that. Today is his birthday. I have to say he does look very fit but, despite that, I can't see him taking on such an active role."

"You're probably right. However, a remuneration package nudging a million a year is quite a motivator. What else?"

"Evelyn Brewster has a will but she hasn't provided us with a copy yet. I asked nicely. Please try and get a copy otherwise we'll have to be heavy-handed and I don't want to do that at the moment."

"I'll try."

"That's it for now. Here are the files on all the family members and household staff. There is more information to come on everyone but there's enough there for you to make a start." He pushed the bulk of the files towards Brent. "Crime scene report, witness statements… this is the autopsy, though we're missing some lab work and I think forensics is getting lazy. We should have everything by the end of the week." He added the other files to the top of the pile.

"Now, then, how did it happen?" asked Brent.

"Death was caused by thallium poisoning. The initial estimate is something north of 2 grams administered through food or drink. Drink is the most obvious choice as thallium is odourless, tasteless and colourless. The way this house is set up it would be easier to slip it in a drink than go to the kitchen and put it in food. Too many staff working there and an outsider would immediately look suspicious to the staff.

The examiner swears there are no puncture wounds on the corpse. Likely the poison was introduced between four and twelve hours prior to death which occurred at 4:31 a.m.. That time is established by multiple witnesses.

The deceased has been an alcoholic in the past. He's been to rehab and it appears that of late he had it under control. However, on Friday he resumed his former habit and was drinking like a fish. From four in the afternoon until midnight, it is known that he consumed two martinis, a beer, a coffee, six to seven glasses of wine and at least five large whiskies."

"That is excessive by any measure. I get a headache if I mix a glass of white wine with a glass of red. Did they carry him to bed?"

"He managed it on his own."

"I am equal parts disgusted and impressed."

"He also had consumed two beers and three glasses of wine at lunch."

"Breakfast?"

"A coffee followed by a beer. He may have drunk more on his own in his bedroom. There was a half-empty bottle of rye on the bedside table. He arrived late Wednesday night."

"Greg, that's enough, thanks. Where does one buy a bottle of thallium tablets?"

"It comes in liquid form and you can get it at the Sadler-Creme factory if you have a key to the dangerous chemicals area. It's used in a process to manufacture electronics."

"That's puzzling. Presumably, Franklin would be the only one of the family with access."

"I would agree, except - every year the trust fund managers like to have a get-together at the Sadler-Creme factory. Two months ago, the entire family went on a tour of the facility. I sent a detective over to find out all he can and told him not to ever come back if he doesn't find anything. I want to know who had access to the dangerous chemicals area."

"This looks bad… a mess, as you rightly say. Give it to me straight… sorry, no drinking pun intended."

"We can't find a trace of thallium anywhere. Most of the family has some kind of personal motive to do away with Franklin but without any immediate financial benefit being derived from his death. He was not liked - although this is only hinted at rather than stated openly. The family definitely has stronger immediate financial motive to want *Evelyn* dead and to have the trust wound up. So, maybe someone missed her and got Franklin by mistake. Or, Franklin may have committed suicide. Also, they are all keeping their mouths shut."

"Any thoughts?"

"Yes. I'm glad you are here to sort it out for us. Now, as you know, you cannot keep our files or copy them because you're not part of the Department. It is against our rules, you might remember, as outlined by Chief Howard. I find I have to leave for about oh, let's say, fifteen minutes. Please, do not let them out of your sight." Greg grinned and left the room.

As soon as the door was shut, Brent took out his cell phone and quickly began photographing every page of interest in every file.

When Greg Darrow returned, the files were neatly stacked at the end of the table. Brent stood looking out of a window at the gardens. He turned around.

"Good. I think I'm ready to start the game. You know, Greg, this Italian garden is an absolute gem of symmetry. It will be beautiful in the summer. Today, it mourns. The cypresses are doing their job."

"Quite often I have no idea what you're talking about."

"Oh, me, too. I can't help myself, really. Um, the grandchildren, where are they and is there anything of interest there?"

"All in the house at the moment. They'll be shipping out soon. Robert Halliday wants to get back to selling cars. Aurelia is stressed over her course load, particularly a paper on Mesopotamia…"

"Ah, yes. MA in history. That gives me an idea. Go on."

"Chloe Halliday is only interested in acting and climate change. The Aimes children, Karen and Brad, are too young. Remember, none of them was present the day of the murder."

"I know what you mean. However, one of them might have seen or heard something beforehand. What did the household staff tell you?"

"Precious little. Marjorie Bellingham is helpful. Jackson the butler is tight-lipped. We've interviewed a total of fourteen staff and haven't got a thing from any of them. There were two women and a man supplied by an agency to wait at the table. All clean and no one noticed anything."

"Surely someone must have seen the mysterious hand come through the curtains, holding a bottle clearly labelled 'poison'."

Brent walked over to a Hepplewhite sideboard and picked up an old Delft vase decorated with a Chinese scene.

He placed it on its lace doily in the exact centre of a mahogany table.

"Should I ask what you're up to?"

"Opening gambit. I'd like to see Evelyn Brewster, if I may."

Chapter 3

Tuesday morning continued

*I*t took some minutes before Evelyn arrived in her wheelchair propelled by Marjorie Bellingham. Evelyn was simply dressed in black. Her only adornment was a dark red jasper cabochon pendant and small black earrings. She was an elegant woman. Her eyes looked tired and were red-rimmed.

"Good morning, Mrs Brewster. Good morning, Ms Bellingham," said Brent. They both returned his greeting.

"I'm sorry for your loss… I hope to be as unobtrusive and sensitive as possible. First, though, I must ask your forgiveness for my unseemly attire. I was away over the weekend, travelling. I received an urgent summons from Lieutenant Darrow and I came at once."

"It doesn't matter," said Evelyn.

"Thank you. I believe we will be more comfortable at the table. Allow me, Ms Bellingham."

"Marjorie, it seems we are to have a tête-à-tête." The companion left the room.

"Where would you like to sit?"

"Just there will do."

"I understand that hip replacements are routine. You'll be dancing soon."

"Dancing? I haven't danced in years."

"Perhaps you'll pick it up again. It's possible, you know."

Brent seated himself on the other side of the table so that he was directly facing Evelyn. He picked up his scruffy bag and pulled from it a cheap ring binder filled with blank paper. He placed pens and pencils next to it. He opened the cover and wrote a few things quickly. Then he stopped, put the pen down to stare at Evelyn with a slight smile on his face. When he held her gaze, without moving his head, he made his eyes travel to the Delft vase in the centre of the table. Evelyn's eyes followed Brent's glance.

"What's that doing there?" she asked.

"I put it there for a reason. I will tell you what this room and the Delft vase have told me. This is undoubtedly your room and very lovely it is, too. This vase dates to the early seventeen hundreds, could be even earlier. The obvious chips around the rim and the base add character but they also tell me that the vase has been used and cherished over the years." Brent picked the vase up carefully. "It has an old repair… it was drilled and stapled back together… probably a century ago. But, and you know this, it has a modern repair… here at the rim. It's difficult to detect but it stands out as incongruous because there are no chips in the area and the reproduced crazing on the repair does not quite match the rest of the vase. I'd say the repair is between two and ten years old. Furthermore, the plastic insert inside the vase is to protect it when filled with water and so you place flowers in it. How am I doing so far?"

"Very well. It was repaired seven, no… eight years ago."

"You encourage me. I think that in such a perfect house as you have, to keep a twice repaired vase means it has great sentimental value attached to it. It is in your room, therefore it is precious to you. You had it repaired by a real artist but you made sure that all the chips were left and, more telling, the old repair using staples was not touched. That can only mean that, to you, the old repair is a part of the piece and it would look wrong without it. From here on I'm guessing, but the vase signifies a special moment in your life. This good old Dutch vase says to me that your husband, George Brewster, gave it to you at a joyful time in your lives. A time you treasure. Perhaps you made a joke about a cracked pot."

"That is quite uncanny. It is as you say. It was when we were first married. We found it in an antique shop on a country road. I was attracted to the vase and we laughed over the curious staples. He bought it for me saying something silly... that there were now three crack-pots in the family." Evelyn smiled gently as she remembered these things.

"I've been admiring your garden," said Brent. "It's the wrong time of year for everything, I know. What I wondered was, where is your flower garden?"

"That is on the west side of the house." She looked at him quizzically.

"I know it's entirely out of season but I'd like to see it, if I may. I like gardening."

"Of course. What do you grow?"

"I have a fledgling garden at the back of my suburban house. There will be roses, phlox, delphiniums... usual stuff. I'm smitten with Cosmos at the moment and I hope to put some in this summer. My gardener, Eric, says we should grow a hardy geranium like Rozanne instead of Cosmos. We are at an impasse. He invests as much time in the garden as I do. It is a very delicate situation."

Evelyn showed interest but she began to look uncertain.

"Are you a policeman?"

"Oh, no. I'm a private investigator brought in to help. As you can imagine, the current circumstances are very muddled, knotty. I talk to people and help tease the strands apart."

"I don't understand. Do you put people at their ease and then ask difficult questions?"

"That's very perceptive of you. I do always strive to be pleasant. I like meeting people. I explained the vase to let you see how I work - how I think about details - to reassure you that I am after the truth of the matter. Franklin has died. Someone killed him or he killed himself. You want to know the truth of that. Not necessarily for justice or revenge, but you must know. I want you to know it, too. Something ugly has happened and it needs to be thoroughly understood to be dealt with."

"To lose him like that…" Her lip trembled until she made a conscious effort to control herself. "You have a very disarming way about you and are almost too honest. You make it sound like a game."

"It is in some ways. The police ask serious questions with serious faces. If I do the same everyone will answer me in the same way, if they answer me at all. I prefer to find out what people are like and what they think. To do that, I must be conversational and pleasant.

You and I must talk about an awful matter. I only wish to find out some of the things you know that may have a bearing on the case. You can stop any time you like but, if you can help me, I hope to bring the unresolved issues surrounding Franklin's death to a conclusion. I'm sure you want that."

"Of course. I think he was murdered… I can't imagine he would kill himself. You do not know the pain I feel on the inside. The pain of losing a son… my first child… If you can help lessen that, I'll play your game."

They talked for a while, going over mundane, technical matters. Evelyn told Brent that she had not seen anyone approach Franklin or do anything to his food or drink. She said that the only time she thought it possible was when everyone was coming to her at the end of the table to welcome her home. Brent suggested that it would have been too easy for the poisoner to be observed in so open a setting.

"Could we go to the dining room in question?"

"Yes, we can. I feel so helpless in this contraption."

"Do you think you could walk there?"

"Oh, I don't know about that. I feel as though I could. A physiotherapist was supposed to be visiting but with all this going on I've cancelled two appointments already."

"Then I have a suggestion. I will be your therapist. The best exercise for legs is walking. You can lean on my arm and, if the distance is too much, we'll have the wheelchair on hand."

Evelyn looked at him. "Let's try, then. Don't go too fast. Promise me you will not pull me about."

"We will proceed at the pace of a cautious sloth. I'll just go next door to find a kind soul to help with the procession."

The soul he found was officer Fletcher. The two men carefully helped Evelyn to her feet. She tried a couple of tentative steps leaning heavily on Brent's arm.

"Any twinges or pain?" he asked.

"No, none. I'm surprised."

"That's good. If you have any problems, shout out. We'll go very slowly. We don't want to do too much as it might be painful for you later."

They left the room. Evelyn was doing well as they went along the passage and this pleased her. On the walls on either side were portraits of ancient Brewsters.

"Quite the family," said Brent, looking at each painting as they passed them. Brent wondered if any of the family he would be meeting soon would have similar features. "Certain facial characteristics seem to be hereditary. Hello, not this one, though. Nor yet this one." They stopped before the two paintings in question. "The nameplate says 'Nathaniel Brewster' and this one is 'Johanna Brewster' and they are painted in the same style. Is there a mystery here? The lady is plausible, assuming she married into the family, but not the gentleman."

"Do you know you're the first person ever to notice that?" said Evelyn.

"Do I scent an intriguing story? Do tell me what it is."

"All these portraits used to hang in the large dining room. I never liked them there but as it was a family tradition I let them stay. George didn't care one way or another. It was such a long time ago. Franklin would have been two at the time and the other children were not yet born. Well, we were having trouble with the fireplace... It smoked occasionally. It wasn't attended to and just before we were to have a very large dinner party, thirty guests as I recall, several bricks and rubbish fell down the chimney and landed in the fireplace. It all got out of control because no one was in the room at the time. A log rolled off and hit a small table with a cloth over it which stood near the fireplace. The cloth and the table caught fire and there was a small blaze with smoke everywhere.

The damage wasn't very bad because the fire was quickly put out, but two portraits were badly scorched beyond repair. I decided to replace them. I bought these two at an auction and they seemed a suitable fit so I had the nameplates from the damaged frames attached to them.

Later, we moved all the portraits out here for safety's sake and the children have grown up believing these are their actual relatives. They've been there so long they seem like family to me now. I've never thought to explain it to anyone."

Brent laughed out loud. "What a great story. I wouldn't tell them, either."

In the small dining room, the scene of the celebration on the fateful night, Evelyn and Brent sat alone, talking. The empty wheelchair was for the return journey. Brent stared at it.

"Do you have an elevator?"

"Yes, at the end of the west wing. An old contraption that has seen little use until recently."

"Hmm." He paused for several seconds. "Franklin was sixty. How would you describe him... his personality... from when he was a little boy?"

"He was a lovely child. You would have liked him. He was talkative... and thoughtful. He liked animals and sports and... I loved him. He was never any trouble. He made himself the self-appointed guardian of the younger children when they came along. He had a particular affection for Laura, my youngest. She adored him. He went away to college... That seems like only yesterday... and he did well academically. He was a great reader of all things. I remember the bedtime stories I read to him. That was such a delight for me and he was so enthralled with the stories. 'One more chapter,' he often said. I couldn't deny him... Sometimes it was two extra chapters." She paused for a long time.

"Where was I? Yes, a change came over him when he returned from college. I think it was just normal growing up. He was not my boy anymore, he was a man... independent from me... which is how it should be, I suppose.

The changes must have been gradual, I guess, and seemed to have been masked during holidays. It was only at the end of college that I fully realized that he was a stranger in the house. Not an unpleasant one, but he was definitely aloof and had become disengaged from the rest of the family.

When he started working at the factory with George he seemed to go from me for good. This is the difficult part. I loved my husband, George. Our marriage was good. Yet there are two things he did that were wrong. George promised Franklin the factory when he was quite young... about twenty-five. I think it must have been his joy at working with his eldest son... and Franklin was a hard worker. George said it would be Franklin's. I disagreed at the time but I could hardly stop my husband from saying what he pleased when he and Franklin worked together. It was a promise of too much, too early, as far as I saw it. Unfortunately, I was proved to be correct. Franklin distanced himself from me and became, well, to put it simply, avaricious.

The second mistake my husband made was in setting up the trust the way he did. I was told at the time that it was good tax planning and I didn't think very much about it. This move seemed only to reflect George's intentions that he'd already made plain. I didn't foresee the problems that would follow. It wasn't that it was unfair as such; it was that it permanently isolated Franklin from the rest of the family. He would be getting more than half the estate with the other half shared between the rest. What jealousies that has aroused. Worse was that Franklin would be receiving an executive's salary while the other children received very little by the family's standards. Because all the children were so much younger, I didn't realize how much acrimony there would be. I really don't know what George was thinking of. I suppose he didn't expect to die early otherwise he would have been able to make changes and there would have been no problems."

"I wonder," said Brent, "if Franklin influenced his father so the trust was set up the way he wanted. Is it possible?"

A long silence followed. "Yes, it is entirely possible," replied Evelyn. "Franklin is, I mean was, a competent businessman. He had shortcomings - two failed marriages and no children. Please don't ask me about them… you'll find out soon enough. But he would consider the trust only as another contract from which to wring the best terms possible for himself."

"Thank you, Mrs Brewster. You have been very helpful. I begin to see a picture. Now, where would you like to go and will you walk or ride?"

"Ride, I think. I feel tired. It has been very interesting talking to you. You're a good listener."

"Ah, is there anything I can get for you?"

"No, don't trouble yourself. Marjorie will look after me. Ring the bell for Jackson."

There was a woven and richly patterned bell-pull by the fireplace. Brent went and pulled it solemnly three times because he had never operated such an instrument before. He returned to stand by Evelyn's side.

"I've remembered something. You'll think it's terribly rude of me, I know. You have a will. May I see it, please?"

Evelyn gave him a sharp look.

"You do not have to show it to me," said Brent. "The police will first request it and then insist it be handed over by legal documents that your lawyer cannot refuse. When they have the will they will then tell me the contents. I'm very sorry that I'm so nosey."

"I don't believe you're sorry." Evelyn smiled slightly. "Marjorie will bring you my copy. I'd rather give it to you than somebody I don't know."

Chapter 4

Tuesday morning to lunchtime

*B*rent walked slowly around the library. He estimated the number of shelves and the number of books on each and came up with the total of twelve thousand books. All the volumes were neatly arranged by size, type, and subject matter. They were housed in built-in, floor to ceiling walnut shelves. The top frieze and the brackets between sections were ornamented with applied carving and gilt rococo figures. It was impressive but not Brent's favourite style of decoration. What appealed to him most were the movable ladders. He played with one, sending it gently back and forth in its track. Gratified by its effortless, quiet movement, he moved it to the section he wanted and climbed up to inspect the uppermost shelves.

Brent liked reading but was not particularly bookish. After glancing along the spines nearest the ceiling he found several volumes that interested him. He examined them. After putting the last one back, he turned to survey the room from his unusual vantage point. Several desks with chairs and half a dozen easy chairs and settees stood on as fine a collection of hand-knotted rugs as one could hope to see. A large old globe in its heavy wooden cradle stood in front of one of the windows. He found the view very satisfying. He watched as Sophia Halliday walked into the room accompanied by her daughter Aurelia.

"Hello," said Brent gently. "I hope I didn't startle you. I'll be down in a second."

The two women were surprised, more than anything else, to see a strange man up the library ladder. They watched him descend.

"There, back on terra firma. My name is Brent Umber. You're Sophia and you are, don't tell me... Aurelia?"

"Hi," said Aurelia. "A detective asked us to come to the library." She seemed amiable.

"What exactly are you doing?" asked Sophia. She was on the verge of ordering him out of the room even though her mother had told her of the nice young man who was working with the police.

"I would be untruthful if I said I was a book collector looking for a rare volume. I couldn't resist the ladder. I climbed it to admire the view. I'm sure you've done it."

"Not since I was a little girl." Her tone implied that a grown man should not be doing such a thing.

"That's exactly it. I'm a little boy at heart. It just so happens that it was I who sent for you. We should have a chat."

"About what?" asked Sophia. She was fifty-five - a tall woman who looked similar to her mother.

"As a private investigator, I'm here to discover who the murderer is."

A stony, uncomfortable silence followed.

"Do either of you know who might have done it?"

Aurelia looked very uncomfortable. Sophia had a worried look.

"No... we have no idea," she answered soberly and with reluctance.

"Excellent. Neither of you two had a hand in it, I'm sure. Now we are free to talk and find out who did. Please, take a seat while I get my gear."

They watched him in silence, sitting close to each other on the edge of a large settee. Brent balanced his ring binder on his knees. It looked to be a cheap oddity in the sumptuous library.

"Usually, I interview people separately. I find them more forthcoming about things. It would be immensely rude if I asked one of you to leave the room. So, this should be interesting."

Neither woman looked reassured by his little speech.

"Right. Aurelia, I'm so sorry that you have walked into this horrible situation. I wish I could turn the clock back and change a few things. I've heard that your master's degree is proving problematic. Is there anything I can do to help?"

"Help me with my degree?" She looked bewildered.

"Yes. Is it the course load? What subject is it?"

"MA in history. I have to write two papers. There's one on Mesopotamia that I haven't even started."

"Mesopotamia, hmm. Hammurabi and the First Babylonian Dynasty would be a good choice - sketchy details - but that gives you a free hand to become inventive. Or you could go earlier and present the competing arguments for defining the Uruk and Ubaid periods. I suppose the problem is the getting down to it and not just the inspiration."

"Did you take courses?" asked Aurelia.

"Not in that epoch. I just read up a little on my own. I'm cursed with a retentive memory."

"Actually, it's the Neo-Babylonian era."

"Nabopolasser! Would he do?"

"Yes. I was thinking of him."

Brent leapt from his chair, upsetting his ring binder, to march over to the ladder. He climbed up and from a shelf near the top took out an old volume. He brought it down with him. Aurelia nudged her mother and pointed to the open ring binder. A page was visible and it had strange symbols and lettering on it. These were Brent's notes on his meeting with Evelyn. He alone could make sense of them.

"Here, would 'Babylonian Statecraft from Nabopolasser to Nebuchadnezzar' be of any assistance? It's a bit dated… first edition, 1879, but Rufus Wallington was the expert in his day, if I remember correctly."

He presented the leather-bound volume to Aurelia.

"Yes… that's a great idea. Statecraft is a good theme."

"Very good. Umber's Frazzled Student Emergency Service doesn't stop there." Brent took out his cell phone, dialled a number, and proceeded to walk about the room. He ended up by the globe and began walking his fingers across it.

"Hello, Fred. It's me. I can't stop but I believe you owe me a favour… A small request in the scheme of things. I have a friend who has to write an essay on Nabopolasser… polasser. Yes… Statecraft… MA… It was due yesterday, so no slacking. What she would like is an overview, a list of pertinent things to include to impress the professor and a fistful of references since Wallington… no, she has that on hand. In hand, actually. Make it a fill in the blanks sort of thing… Excellent… Email it to me and I'll forward it on. Nearly forgot. Has Rosie given birth yet?… How many?… Six! I'll take one… How much?… That's daylight robbery… No, it's for a very young friend of mine who would love and is in need of a Golden Retriever puppy… I have to go. Don't forget the notes on Naby… Talk to you soon."

He came back to the women who had heard every word.

"That's settled. Fred, who happens to be an eminent history professor with a sideline in Goldens, will do the heavy lifting for your essay. You should have it later today."

"Are there not rules about ghostwriting?" asked Sophia.

"It's a grey area, mom. But I'll be writing it so there's no plagiarism, and ghostwriting doesn't enter into it. Thank you, Mr Umber. You've saved my life."

"You're welcome. Please, read your statecraft while I talk to your mother. We can chat later."

Aurelia went to a distant part of the room and settled down to study.

"It was almost as though you planned that," said Sophia.

"It's just possible that I did. I climbed the ladder looking for books suitable for Aurelia's studies."

"Thank you, anyway. Aurelia has been stressing over deadlines and this terrible business brought her to tears."

"It is terrible. Did you cry over it?"

"Why do you ask?"

"Because you are... defensive. Your mother wasn't when I spoke to her. From what I've learned, I should imagine you have had bad feelings towards Franklin. Now that he is dead, murdered maybe, you are ashamed of those thoughts. The trust document was appallingly short-sighted."

"You're right, of course. I suppose I hated my brother. Now that he's dead I find I don't. It was only while he was getting away with it all... I pity him now."

"So, I take it there are more things than the trust that have caused problems. His drinking, for example. Careless, hurtful words? Belligerence?"

"Yes, there were those."

"Then there's something else? You can tell me. I'll make you a promise. If your story does not help the case I'll not mention it to the police. You must see that, until they have a real suspect, you are all suspects in their eyes."

"I know. But I can't trust you. Not with this. Not now."

"I understand. I would do the same... for a friend. We can talk about something else. Um, how was the dinner party that night?"

"Well, it was a little stuffy... as it usually is. Mother enjoyed herself. She likes to see all the family together."

"Whose idea was it?"

"Franklin's..."

"Why do you hesitate?"

"I wish you were a police officer - you wouldn't ask such awkward questions."

"Meaning...? Do I understand that there was bad feeling on that night? Before that night?"

"What happens if I don't answer you?"

"I'll get bits and pieces from everyone else and then I'll come back to you again."

"I think I shall tell everyone not to talk to you. You may have charmed Mother but don't think you can get away with it with the rest of us."

"Why take that attitude?" asked Brent, smiling.

"Why are you smiling? Did I say something funny?" asked Sophia.

"Yes. You're trying to be dignified and there's nothing wrong with that but trying to maintain privacy and family reserve in the face of a murder investigation is making it unnecessarily hard for you. I would rather we be on friendly terms and you tell me what I need to know."

"Have you ever considered that I might not want the murderer to be caught?"

"No, I haven't. That's very interesting, though.... What makes you believe it was murder?"

"I can't believe Franklin would commit suicide. It was not in his mental make-up. He wouldn't do that."

"Perhaps he was depressed or had mental issues?"

"Depressed? Yes, I think he might have been depressed. No mental issues, unless being selfish and greedy are mental issues."

"Greedy in what way?"

"He wanted this house, the company - everything really. It wasn't for the value alone. I think it was more than that. I believe he wanted to exclude the whole rest of the family. He thought we were all hangers-on and he was the only one working towards the good of the Brewster name."

"I see. But, ah, he had no children to inherit from him."

"You didn't know my brother. Despite his age, he would have fixed that - probably with a mail-order bride or some such scheme. He would have married if he needed to. There was a hint of an illegitimate son years ago.... He would be late twenties by now. What his name is or where he lives, I couldn't tell you."

"This is the first I've heard of him having a son so I couldn't tell you, either," said Brent. He was thoughtful for a moment. "Could you excuse me while I make a quick call? I don't think the police know about this."

Sophia nodded in reply.

Brent called Greg Darrow

"Hi, Greg. Did you know that Franklin had an illegitimate child?"

"No, I didn't," replied Greg. "We haven't got all his papers yet. His lawyer is going slow and there's a safety deposit box we haven't been able to access. If there's a will it might show something. Got a name for me?"

"I haven't," said Brent. "I was hoping you'd have something. Talk to you later." Brent put his phone down. "Sorry about that. You do realize that it might have a bearing on the trust disposition?"

"I'd never given it any thought. I suppose it would."

"I think it goes along the lines that if the son is named in Franklin's will then he can inherit from his father. If he is not named, is not a dependent, has been adopted, or a few other things like that, then he will have no right of inheritance. Even if he *is* named in Franklin's will, he would be precluded from receiving anything from the trust."

Brent watched Sophia as she received this information. As far as he could see she showed no outward surprise or distress which left him wondering if she already knew of the possible changes to the disposition of the estate or, if it was news to her, if she just did not care.

"Does any of this make a difference to you?" asked Brent.

She looked at him searchingly before looking away. "Some years ago I did the calculations and realized I would be receiving something like seventy million after taxes. It's only ever gone up since then. As it is already, my family is comfortably off without inheriting anything. We're not wealthy but neither do we need anything else. I would say we were content. The one thing I have always wanted out of all these dispositions was this house for the simple reason that I was happy growing up here.

You should understand that this estate costs a lot to run each year and the staff is very much like family. Having said that, I would prefer things continued as they are and to see Mother live on here for many more years."

"That is an awkward situation to think about," said Brent. "So you would rather everything stay as it is now and the extra money from Franklin's share of the trust has little meaning for you?"

"Do we have to discuss this?"

"I'm sorry but we do."

"Then I would rather have it as it was a week ago before Franklin died. If I had known, I would have behaved so differently towards him. I didn't like him for many reasons but he was my brother and he was a decent person once. He was far more suited to running a company than any of the rest of us would ever be.

As for the shares in the company and the extra money? I don't know. I've persuaded myself I don't care about all of that but I suppose I do.... like the majority of people would.... I suppose it will work out to about another two hundred and fifty million after tax."

Her demeanour remained unchanged as she spoke.

"I think I understand what you're saying," said Brent. "How much money is enough? When a person has enough the question ceases to be meaningful.... What will you do now?"

"I've no idea. I feel like I'm in suspended animation. I can't grieve... I feel guilty about that.... I feel emptier than I did... I've always felt a little empty... Why am I telling you this?"

"Probably because you've needed to tell someone but the opportunity hasn't arisen."

She laughed. "You could be right.... Changing the subject, you would not believe how difficult it was to get Aurelia to study at school. Now, look at her. As quiet as anything, reading about Mesopotamia... Totally absorbed. I wish I could be so absorbed in something like that."

"Find something that interests you, if that's what you would like."

"It only ever looks like filling in time.... I guess you were up the ladder looking for a suitable book for Aurelia to keep her quiet so you could talk to me privately."

"You make it sound very calculating on my part. It worked out well, though, don't you think?"

"I suppose it has.... How does what I've told you help in any way?"

"Helps me understand what motivates you. Think about this, Sophia - you say Franklin would not commit suicide. If you are correct and it would be better if you weren't, then it means there was a murderer in the house that night. A finite number of people had access to him. The more I can believe in each person's innocence the more likely I am to find the murderer for the simple reason that I cannot believe in that person's innocence."

"Where does that leave me?"

"It's early yet. Nothing you have said alarms me but I can't say more than that."

"At least you're more forthcoming than the police were…. I didn't kill him…. I know that means nothing but I want you to hear me say it. It's on record now. The police didn't ask me and all I wanted to do was scream it at them."

"I think I would feel the same way," said Brent.

"Why would you?"

"Ah, now that's my secret. If you tell me yours, I'll tell you mine."

"Well, I can't. Though I've half a mind to make something up to hear what secret you will tell me in return. Give me a hint."

"Did you ever do something wrong and want to confess but couldn't because you were afraid of the consequences?"

"Not since I was a small child." Sophia smiled for a moment and then stopped smiling. "Oh, I see."

"Changing the subject once more, I have a degree in History which was why I thought I could help Aurelia in her current predicament. I saw what she was studying and hoped that a large, old library like this might have a copy of Babylonian Statecraft. It was very popular in its day. The gentleman I spoke to was my professor for a while."

"You talk to your former professor like that? He sounded like a friend."

"He is. I was in reverential awe of him while he taught me. We've kept in touch since I finished my studies. Once, I helped him out of a difficult situation and he swore undying gratitude to me. That is another secret, though." Brent smiled. "One I cannot tell to anyone."

"Very interesting… There's the gong for lunch… I'm sorry I can't tell you everything but there it is." Sophia stood and turned to call to the studious Aurelia who had not looked up when the gong was struck. Brent stood up also.

"Aurelia… Lunch. Bring the book with you," said the mother.

"Lunch? Okay," said Aurelia.

"How's Mr Wallington?" asked Brent.

"Fascinating," said Aurelia with a smile. "Thanks."

Chapter 5

Tuesday after lunch

Someone had thoughtfully instructed the kitchen staff to provide all the police on-site with a variety of very well-made sandwiches which, when served, were greatly appreciated by the recipients. Brent was also included in the number. Greg Darrow had left the house so Brent ate alone and wrote up his notes or reviewed documents as he did so.

It was about two-thirty when he went in search of someone to interview. One of the staff directed him to the lounge. There in the huge room, Brent found a lone occupant. The young 25-year-old man was sitting on a couch, playing a game on his cell phone. Brent came close to him before speaking.

"Hello, Robert. I was told I would find you here."

"You're with the police, right?" Robert Halliday looked up with difficulty - his eyes wanted to stay on the game. He had short hair and piercing blue eyes. Brent noticed that his pupils were dilated.

"Yes, I'm helping them. I wondered if I might talk with you for a few minutes."

"Sure." Robert resumed playing.

"Have you noticed anything strange in the house since you arrived?"

"Strange…? No." He moved his thumbs rapidly.

"You haven't noticed that the police are in the house looking for a murderer?"

"Ha… Like I told the real cops… I don't know anything. I just want out of here."

"I'm sure you do. But you're not going anywhere because I can pin the murder on you."

"What?" Robert put the phone down.

"Oh, yes. You're a prime suspect. You're avoiding questions put to you by the police and myself. This is very suspicious behaviour in and of itself. You have a strong motive to commit the murder and, whatever alibi you think you have, the police and I should be able to break it. The murderer is in the house and I see no reason why it shouldn't be you."

"You're crazy. I wasn't even here on the night."

"Weren't you? It's barely a two-hour drive from where you live to here - a four-hour round trip. You know the house. You have a motive - money. Simple as anything for you to get in, spike a drink, and get out again. If you were seen you would say that you had arrived early - a perfect cover. But you weren't seen… and that's how you got away with it."

"I wasn't here, I tell you. I have an alibi…. A solid one."

"Ah, but for what time? You see, it has to cover a very specific time. Does your alibi cover it?"

Robert, seeing the trick in the question, hesitated before speaking. "I'd better call a lawyer." He picked up his phone.

"That's a little premature for the murder charge but not for the illegal possession of a controlled substance charge that you are about to be slapped with. Call anyway, but remember, lawyers' hourly rates are quite high."

Robert's hand dropped. He placed his phone on the couch beside him. "Look, is there any way around this? I didn't do it."

"You simply have to give me your full attention and answer truthfully, as far as you can. If you can't do that, then I promise to make life very difficult for you."

"Okay, then. What do you want to know?" Robert set his phone aside on the couch. He had a mocking, challenging look on his face.

"Did you go on the tour of Sadler-Creme in October?"

"Naturally. In this family, we all behave ourselves so we can get the biggest payout possible when they're all dead."

"Do you want them to die?"

"What's that supposed to mean?"

"You're looking for a big payout in the same way as everyone else. Your time is valuable to you. You have just given me the impression you want everyone dead who stands between you and your share."

"I never said that."

"In words, no. In attitude, yes you did."

"No… No, I didn't," Robert spoke slowly and deliberately as if explaining a complicated matter. "Want I meant was, the family plays the inheritance game."

"On the tour, did you or anyone else go near the Dangerous Chemicals Area?"

"I remember we passed by it but it was locked up."

"Which one of them killed your Uncle Franklin?"

"We call him Uncle Frank and no one killed him. He killed himself."

"So, as far as you know, no one deliberately poisoned Uncle Frank?"

"You got it."

"Supposing someone meant to kill your grandmother and got your uncle instead."

"That's impossible. Who would want to kill Nana?"

"I would guess someone who needed money in a hurry or didn't want to wait for their share any longer. Someone like you."

"Why'd you bring that up again? I thought we'd settled that I had nothing to do with what happened that night."

"*You* may have settled it in your mind but we're far from settling it either way in mine. You're a young guy who displays no emotion. You have a drug problem…"

"I do not have a drug problem."

"You're a guy with a drug problem and maybe you owe somebody some serious money. The police will be checking into all of that. If you have bad connections they'll find out."

"Dude, I get depressed once in a while… That's it. Nothing serious, so back off."

"That had better be true, for your sake… Did you love your Uncle Frank?"

"What?"

Brent did not answer and left his question hanging. The silence worked away on Robert, inducing him to speak. It took many seconds before he answered.

"I don't know what love is exactly," he said at last, "but when you grow up with someone always there or always in the background… you get used to the idea of him being around and being a part of your life. When I was little he was very nice to me… Yeah, very nice… That's the Uncle Frank I'm going to remember… Recently, we had no time for each other."

"Was that your doing or his?"

"Both… I'd say it was both of us… The family was against him… Mom's got this big secret about wicked Uncle Frank… I don't even know what *that's* about. But he didn't do himself any favours, either… Families can be so weird… The smallest thing gets remembered forever. Make a mistake and they'll bring it up… No, it's worse than that. If you make a mistake there's no discussion… They *don't* bring it up but they always look down on you."

"Why, do they do that to *you*?"

"I didn't say that."

"Come on, Robert. You don't have to tell me if you don't want to but something's hurt you."

"You got that right." A deep frown settled on his face as he stared at the carpet. He crossed his arms. "Okay, why not? Confession's supposed to be good for the soul.

I first heard about the trust when I was sixteen. Can you imagine what it's like to know you're going to get ten million bucks and more sometime in the near future? I mean I was *sixteen!* I had that ten mill spent so many different ways. The things I wanted to do if I'd had the money back then!

So guess what happened? Guess which kid thought he didn't have to work at school any longer? Guess who dropped out of school and started getting into trouble? Guess who lost friends because he talked like a big shot all the time…? You're looking at him.

Because I didn't do well in school, what happened next? The family's so disappointed with me. I had arguments with mom and dad all the time… The look of disappointment on Nana's face… I didn't do what the family expected me to do all because of ten million bucks that I didn't even have in my hand.

Then there was Uncle Frank… he just gave me the cold shoulder. He thought I was a dummy. I was eighteen and the family is pitying me because I wasn't going to college.

That's their fault, not mine. Afterwards was my fault, not theirs. There's a period in my life I'm not proud of but I grew out of it and it was a close call for me. That's not part of this story.

Anyway, by twenty, I realize I have to do something to turn myself around. I'm interested in cars and I get good at selling, working in a few different retail stores. I decide to make a career out of sales and do it properly. I went to all the right seminars and listened to all the sales pitch gurus. I was hungry to learn. I learnt so much I can spot the good guys from the con artists. Let me tell you something, it's the con artists who charge the highest prices.

Today, I'm a self-taught salesman and I'm very good at what I do. I like working and I work hard and smart. Do you think my family recognizes any of what I've done? I make more money than my dad. Does that change anything? No, it doesn't. No, I made the mistake of dropping out of school and there's no forgiveness for that in this family - ever.

Now you know why I have a chip on my shoulder and why, while sitting around here, I'd rather be playing a game than talking to anyone.

Tell you the truth, I'd like to be back selling cars. I have a great time with many of my customers, and the people I work with at the dealership appreciate me and value what I can do for the team."

"I completely understand all of that," said Brent. "Have you ever explained all or any of that to anyone?"

"Like, what's the point? You think Nana cares about me? You think she'll listen to a car salesman complain about his life?"

"She might, particularly because of the way the trouble started. What's the worse thing she'll do to you?"

"Not listen… Not understand."

"Oh, I think she'll understand. What do you want from her, then?"

"For her to be proud of me."

"Tell her your story and see what she does. I'm sure Evelyn has no idea about any of this. You have nothing to lose and maybe a lot to gain if you do speak to her."

"I don't know… Maybe I will one day… when this situation has blown over."

"Hi, Karen. My name is Brent. I work with the police." He had found the Aimes daughter sitting in the conservatory. She was on her phone. To Brent, she looked younger than fifteen as she sat curled up in the corner of a settee. Her polished fingernails were different colours.

"Oh. Like, do you want to speak to me?"

"For a few minutes, please."

"No problem." She shut her phone off.

"It is so lovely and warm in here," said Brent. Karen watched him warily as he sat down in a rattan armchair. Her eyes were on him while he stared at an orange tree in a massive clay pot. Then he turned to her and said, easily and slowly,

"I don't bite. In fact, I believe I can honestly say that I have never bitten anybody, even as a small child." Karen laughed. Brent continued, "There are a few people I know who deserve to be bitten. How about you? Anyone you'd like to sink your teeth into?"

"Not really. That's, like, so weird to think of biting someone."

"I suppose it is. How about your brother, Brad?"

"Yeah… I could totally bite him." She became animated now.

"I see. Please don't do it before I have my interview with him, though. I'd feel so guilty if he were covered in band-aids." Brent looked back at the orange tree. "You must know that I have to ask questions. Sometimes it's easy and sometimes it isn't. So, I need your help."

"In what way?"

"Have you seen anything that doesn't look right to you? Let's say, in the last few weeks, right up until now." He got up to look out of the window.

"Like a clue, or something?"

"That's right. Anything that has stuck out as wrong, unusual or puzzling."

Karen shook her head. "No… no, nothing."

"What did you call your uncle?"

"Uncle Frank. I didn't see him very often."

"He was probably busy with the factory most of the time. Did you like him?"

"He was kinda hard to talk to. Like, he didn't know what to say. Dad says it's because he doesn't like children, but…" She stopped and shook her head.

"Oh, Karen. Don't leave me hanging. But what?"

"If he didn't like children why did he buy me such nice presents?"

"I would say because he liked you."

"He gave me a really good camera one year. Oh, yeah, he gave me this huge, and I mean huge," she extended her arms to show the size of it, "doll's house that opened up at the front. It had everything in it. I loved it."

"That was nice of him. I'm glad you told me. You see, I'm trying to build up a picture in my mind of what Uncle Frank was like. To do that I need to find out all I can about him."

"Do you know who the murderer is?"

"Not yet. We're still in the early stages of the investigation."

Karen re-positioned herself on the settee so that she was kneeling. Her eyes were dancing. "You must have a suspect. Who is it?"

"If we did, I wouldn't be allowed to tell you."

"You do, don't you?" The light and animation then faded from her face. "It's one of us, isn't it?"

"It isn't you, of that I'm sure. It probably isn't your brother, although he surely deserves to be bitten. And I promise to come and tell you that it isn't your mom and dad as soon as I've spoken to them."

"I know! Check the security cameras. The suspect has to be on those."

"That's a good idea. I wonder if the detectives have looked at the recordings." Brent moved to the orange tree and examined it closely.

"No, they will have done that already. It's, like, in every crime show. It's the first thing they do."

"Oh, I see. Have you ever thought about being a detective?"

"I wouldn't mind. Looks exciting… but the ones in the house… they don't look like they're having fun."

"That's because they're busy. They have to concentrate on their work."

"But you're not like them."

"No, I'm not. They work according to police procedures. I work only to build a perfect picture of the crime in my mind. Right now, I'm only roughing in things here and there on the canvas. Later, I'll have the scene of the crime finished. Then, in my mind you understand, I'll have a series of portraits of all the people who could have committed the crime. One of them will be the right fit. One face will fit in the picture and the others will look wrong."

"One of us will be the murderer."

"That is likely to be so."

"Like, your asking about Uncle Frank because you, like, have to know the character of the victim so you can understand who the murderer is?"

"Very good. That is exactly right." Brent returned to the armchair.

"Well? Aren't you going to ask me some questions?" asked Karen.

"If you hadn't noticed, I've asked them already."

"You did?" She looked very doubtful.

"Not very impressive, am I?"

"Like, not at all."

"Ah, you put me in a difficult situation. I should try to maintain my reputation - it's very important to me. Yes, I have it. I think I have it… You have a boyfriend, true or false?"

Karen coloured very slightly. "Ye-es."

"Good. Fact number one is established. Now, how is your schoolwork doing?"

"Don't ask."

"I have asked. Fact number two is established - grades are going down. If you were involved in a crime, or if I thought you were, I would need a couple more facts but in your case they are none of my business. So, for demonstration purposes only, I will act on my hunch now." Brent took from his pocket a pen and a couple of his own business cards. One of the cards he handed to Karen along with the pen and said, "Sign your name on the front of the card."

Intrigued, the girl obediently did so and handed the pen and card back to him. Brent then wrote a few words on the back of the same card and put it in his wallet for safekeeping.

"I have written down my detective's intuitive hunch regarding Ms Karen Aimes. Now, who is your best friend?"

"Er, Milly."

"And do you have a second-best friend?"

"Oh, that would be Sandra."

Brent quickly wrote a few words on the back of the other business card and then handed it to Karen. He had written,

'Luncheon date, early March, Karen, Milly, and Sandra.'

"In three months you will keep the luncheon date. We will be properly chaperoned by Milly and Sandra. I will clear it first with your mom and dad. We will go to a very expensive restaurant where one needs an interpreter to explain to us what is on the menu. Anyway, while we are lunching there, I shall surreptitiously slip you the card on which I just wrote my hunch and you will see for yourself what a great detective I am! As a bonus for you and your friends, I will entertain you with hair-raising stories of how, not once, but twice, I have nearly been killed by assassins and only my wits and dare-devil action saved me from an untimely end."

Karen was too stunned to speak at first - her face showed it plainly. Then she burst into a fit of laughter that had her clutching her stomach with one hand and covering her mouth with the other.

Chapter 6

Tuesday afternoon continued

$\mathcal{W}$alking along a corridor, Brent met Detective Alice Bates coming the other way.

"Excuse me, Officer Bates. Do you know where I can find Brad Aimes?"

"You'll probably find him in the small sitting room on the second floor of the west wing."

"Thank you. This house is so big I might have lost an hour looking for him."

"How's it going?"

"I'm trying to see all the grandchildren first before they scatter in different directions. I haven't begun with the prime suspects yet. Spotted a few of them here and there. One thing strikes me, I haven't found many expressions of grief over Franklin's death so far."

"That's right. The deceased kind of brought it on himself. He pushed the family away and wouldn't let them participate in a wealthy company."

"I suppose so. Now the family seems disjointed, having had to fend for itself, as it were. Thanks again, Officer Bates."

"Call me Alice."

"And I'm Brent. Have you got any ideas on what happened that you can share with me?"

"A couple. I don't see how it was possible to introduce thallium at the dinner table. Everybody at dinner stood near the deceased at some point. I can't see any of them taking the risk of being seen tampering with his food or drink."

"No, it doesn't seem plausible. Technically it was possible, but not likely. It would be more sensible of the murderer to get Franklin on his own. The problem we face is that the time frame is so extensive that everyone had access to him. Some of these opportunities were witnessed by others but we have no idea how many could have gone unnoticed."

"Yeah. What with no physical evidence, we'll have to wait until someone breaks down."

"True. What was your other idea?"

"I don't see it being a suicide. He had to know the effects of thallium because of the Safety Data Sheet required at the factory and he could easily have researched it elsewhere, too. He wouldn't off himself in such a painful way."

"I'm with you there. Just from the reports, it doesn't look likely that thallium would be his way of doing things and, from what I've learned since, he hasn't even the profile of a suicide."

"Okay. Why?" asked Alice.

"Franklin was closer than ever to achieving his goal of complete company control, at which point he would have been able to sell it even, if that's what he wanted. He was isolated from most of the family and yet still had some influence with his mother. I've read her will. Did you read the copy I gave Greg yet?"

"Yes. He gets the company because the trust is wound up upon Evelyn's death. However, he's an equal beneficiary with his siblings as far as the rest of the estate is concerned."

"Exactly. If he had been out of favour Evelyn would have cut him out of her will or reduced his inheritance. So, unless something has happened recently and she hadn't got around to seeing a lawyer, he was in good standing with Evelyn."

"Yeah, I get it."

Brent smiled. "Look, I don't want to hold you up. The way I work is on the slow side but if anything crops up I'll let you or Greg know immediately."

"Sure. I'll do likewise. See you."

He watched her walk away for a few moments and thought to himself, *Why is it that whenever I meet a competent woman, she's married?*

Brad Aimes, the fourteen-year-old recluse, was occupying his temporary hermitage. Wearing large headphones, he typed on his laptop. He was sunk down low in an armchair to one side of the window with his legs dangling over its cushioned arm. The Art Deco room was small and intimate - a relic of the nineteen-twenties and thirties. An old floor-model tube radio stood against a wall. On top of it was a chrome-plated statuette of a leaping gazelle.

Brent came in and sat down in the armchair on the other side of the window. He said nothing and made no acknowledgement of the boy. Brent took out his cellphone and began reading something on it. He could hear music emanating faintly from Brad's headphones.

The boy looked at the man and straightened up in his chair. He looked at his screen again. His typing slowed down. After a minute, it stopped.

Brent put his phone down, reached forward, and tapped Brad's foot. When the boy looked at him, Brent pointed to the earphones. Brad pressed a key and pulled the headset down around his neck.

"When I was your age I hated everyone."

Brent picked up his phone again and leaned back into the chair in one easy movement. He started reading police reports. Brad stared at him. Seconds passed and the room was still.

"You should ask me why," said Brent who continued to read.

"Why?"

"Because no one understood me… Everyone told me what to do… Nobody loved me." The silence returned. Brad unconsciously fiddled with the cord of his headphones.

"What I did was shut everyone out… Also, I got into a lot of fights. A lot… Then someone gave me a real beating so I stopped doing that. I went further into my shell." Brent put his phone away.

"I went down inside myself because it was the only place I felt free. But there's no light or air in that place. Just endless days of the same old darkness. Do you want to know how it happened?"

"Yeah, I do."

"I was a foster-child, pushed from one home to another. My father had gone, run out on us, and my mother was not in a fit state to take care of herself, let alone me. All I wanted was for them to be back together and have a happy home. Wasn't possible. Some foster parents were okay, others did it for the money. One couple were like devils. I ran from that place. Ran from a few homes with no real idea where I was running to."

"What did you do to get out of it?" asked Brad.

"It took time… nearly two years. I hated not knowing which way to turn and just reacting to stuff. I had to change and I knew it. I caught up on the schoolwork I had missed. More importantly, I decided to play the system's game and get myself set up so that I wasn't dependant on others. I had to raise myself and counsel myself and I made a lot of mistakes but at least I was making a path forward. Do you know what I mean?"

Brad sat up in his chair and put his feet on the floor. "Kind of. *I* feel trapped. I don't think anyone likes me."

"School?"

"Yeah. I've been bullied but it's not so bad now. I'm scared to talk to anyone so I don't."

"I know how that feels." Brent looked out of the window. "I wanted friends and family. I wanted someone to talk to who would listen to me and understand. I wanted someone to guide me. Some tried, like counsellors and social services. I didn't listen to them. You can't be friends with a social worker when you think that you're just another case to them. That was a big mistake on my part. Probably the biggest I made."

"I've seen a guidance counsellor. Mom is thinking I should have therapy. I don't want to."

"There's nothing wrong with you, Brad. You just need a plan. There are all types of people who will help you decide what that plan looks like. Talk to them. Hear what they have to say. From what they offer do what works for you."

Brad nodded his head, then said. "Then there's my dad. We don't get along. He puts me down."

"Doesn't surprise me. I should think he wants only the best for you but says it in ways that sound like if you don't do what he tells you you're an idiot."

"Have you met him?"

"Not yet. When I talk with your Dad I'm going to fill him in as to how the situation stands. I'll make him see reason if I can."

"You will?"

"Yes. I'm on your side."

"Don't get me in trouble, though."

"I won't, I promise you. What you should know is that it seems some parents forever see their children at age six or eight. They never reshape or update their attitude properly or fast enough. Your dad loves you or he wouldn't bother with you. He wants you to be six still and carry you on his shoulder as he used to. You're growing up and he sees an idyllic time in his life has slipped away from him. Now you are fourteen, about the same height as your dad and you're just too heavy to lift."

Brad smiled. "What do I do? I don't like everything being like this."

"Learn to talk to people... I've got an idea!" Brent sat upright. "You like pizza, don't you?" Brad nodded. "Then give me a minute here and we'll get a couple in... and drinks with them." Brent searched on his phone and found what he was looking for. He dialled a number.

"What toppings do you like?" he asked, as the number began to ring. Brad told him.

When the order had been placed, Brent said, "I so want to see the butler bring pizza to us."

"He probably won't," said Brad. "It'll be someone else. But it would be really funny if he did." He quickly stood up and said in a plummy voice, "Pizza is served, gentlemen."

Brent smiled. "That's really good. It sounds just like him."

After pizza and a long chat with Brad, Brent was out in the corridors with a measuring tape and notebook in hand. He drew out a floor plan for both wings and, taking each in turn, measured distances between rooms and checked doors to see if they squeaked when being opened or were noisy when being closed. He was building a framework in which the theory that one of the inhabitants went to Franklin's room and administered the fatal dose of thallium might be plausible and make sense.

He had the name of the occupant for each room so he added them to his floor plan. The exercise in itself yielded no startling revelations except that only a single door had a barely noticeable and very slight squeak. What did happen to Brent was that he began to forget why he was testing doors in the first place as he began to admire the doors themselves and the mouldings surrounding them and the craftsmanship of more than a century ago.

Brent had been warned. Chloe Halliday was difficult to talk to. He was once more sitting in the library, waiting for her to arrive. The lights were off. The sun was going down and the few clouds near the horizon had turned pink. This fading December light made the room fill up with dark shadows, almost as a tank is filled gradually with water. The rays of the sun seemed also to bring out the smell of ancient books. Where the light fell on their spines it painted them in rich hues but the effect was transient, changing and diminishing all the time as the sun sank and the light failed.

He thought of it as twilight in the Brewster library and the twilight of the Brewster family itself. Unless the remaining son, Jimmie, unexpectedly produced a son, there was no Brewster left to continue the name. When the Hallidays eventually moved into the family home, what would they do? Would the books be sold, dispersed to private collections, and no longer be the unique assemblage of culture and letters that it was? Would the heiress, Sophia, insist that all remain as it is? She could afford to do so. If Sophia showed any inclination to sell off the house because of its recent association with a violent death, Brent thought he might have trouble stopping himself from telling her that she simply had to keep everything intact. He knew he had no say in the matter but he was saddened by his thoughts.

He liked old things to continue on together, in their rightful place. Once, he went to buy a painting to hang in a particular spot at his house. He found a work that was reasonably priced and seemed to be perfect for the chosen place. There were two other paintings available by the same artist. He did not need them. Because the paintings were produced by the same artist and had been together for more than fifty years, Brent could not bear to separate them. He bought all three.

At a desk, he switched on a lamp. Deciding that more light was needed, he went to the door and flipped several switches. The room was thoroughly lit now. The library became a palace of erudition filled with a rich, glowing blend of golds, browns, and reds - a store of intellect, culture, and refinement, printed over four centuries but spanning four millennia. Here were present millions of pages - the expressions of thousands of minds ready to communicate the thoughts, secrets, certainties, and uncertainties of expired ages. And in the house where this treasure trove lay, a clever murder had been committed.

Even if Franklin Brewster had read every word contained in the library, would he be alive today? Brent wondered, and then doubted it. Such wisdom as might have been gleaned had never been sought here by Franklin.

Franklin did not seek in this library for answers. He would have found them had he been teachable, but he had not even looked. Indeed, Franklin had no questions requiring answers from this place because a greedy, controlling disposition had arisen in him that isolated him from wisdom. To make money is more important than human relationships - this became his mantra. And there is no truly wise person on record as having said that such is the path to truth and enlightenment. They usually said the reverse.

He surmised that if Franklin did have, after all, one question that required answering, it would have been, 'When will mother die?' Had Franklin become impatient and intended to kill his mother to seize what he desired, only to have the plan go wrong and become the victim of his own bungling attempt? Brent, so far, had no evidence at all of this being the case and no witness had said anything to support such a hypothesis. If it could be proved, however, Franklin as both killer and unintended victim of his own actions would be the most satisfying of all outcomes: the murderer murdering the murderer. Brent wanted it to be so. He was beginning to like too many people in the family and wanted to protect them from that second calamity that would surely follow if Franklin was a victim only. He wanted to save them from the protracted torture of a trial.

"Shall we sit at the table?" asked Brent pleasantly, extending a hand towards it.

"Fine," said Chloe Halliday.

"I'm sorry to put you through more questions but it is necessary, as you can appreciate."

"Whatever. I don't mind." Chloe was a tall young woman, eighteen years old, with long black hair. Her voice was well-modulated and she wore many silver rings on her fingers.

"What did you call Franklin?" asked Brent.

"Uncle."

"Did you have a pet name for him?"

"No. I didn't see him very often."

"When you did see him, how did he behave towards you - around birthdays, and such."

"I think," Chloe gestured by extending her hand, palm upwards, moving it expressively to accentuate her words, "he remembered my birthday when I was small. After that, mom and he had arguments. There was much bad feeling between them. I don't know what the cause was."

"I see." Brent wrote in his ring-binder. From the tip of his pen flowed ideograms, shapes that encapsulated something Brent heard in the conversation and thought important. When somebody peered into his notebook, as inevitably was attempted from time to time, Brent's notations gave nothing away.

"Is that an ancient language?" asked Chloe as she watched him.

"No, it's modern - about three months old." He finished. "Sorry about that." He looked up and smiled at her. "Now, what do you feel about Franklin's death?"

Chloe composed herself. Then, slowly, she brought a hand up to her forehead, lowered her gaze, and said softly and with feeling, "It is the most horrible crime… I am sickened by it." She raised her head suddenly, her heavily-ringed hands were extended pleadingly, her face became a mask: imploring and distressed. "What person, what evil mind, could think of such a cruel method? I ask you, tell me if you know, that I may ease my mind… who is this slayer of men?"

Realizing what she was doing, Brent replied with a stern demeanour and a hard edge to his voice, "I am disadvantaged. I know not the man-slayer. Yet, I am on the hunt, like a dog. I sniff the ground here and there and, upon my oath, once finding the scent I shall wed myself to it. Then shall I remorselessly pursue my quarry 'til the slayer be brought to earth."

"That's good," said Chloe. "Usually, I get odd looks, or 'Stop it, Chloe', when I put on an act."

"I'm sure you do. I have read that you're studying drama. What methods are they teaching you?"

"Script analysis to stay true to the scene, emotional impulse, and immersing oneself in the life of the character to be portrayed. Do you act?"

"Nearly all the time. I'm of the make-it-up-as-you-go-along school. I had acting lessons, oh, ages ago and, although I thoroughly enjoyed the experience, it wasn't for me."

"I've always wanted to be an actor, ever since I was a little girl. It's my dream."

"I'm glad you're making progress towards achieving that. I hope you realize all that you want to accomplish." Brent paused. "Um, do you have any ideas as to who could have committed the murder?"

"So… it's not an outsider?"

"Doesn't look like it. I wish it were."

"Well… ah, it's so difficult. If I say I've seen something you'll go after them, won't you?"

"That's right. I'll go after them to prove innocence or guilt. I need your lead, though. The murder was premeditated. It was a heartless killing. That is what you should focus on. The temporary discomfort of a family member is little compared to the danger of leaving a murderer at large. This person may have killed before. He or she may kill again. The rest of the family is at risk, hence the police presence in the house day and night. But that can't last forever and we all need to find a quick resolution."

Chloe began nervously twisting the rings on her fingers. Brent watched her.

"I… I don't know. I overheard a part of a conversation. It came back to me when I heard that Uncle had been murdered. I can't tell you who, I just can't do that. But one said, 'What shall we do?' The other person replied, 'We have to remove him.' They stopped talking when they saw me come into the room." She looked at Brent and there were tears in her eyes and she looked wretched.

"When did this take place?"

"At the Trust Fund meeting, in early October."

"How did these two persons react when you interrupted them. Describe it as a stage setting."

"They moved… let me see… I entered Stage Right; they were standing Up Centre. One met me Centre Stage; the other moved Stage Left."

"When you spoke together, what was it you discussed?"

"Something ordinary, I think… yes… what a chore it was to attend this annual meeting, because…. Whoa! You're so tricky."

"I had to try. Don't blame me. It's the job that makes me do it. The words you heard likely were those of a commonplace conversation made pregnant with meaning by what has happened subsequently. If you change your mind, please, please, please tell me at once. As I tell everyone, I keep the information in strict confidence and only pass it to the police if it's necessary in order to catch the murderer. Will you promise to do that much?"

"I don't think I'll change my mind. If I do, yes, I will let you know."

"Complete change of topic. I would absolutely hate to see this library broken up and parcelled out. It looks so complete, so right, as it stands."

"Who's thinking of doing that? They can't do that!"

"Wonderful, wonderful. You have eased my mind. As I was sitting here, alone, I had fears, vague at first, then deepening, that the death knell of the library might be sounded someday."

"Not in my lifetime. Mom won't either. She loves this place. Though, I don't know what she thinks now after what has happened. She doesn't use the main staircase anymore."

"I see. Quite understandable. I avoid it, too. Now, if you don't mind, can I ask you about your rings?"

"My rings...? Sure." Chloe extended her hands for him to see. Brent leaned forward.

"I like that garnet," said Brent as he studied each ring carefully. "Those Celtic designs are so interesting. That's a tourmaline... jet... peridot... and what's this one, a zircon?"

"Yes, it is. I like silver... suits my budget." She laughed.

"You have done very well. You have a couple of spaces left. Why do you like to wear so many rings?"

"Each one means something to me. A couple were gifts, but when I did well at school I treated myself... that type of thing."

"Good idea. A reward and a memento at the same time."

"You're not wearing any jewellery."

"I have some. I had just taken up gardening and took off a ring I habitually wore so it wouldn't be in the way. That seemed to break the spell. I wore jewellery less and less... Now, rarely, if at all. I still very much like precious stones and the craftsmanship that goes into them."

"You should see Nana's jewellery, then. She has some fabulous pieces. There's one un-believable diamond ring... it flashes fire in any light."

"Sounds lovely. Evelyn was wearing an excellent pendant this morning that suited her perfectly."

"Nana has always dressed beautifully. She's showed me her clothes from when she was my age and up. They're gorgeous. We have often talked about where she went and what she wore for hours and hours. Nana has so many interesting stories and I curl up next to her and listen."

"Are you one of her favourites, then?"

Chloe gave a little laugh. "I guess I am. She's nice to all of us but we do get along very well."

Brent smiled. "That's very nice," he said. Chloe did not notice the wistful tone in his voice.

Chapter 7

Tuesday evening

"*E*xcuse me," said Brent quietly. "We haven't been introduced, I know, but you must be Laura Aimes." He was speaking to her from the doorway of the ground-floor study while Laura sat at a lamp-lit desk, staring at a paper in her hands. Even though Brent had been soft-spoken she still gave a small start.

"Yes, I am."

"I didn't mean to startle you. My name is Brent Umber."

"Oh, yes. Of course." Laura had difficulty collecting her thoughts. "Karen was telling me... I didn't understand... you're taking her to lunch? Is that right?"

"Only with your permission. I can explain it to you. May I sit down?"

"Yes, please do."

Brent sat down on a chair beside the desk. Laura, sitting in a high-backed swivel chair, looked like a professional consultant while Brent, sitting upright in a side chair, seemed to be her client.

"I'm a private investigator who, from time to time, assists the police in situations like the one we're in now. My focus is on finding out who is the most likely person to have committed the crime. My methods are different from those used by the detectives. They want facts and evidence. I look for nuances and traits. Our goals are the same." While he spoke, Laura was nodding her head slightly as she listened. It was a habit of hers.

"I interviewed Karen and she was very entertaining."

"Karen was?"

"Yes. I have an ulterior motive behind this luncheon date. I talk to all kinds of people about all kinds of things and many of these conversations take place in stressful or very awkward situations. It is a self-imposed requirement for me to understand what motivates the different categories of people I meet. I need to understand what drives them.

There is one category of humanity with whom I am not particularly familiar. When I was a teenage boy I found teenage girls to be thoroughly inscrutable. They mystified me then and, even now, the mystery is just as impenetrable to my mind as it ever was. I rarely meet teenage girls in the course of my investigations but the next case might be full of them for all I know. They are an alien race to me. Seeing as they walk among us, I find it necessary to learn their ways and motivations. I need to study them in the wild, so to speak. This will allow me to compare the behaviour of what I will observe of Karen and her friends with what I observe in the course of my future investigations. Strange as it may seem, I would appreciate the chance to capture and gently interrogate the three girls before releasing them back into your care. Also, I think it would be fun."

Laura stared at him. Then she burst into carefree laughter, much as her daughter had done.

"Is that the real reason?" she asked when she was sufficiently recovered.

"Yes, but there is also a second reason. My honour as an investigator has been impugned by Karen. She's unimpressed by my abilities. I'm taking a chance on you -

that you will keep my secret. I have set her a challenge. I've gambled on a hunch that her current romance will not last. I didn't tell her this. She is to tell me what my hunch is in three months time. She can't see what I'm thinking now because she undoubtedly believes that her love is forever, but she *will* see in three months when the youthful romance has ended. I may have to bribe the boy in question to clear out if it looks like I will fail. By hook or by crook I will restore my honour. She will get a decent lunch and be entertained, I hope, as will her two friends."

"I'm sure they will be entertained." Laura was smiling. "However, it looks like you understand them quite well as it is."

"Not nearly well enough and, en masse, not at all."

"Oh, why not. I'll persuade Steve to agree to it. I'll talk to the other parents, too. I will keep your hunch a secret."

"Many, many thanks. I'll let you know the restaurant, time, and date well in advance." Brent leaned back in the chair. "Tell me, what was it like to grow up in a house this big?"

"I've never really thought about that. It was normal for me… I didn't have anything to compare it to. I love the house because it's my childhood home. I suppose the thing I liked the most was that this house was its own little world, away from everything. The staff had a daily routine and it was nice to see them about. There were a few who were very good to me… even spoiled me." Laura smiled as memories came back. "It was so peaceful and reassuring… I know, I'm looking back with an adult's view of such things but there was always a sense of peace, and… oh, I don't know what… certainty, perhaps.

Mother and Father were very loving. I think I was a Daddy's girl. I used to come in here and he would be working… in this very chair. Even if he were busy, he set aside the time to sit me on his knee and watch me draw or we would play games. I must have been three or four... That is probably my earliest memory. He didn't seem to mind how often I disturbed him. I came in here earlier this evening just because this room reminds me so much of Daddy. You see this?" Laura held out the page she had been holding earlier. "That is the last thing he wrote, as far as I know."

Brent took the page. It had yellowed with age. The writing was in an infirm hand and was an invitation being extended to a friend of long-standing who lived some distance away, asking if he would like to come and stay for a few days. It had never been sent.

"Thank you," said Brent, returning the document. "I like this house. What do you think about Sophia getting it under the terms of the trust?"

"Oh, rather her than me. She wants it and I like to visit. A perfect arrangement as far as I'm concerned because I wouldn't have to tell other people what to do."

"That would be a burden if you didn't want to run such a huge house. I suppose Franklin didn't see it the same way."

"At first he didn't seem to mind. Later, it became an ugly issue. He and Sophia had a terrible argument about it once. I never understood how or when he changed."

"How was he towards you when you were young?"

"He was always so good to me. He was much older but didn't mind me following him about. I was like his shadow. When he was at college and came home for holidays, he spent time with me but, of course, he had work to do and friends to see. He was becoming a man, so he had less time for little children, not that I resented it. I was always thrilled to see him. I would watch for the car that had been sent to bring him from the station.

Once, I waited for him for two hours because the train was delayed. I fell asleep waiting. I was informed the next day that he had carried me upstairs to bed. Then, in his final year, a change came over him and he took a lot less interest in my little affairs."

"I think that's natural," said Brent.

"I suppose it is. Yet, from that time on he became more remote. Over the years he became less friendly to the point of indifference, until… until last week." Laura put her head down and began to cry. She reached for a handkerchief. It was obvious she had been crying a lot recently.

Brent had the urge to put his arm around her shoulders. "It must have been a terrible shock. His death seems to have affected you the most."

"Has it?" she pulled herself together. "Sorry about that."

"Don't apologize. I feel I might need a handkerchief as well."

Laura smiled weakly at the silly remark. "I'm the emotional one… the others are grieving, too. They don't show it. His death doesn't surprise me. I've always been aware that he was drifting away from us all and, once, it struck me that he would drift so far that it would be as bad as his death. What makes it so much worse are his last words to me. They were cruel and insulting. For no reason that I can see, he forbade me to speak to him again. This, from the boy who carried his baby sister upstairs because he loved her."

The room was quiet. Outside, in the dark, someone walked on the wet gravel driveway and the crunch, crunch of their progress could be heard.

When the footsteps were no longer audible, Brent said,

"I don't know the truth of the matter. I wonder, though, if Franklin had some type of premonition of his demise. It might be that he chose to wound you with his words to preserve you from the greater wound of grief."

"Do you think so? I might find some peace of mind if I could believe that."

"It's only a thought on my part. I have no proof. Yet, I don't see why not. Franklin may have understood that somebody was against him and that his life was in jeopardy. Even if he were not aware of that he may have known of something else that was so detrimental to him personally that he thought it best you be fully separated from him."

"Is that likely?"

"Possible, I would say. Why would he forbid you to talk to him? People's actions and words usually have a reason behind them. It seems logical, to me at any rate, that Franklin would only speak to you as he did because he felt he had a valid reason to."

"He was drunk, you know."

"Yes, he was. What sort of drunk? Talking incoherently and stumbling drunk? Looking for a fight kind of drunk? Or was it all-filters-removed drunk whereby he could function, communicate, have some reasonable, although distasteful, motive behind his words and speak them because he couldn't stop himself?"

"Oh, definitely the last condition."

"Then there was a reason for him to say what he did. A bleary, drunken, sodden reason. Nonetheless, it crossed his mind to utter certain words, he did so, and, technically, walked out of your life. You do not know why he did it. I do not know why he did it. He knew why he did it. I'm inclined to impute a good motive to his bad words, otherwise he would have been depraved to have attacked you so arbitrarily and for no reason at all."

"He was greedy," said Laura, " but, I think, no more than that... Although he has treated several women badly... I can hardly believe that of him."

"I think those instances were for different reasons entirely. You were his sister and he knew you still had a great deal of affection for him. So you see, as far as we can fathom the matter between ourselves, Franklin spoke on purpose."

"Oh, goodness. You have given me something to think about."

"I'll leave now. There are some things I have to do. Thank you for being so forthright."

"I should be thanking you. Goodnight, Mr Umber."

"Goodnight."

Chapter 8

Later Tuesday evening

*I*t was just before nine. Brent and Greg were sitting alone, eating dinner in the servants' dining room.

"This is good food," said Greg. Brent nodded. "Found anything?"

"Nothing you don't already know. Karen and Brad didn't have anything. They're in the clear."

"Well, I know *they* can't be suspects," he said in surprise.

"I'm only being thorough in my reporting. Robert is interesting. I can see *him* as a possible candidate. There is a narrow technical window of opportunity in his alibi but it is not a practical one. I consider him an 'unlikely'."

"There's something wrong with that guy," said Greg. "No record… I get the feeling he should have one."

"Struck me much the same way but I think he has reasons for acting the way he does. Aurelia - I haven't finished with her - but she's definitely a low-likelihood candidate and has a solid alibi."

"What's in this sauce? It's so rich."

"A pint of cream, I should imagine. Evelyn is my only high-likelihood candidate at the moment. She has a disciplined and thoughtful mind. She had opportunities. Her motive would be grounded in family honour and so on."

"I don't see it," said Greg. "There's that companion on hand all the time."

"Companions can be sent away on errands."

"Yes, but she was in a wheelchair."

"She can walk slowly."

"Her only real opportunity would have been at dinner with everyone watching."

"Let's discuss that. My opinion is that the dinner table, with them all seated around, is the best and worst of crime scenes. It is the best because the thallium can be introduced in a public setting and the suspicion of guilt is later spread equally among all the diners. Similarly, the murderer can actively reduce the danger of being exposed by engineering events in order to seem the least likely person to have committed the crime.

The dinner table is the worst place for the crime to occur because any slip-up or any odd behaviour on the part of the murderer will potentially be seen by multiple witnesses. Therefore, the murderer, if he or she chose to introduce thallium at the dinner table, would have to manage to do it in an anonymous way - a way that he or she could be sure would not be seen."

"I agree with what you say. How does any of that apply to Mrs Brewster?"

"Elegant Evelyn, in her finery, sits at the head of the table. She is the natural focus of attention. She is the grande dame. That is her place. She is comfortable in it. The victim, Franklin, sits at her right hand. Her wine glass is to her right. Franklin's glass is to his right. It is beyond her reach. She must reach across him to tamper with his wine. She must reach in front of him to put thallium on his plate. She will be seen. Also, she has been wheeled up to the table by Marjorie Bellingham. No chance there."

Brent resumed eating.

"Oh, you're kidding me. You've disproved your own theory."

"No, I didn't. I discussed the strengths and weaknesses of the dinner table as a crime scene. It would be the worst place for Evelyn and she would have no chance there. However, Evelyn and Franklin occupied rooms on the same floor. She walks to Franklin's bedroom when he was out, puts thallium in his glass. She then adds a half-inch of rye on top of the thallium and leaves. Later, when Franklin returns, what is the first thing he does?"

"Drinks the rye."

"Exactly. When he goes down to dinner early, no doubt with a thirst for something other than rye, Evelyn hears his door shut. That is possible - I checked. She dismisses her maid as per your reports and returns to Franklin's room. She sees the rye has gone so she washes out the glass in the adjoining bathroom. She returns to her suite and presses the button to summon Ms Bellingham to her. I think she could do it in under three minutes per trip.

I experimented with a similar set-up and by walking slowly. A four-minute gap between the maid's departure and Ms Bellingham's arrival is all but a continuous alibi and the gap is small enough to be made to disappear. The maid's witness report states she left at about ten to seven. She also saw Franklin in the corridor ahead of her. Ms Bellingham says she arrived at 6:52 p.m. by her watch because she was expecting a summons any moment. Evelyn says she rang the bell immediately after the maid left the room."

"Possible... the way you put it."

"I need to talk to Marjorie Bellingham before you question her again. It's too late now but I'll see her first thing tomorrow."

"Okay. Remember, it was Bellingham who sat on the deceased's right at dinner. What about the others?"

"I can't say anything about Sophia just yet. I warn you, I've sworn myself to secrecy with a couple of people. Franklin has done something bad, probably criminal. I don't know what it is. I can guess but, until she tells me, I can't work it into the picture."

Greg puffed out his cheeks and blew out deeply.

"I know you find it annoying. I'm sorry, but I have to earn people's trust first. If I have to give my word, I will keep it. I tell them all that if the information they've given leads to the murderer I will use it. If it doesn't, I will tell no one."

"Very well. It's the reason why you're here. Brent, I'm forever in your debt but I have to run the investigations the way I'm supposed to. You understand that?"

"I do. Let's not talk about debts again. Anyway, Sophia has more to tell but I haven't got near it yet. Also, I have to talk to her about the library."

Greg shook his head disbelievingly and smiled. He had worked with Brent on three cases in the past - one being his own case - and knew the private investigator's methods, which were not his methods. He well understood that Brent blended personal interest with his casework. It went against the grain.

"Aurelia… I can't fit her in anywhere. She has a weak alibi but the stress over her studies is real enough. Very low likelihood. Laura is a different case. Her character proclaims her innocence but she had two motives - money and a sense of injury over what Franklin said to her. She could commit the crime - plan it, and so on - but it is so unlikely. Her grief is real. It has no taint of being remorse over her killing her brother. It would be so far out of her character. She had opportunities - they all did. If she is the murderer she has fooled me completely."

"Who else did you see?"

"Chloe was the only other one. If this crime required any acting she would be the prime suspect. You must have seen that for yourself. She has a potential lead but she is being coy about telling me what it is. I think she chanced to hear a conversation that was about a mundane, private matter that she has made more of than she needs to. Besides, if there were anything in it, we would then need to look for two murderers and not just one. I hope to get to the bottom of it through other avenues. She inadvertently narrowed down the field before she spotted what I was doing. She called me tricky. That wasn't very pleasant."

"You *are* tricky."

"I know but to be called out on it by an eighteen-year-old makes me think I need to overhaul my technique."

"We have to start another round of interviews tomorrow. I don't want to crank up the pressure just yet. Who do you want to see next?"

"Ms Bellingham, as I mentioned. Jimmy Brewster and Merrell Fortier… for some unknown reason I wish to see them together. What do you think?"

"Might get something extra."

"Yes… I'll try it. Then Mike Halliday, Steve Aimes, and a further meeting with Sophia. Then Lloyd, who stands alone. That will probably be the lot. I'll get to the staff and do follow-ups Thursday. Probably, an all-nighter Thursday to put it all together… I should be finished on Friday unless there's some outside work to be done."

"The funeral is on Thursday."

"Oh. In my zeal to look like a productive asset to the police, I had forgotten all about that. I'll have to rearrange my schedule. Are you attending the funeral?"

"Yes, in a discreet manner."

"Mind if I tag along in your car? I can be discreet sometimes. Also, my old Jeep won't look right in a funeral procession."

"Sure. You know, I can't believe that old death-trap is allowed on the roads. The traffic police should look into it."

"They probably will one day. Before he writes the inevitable ticket I will merely say that I know Lieutenant Greg Darrow. At the mention of your name, the officer will give a smart salute and apologize for bothering me."

"Buy a new vehicle. It's not just you on the roads."

"To reassure you, I have just had the brakes and steering done, at tremendous cost. I love my Jeep. My mechanic, Boris, is an artist. He assures me that it is as good as new. Anyway, I can't afford a new vehicle on the irregular income the police department pays me. All this is more of a labour of love hobby with me."

"Okay," said Greg, getting up from the table. "I have a report to finish off. I'll see you tomorrow. Where are you staying?"

"I booked a room for the night. I have some reports to write up, too, so I had better be going."

They left the dining room together. Greg went to the office; Brent decided to wander around the house before leaving. He switched on lights in dark rooms. He found the ballroom and discovered it was an ornate work of art by which he was immediately transported to a different age, one filled with dancing figures. Musicians playing, the rhythmic sweeping motion of elegant black-clad men accompanying brilliantly dressed women across the polished wooden floor, the soft light from three chandeliers bathing all in a golden glow - this marvellous sight is what he imagined had so often transfigured the now empty room.

From there, he went to the large dining room. This space was in the style of a baronial hall and a good-sized one at that. There were three tables spread out - two long parallels for the lesser lights and a shorter one, at right angles, for the seating of visiting dignitaries and senior family members. Impressive though the space was, Brent found it possessed a forbidding character, particularly in its now empty state. He would change the room if he owned the house. He found it odd that if this hall was the inspiration for the naming of Hill Hall, it was also his least favourite feature of the house. It unexpectedly crossed his mind that it should be converted into spaces for disadvantaged people.

From there he went to the small dining room. This room he found pleasant and well-appointed in an old fin de siècle way. He tried to recreate the scene of the previous week. The diners, seated at the table, came to his mind as shadowy and unformed, even though the room was bright. Staff stood back discreetly against the walls, watching the table like hawks, ready to assist a guest, refill the half-empty glass of wine or water, remove the empty dish within seconds of the food being eaten, asking if more of something was required. The diners were under continuous scrutiny while they sat. Their progress through the dinner was marked very carefully by the staff. It seemed impossible that thallium could have been thrown onto food or dropped into a glass without the action being noticed.

To Brent's mind, one person was well lit by clear light in vivid contrast to the semi-formed figures that surrounded her. It was the matriarch, Evelyn. She shone. She even looked radiant and happy. "Why is that?" he wondered aloud. He had no answer for himself.

He went to the foot of the stairs and stood next to the place where Franklin had come to rest. All marks of the tragedy had been erased. Brent looked at the topmost stair. It was a long, hard flight down. The autopsy had revealed that Franklin had received head injuries - severe enough to be fatal if not attended to immediately. The cause of death on the certificate, however, was thallium poisoning.

"Speak to me, Franklin," said Brent softly. "Why did you throw yourself head-first down the stairs?" The private investigator had already made an observation, in the form of two questions, in the report that he had started. He had written, 'Was it the pain? Or did he feel he needed to ensure his own death in case he might be revived?'

Brent left Hill Hall for the night but not before switching on the great chandelier that he had so admired earlier. He looked like a child gazing up at the blazing light. He switched the light off and, having gone out, shut the door quietly behind him. A patrol car, with two officers sitting in it, was parked outside. He waved to them and they waved back.

He climbed into his Jeep. When he drove away down the gravel drive, the car sounded a bit noisier to him than usual. He was disturbing the peace of the place. Brent thought, *I must get the exhaust system fixed when this case is over.*

Chapter 9

Hill Hall, Wednesday, 7:30 a.m.

*T*he weather had turned colder. The dusting of snow that had fallen overnight had been scooped into piles by the gusty wind. Yesterday's puddles had turned to ice. There was a single media vehicle outside on the road with nobody inside. Brent pulled up to the gate which slid open for him after a delay of a few seconds. As he passed the gatekeeper's house he saw an empty patrol car parked among the vehicles next to it. Brent smiled to himself. Everyone was sheltering from the cold.

Today, he entered through a side entrance of the house that was closer to the office. Greg Darrow was already there with the officer who had been protecting the premises overnight and was now signing out from his shift.

When they were alone, Greg told Brent that the detective who had been detailed to investigate the Sadler-Creme factory would be finishing up today.

"He's found out a lot but most of it is not of great value," said Greg. "The record-keeping controlling the thallium looks in order. We'll get the report later. However, it was no secret that the deceased had had a long-term affair with a married woman working at the company. She left a couple of years ago. There is also a vague rumour of a more recent incident that occurred about four months ago. A female employee in her mid-twenties was connected to an as yet unknown extent with the deceased. They were seen together outside of the office. She left suddenly and many at the factory believe that Brewster's lawyer paid her off and had her sign a non-disclosure agreement. She wasn't paid out of company funds."

"I wonder which way that should be interpreted," said Brent. "Is it Franklin the villain or is it that the young woman had incriminating evidence and wanted a payout? Maybe it's a blend of the two. Will you follow up?"

"Yes, both women will be contacted. The latter is too important to leave out but I can't see where it would fit in."

"Neither can I. You never know, though." Brent took out a USB drive from his pocket and gave it to Greg. "You'll find my report of yesterday's activities on there. There's also a grid of the potential suspects with their relative strengths and weaknesses as to their ability, opportunity, and motive to commit murder. I'll update that daily."

"Thanks." Greg took the drive to copy the data before returning it.

Although early and prepared for the day, Brent could not get started on any interviews until the members of the household were in a fit state to be interviewed. He felt great urgency to talk to them but there was no *real* urgency within the larger scheme of the police investigation. The leisurely pace at which the household was washing, dressing, and eating irked him. He wanted them to get a move on. They, on the other hand, having little to do and nowhere to go, were behaving as though they had all the time in the world. While he was forced to wait, Brent decided to poke about a little at Hill Hall so he could at least give the appearance of being an investigator.

In such a beautifully appointed house it was easy for him to become forgetful of the actual reason for his presence. In the lounge, Brent studied a massive painting by George Inness, dated 1882. The title on the discreet brass plate declared the obvious - 'Harvest in the Valley.' Brent looked long at the captivating painting. It was set in a shallow, glowing valley of ripe golden fields with, scattered through it, a few small figures of people and animals, working together to bring in a grain harvest. The panoramic, late-afternoon scene had to have been glorious in its day. Inness' smooth brushwork and use of a rich palette of colours had captured its essence. Brent was seeing what the artist had seen and, appreciating Inness' choice of beautiful view, was enjoying his careful and loving attention to making the vista come alive on the canvas.

Turning from the painting, Brent scanned the lounge and thought over the scene that had occurred here when Franklin was last seen alive by the family. It was difficult to imagine how a murderer, harbouring such dark intentions, could stand before such a bright and glorious depiction of innocent endeavour.

It was a supremely beautiful house and a hideously ugly crime. With a final thought and wish that he had been present himself in the lounge that fateful night to witness the interplay between the various people, he left the room to go and 'investigate' elsewhere.

In a hallway on an upper story, Brent stopped by a leaded glass casement window. As with everything else he examined in the house, the quality and design were exceptional. In this instance, it was the elegance of simplicity that attracted his attention. He ran a finger along the gently curving handle. Looking through the old glass of the lights, Brent had a slightly distorted view of an asphalted parking lot beyond which lay lawns and mature trees. Further away, the disorderly fringe of a leafless forest marked where the hill began to descend. In the distance were more hills. Brent thought that George Inness would not choose today to paint this scene.

Looking over the cars parked below, Brent began wondering who in the house owned each of the vehicles. While he was looking, he saw a man appear - heading towards a new, red Camaro. It was Robert Halliday. He had his bags with him. Brent thought over the possible reasons for him to have to leave early. The Brewster family had elected to stay put to accommodate the police in their inquiries. Now, Robert Halliday had decided against staying and was already getting into the driver's seat of his car.

At first, Brent sympathized with Halliday's desire to be gone but then decided he needed to know the reason for the man's early departure. Had something happened? More as a knee-jerk reaction than anything, Brent determined he would find out. He ran down the stairs and, stopping only long enough to get his jacket and bag, went quickly to his Jeep. Halliday was already part way down the long drive. He, more so than Brent the day before, was treating the long stretch of private road like a race-track.

By the time Brent got out on the road the Camaro had rounded a bend and was out of sight. Having come this far, Brent drove on in the direction he had seen the car take. He knew it to be likely that Halliday was heading home or to work. Home for Halliday was the other side of Newhampton while the car dealership at which he worked was nearer but not by much.

It crossed Brent's mind to question himself why exactly he felt the need to chase down Halliday. It struck him that either the guy was guilty and was making a run for it or else he was just being innocently foolhardy. But, there again, if innocent, why would he bolt and draw attention to himself in this way? When the Brewsters were all staying put, one of them leaving suddenly would be bound to raise questions. The singular action would draw attention and look suspicious. Halliday surely had to realize this and yet he had gone anyway.

Brent sped along and within a few minutes the road changed from a winding single lane to two straight lanes travelling past suburban sub-divisions, gas stations, and small plazas. The volume of traffic gradually became much heavier. Closely spaced traffic lights appeared with regularity. At first, Brent made it through two green lights. A red light brought him to a halt. Being at a slightly higher elevation, Brent could see a red car also stopped two traffic lights ahead. He was almost sure it was Halliday's car. There was nothing to do but wait for the lights to change which they soon did. As he began moving again, the light changed to green for the red car, too. Almost immediately it pulled off the road and into what proved to be a small plaza. This pleased Brent greatly - as long as it also proved to be the correct vehicle.

Halliday's car was parked outside a coffee shop, a clean and comfortable place without any pretensions towards upmarket ambience. The prosaic choice to stop for a coffee seemed to dissipate some of the suspicion Brent had been attaching to Halliday's actions. However, when Halliday, now seated at a table, caught sight of Brent entering the restaurant, he did not look pleased to see him. Brent ordered a coffee at the counter.

"Do you mind if I join you?" asked Brent as he approached the table.

"Like, what is this? You followed me… why?"

"Your leaving suddenly looked suspicious to me." Brent sat down. "Did you tell anyone where you were going?"

"No. It's no one's business but my own."

"Well," said Brent, "it's your business and it's my business. So, why did you leave?"

"Look, Umber, you said some things that made sense yesterday but that doesn't make you my babysitter."

"That's true. But I do think you need one. Have you considered the optics of your behaviour? I have no idea what the police will think of it. Maybe they haven't noticed yet but, when they do, they'll ask you why you left without notifying them."

"I don't *have* to notify them. I'm not under arrest. I can do what I want."

"Yes, but the police are very sensitive to being snubbed. They're kind of touchy about it and, at the moment, they'd really like to arrest someone."

"I didn't do it and so I have nothing to worry about."

"That's true. You have rights and you're exercising them. You're also wasting their time because they now have to look into *why* you left abruptly. The whole family is playing along nicely and you don't want to join in. That breeds questions - especially when you left in such a hurry. How fast were you going down the driveway? And you had to be moving along pretty quickly the whole time. I know I did to keep up with you."

"I like driving fast."

"I understand but the police have strong views on that, too. Luckily, you didn't get a speeding ticket but you were well over the limit more often than not and, when you weren't, it was because commuter traffic was holding you up. Are you running away?"

"*No,*" said Halliday emphatically and with a pained expression. He stared hard at Brent before turning his head slowly to look out of the window. "It's the house. I don't fit in… kind of like it rejects me. It was fine when I was a kid and I used to brag to my friends about going there. They didn't believe me at first. When they did understand that my family had this big, important house, then I was treated differently. You can't win. How come I'm telling you all these 'poor me' stories?"

"Maybe this is the first chance you've had to tell them. I wouldn't make too much of it anymore. It's in the past and you'd probably do better to address current issues which, I'm sure, can be fixed easily enough. Why did you leave?"

"Look, I didn't do it but somebody did. I got to thinking about it… You suspect me but you probably also suspect mom and dad… I'd prefer it if you'd suspect me and leave them out of it. Dumb, eh?"

"On one level, yes. On another, not really." Brent sipped some coffee. "This is quite good."

"Yeah, this place is part of a small chain. There's one I go to regularly near the dealership."

"Okay… What do you want to do now?"

"There's no point in my going back."

"No, I suppose not."

"Do you believe me?" There was a slight clipped compression in the way he spoke which suggested he was still adversarial.

"I've heard what you've had to say and I don't disbelieve you. At best, you're a long-shot as a suspect. I have to talk to everyone first and see who fits in where. Believe it or not, I want you to be innocent. You say you are. I don't know that yet for a fact. If our roles were reversed, what would *you* think of *me*?"

"Huh, I don't know. That you're acting like an idiot but you couldn't possibly have done it?"

"Right. Who did kill Franklin?"

"Well, I'm not going there."

"Fair enough. But I have to because it's my job. Anything that looks exceptional or interesting I have to chase down and categorize one way or another. That's why I'm here drinking coffee with you."

"But don't you go by alibis and evidence."

"Of course, I do. You have an alibi. It's been checked - it's probably *still* being checked. That's police business and I'm not needed for that. My job is just to gain some insight the police might not be able to achieve.

I'll put the process to you plainly. Until the police arrest someone you are a suspect. Before that occurs, I will rank everyone - from the least to the most motivated to have murdered Franklin, alibis not withstanding. I don't have a big career in murder investigations but, so far, it has worked out that, by the time I've finished what I do, I know who the murderer is. Proving it - that's up to the police."

There was a long silence while Robert digested what he had heard.

"Outside of the family everyone calls me Rob." He extended his hand.

Brent shook hands with him. "Pleased to meet you, Rob."

Chapter 10

Wednesday morning continued

*O*n the return journey, Brent reflected that Rob Halliday had given away something. If he were indeed as innocent as he claimed to be, then his motivation to leave and draw attention to himself meant that he believed his parents capable of murdering Franklin. Sophia sprang to his mind as the most likely candidate of the two - if they were not in collusion. Sophia had her secret and Brent needed to know what it was.

By the time Brent arrived back at Hill Hall, the household had breakfasted and were variously going about the business of whiling away the rest of the morning. Brent had first summoned Marjorie Bellingham away from her duties. They were now in a sitting room where they could not be overheard. This room, Brent decided, had to be the most comfortable in the house. The grey-green overstuffed armchairs were a delight to sink into. He sank back into his while Ms Bellingham sat on the edge of hers. She did not look comfortable in any sense. Ms Bellingham, 38, was evidently a well-educated woman and had no criminal record. She seemed, on paper at any rate, to have enjoyed a quiet, uneventful past and to be likely to continue to do so. She lived at Hill Hall.

"This is a terrible business," said Brent. He paused for a while. "The family will be badly hurt by this for a long time."

"I can't imagine they will ever recover," said Ms Bellingham. Her face was taut and she fidgeted with her hands.

"If it can be settled quickly and completely the healing process can begin." Brent sat forward in the armchair. "Would you mind if I call you Marjorie?"

"Um, no. Please, do."

"Then, Marjorie, you must call me Brent. Agreed?"

"Yes."

"Good. You know, I imagine that it is very difficult for you at present. Every other person in the house has someone to talk to... someone they can confide in. Do you have anyone?"

"Not a friend as such. There are people here, the staff you know, who I'm friendly with and we talk... a little bit, anyway. I don't know what I'd do without social media."

"That's good. How are you coping personally?"

"Holding it together... and that's about all. It helps I'm attending to Mrs Brewster. I can focus on her and forget what I'm feeling."

"Ah, because she's Franklin's mother, of course."

"Yes. She really is an admirable woman."

"In what way? I don't disagree with you at all. I'm only curious as to what you mean exactly."

"Well, she's not showing her grief in public. You might have observed that. In private, she's had some very distressing moments."

"I see. Yes, she would be like that. It must be very hard to keep up appearances. I'm not sure I could do it."

"Neither could I. I would run... far away and break down completely."

"Where would you go? A desert island or a mountain top retreat?" asked Brent.

"Oh… I hadn't thought that part through… I was only speaking generally."

"I think I would go to a desert island. For me, the main attraction of a desert island is that it doesn't seem to involve any work - at least, that's how I imagine it. You only have to walk leisurely along the shore and get fruit from the trees and fish from the sea. Whereas you do have to climb a mountain and carry things up with you to get to the retreat."

"Surely, you have to get to the desert island, too. I always thought that meant a shipwreck or a long voyage." As she said this, Marjorie looked quite serious.

"I suppose it does. Looks like there is work or calamity even in Utopian dreams."

"I can't imagine not working. I would go insane not doing anything."

"Really? You're probably right but the thought of a few weeks of total inactivity and warm weather is very enticing to me in this December gloom."

"A holiday is different because it is finite. I think, if I ran away, it would be to an old-fashioned farm deep among green, rolling hills."

"I like that idea. It would be so neat. With cows in the fields and horses. Oh yes, there would have to be horses. They are so noble."

"Yes, they are. I'd want a flock of geese, a few ducks, chickens, and a goat. The thing that impresses me most about a farm is the predictable routine. I could just do the work and clear my mind in the fresh country air."

Brent did not say that farm-work was probably far more exacting than Marjorie realized. Instead, he said, "Where would Evelyn Brewster want to go to? I should ask her."

"I wouldn't do that."

"No? All right, I won't ask her. She probably wants to tough it out, anyway."

"I think she does. She recovered very quickly from her… anguish."

"Anguish. Did she feel anguish when she saw Franklin's body?"

"Yes. I went to see what the commotion was about. Several of the others were coming out of their rooms. I got to the gallery. As soon as I saw him lying there I froze on the spot. Franklin was lying in a pool of blood. It looked… it looked…"

"Ridiculous?" Brent moved a little further forward.

"Yes, that's it. That is exactly it. I didn't move for about a minute. I knew he was dead but I was also half-expecting him to stand up again. Then I seemed to come to my senses and I rushed to Mrs Brewster's suite. I was the one who told her. I said Franklin had fallen down the stairs and was badly hurt. She insisted on seeing him."

Brent nodded his head.

"I knew he was dead but I couldn't bring myself to blurt it out right there and then."

"No, I couldn't do that, either," agreed Brent.

"So, I thought I would say it little by little to lessen the shock of the news. Only, I think my face told a different story. She caught on immediately. 'He's dead, isn't he?' she asked. I couldn't stop myself. I burst into tears. I managed to reply, 'I think so'. She didn't cry, not then. Nor when she saw him… although I could tell it hit her hard. Later, as the dawn came, I overheard her dreadful sobbing. I went in to see if I could help but she sent me away. She managed to pull herself together but it was heartbreaking to hear while it lasted."

"Marjorie, after you first spoke with her," asked Brent, "did anyone else talk with Mrs Brewster?"

"Jimmy came in first, followed by Sophia. Mr de Sainte Croix came to her suite later to say that the police were on their way. He was very gentle towards Mrs Brewster. She was still too upset and sent them all away. I tried to sit with her but she told me to leave, too."

"I should imagine that Laura Aimes took Franklin's death very hard."

"I heard she was angry... angry with Franklin. I don't know why she should be like that."

"It does seem unusual. There's probably a reason behind her behaviour. I take it her husband stayed with her to calm her down."

"I think he did... I'm sorry, I can't seem to remember that night very well... only pieces, jumbled together. We all thought Franklin had had an accident."

"Of course, that would be the natural assumption. I know Mike Halliday was with the butler seeing to things and waiting for the police to arrive."

"I don't know."

"When it came out that Franklin had been poisoned, how did Mrs Brewster take that news?"

"She was horrified."

"Over the fact of it being murder or the painful way he died?"

"Both. They both hit her hard. Then she seemed to recover and become all stoical again. She's been like that ever since. Mrs Brewster feels the pain of her loss, I know she does; I see the sorrow in her eyes, but she's not bowing down under her burden."

"I like her spirit. I wish I had a fraction of it. How is she towards you now?"

"Much the same as ever. Mrs Brewster doesn't take me into her confidence - she never has. Sometimes she asks my opinion about ordinary things but yesterday, out of the blue, she asked me who I thought the murderer was."

"What did you answer?"

"I said I had no idea who it could be. I still don't. Not really."

"Not really? Yes, I think if I were in your circumstances it would be apparent that someone had to have poisoned Franklin. Like you, I would not be able to stop myself from thinking who it might be."

"It's too awful to think it was someone in the house… in the family."

"It is awful. The police are doing their best to get past this stage. We *must* get past this stage or there will not be a Brewster family left. If you are aware of anything that might make matters clearer, I beg you to tell me. If you have any useful information it will be a great help. And don't worry that your suspicions might convict the wrong person. Suspicions don't convict; only hard factual evidence can do that. The police do not want a conviction only. They want to convict the murderer and have him or her removed to a place where no further harm can be done."

"I know that. I know you are right."

She leaned back in the armchair and was quiet for a few minutes. Brent leaned back also and looked out of the window. He was aware she was coming to a decision.

"It's Jimmy," she said. "I have heard, you can't help hearing sometimes, that he's in financial difficulties. I don't know how Franklin's death benefits him directly… though it does in the long run. Just knowing that about Jimmy has made me look at him differently. I can't help it. Since the murder, he's been strange - quite nervous and distracted." She breathed a long sigh. "I hope I've done the right thing by confiding in you."

"I say that it is the right thing. I'll be talking to him later and I'll draw my own conclusions. If Jimmy is nervous I will see that straight off. I might have put his anxiety down to his being questioned. Some people inevitably get jumpy. You have told me how long he has been nervous. That will save valuable time. What about Merrell Fortier, though? How does she seem to you?"

"Ms Fortier? I'm not sure… I've only met her once before." A wary tone had crept into her voice.

"That's good. If you compare Ms Fortier's demeanour on her first visit to how she has conducted herself over the last few days, what would you say was different?"

"I have never really spoken to her outside of a few conventional interchanges. She looks the same. I haven't noticed any difference."

"How does she strike you, generally speaking?"

"I think she is after money. She's not Jimmy's type. I had better not say any more."

"Oh, I see. She doesn't fit into a place like this. I saw her, from a distance, and I got the distinct impression she was a visitor, untouched by what has happened. It was only an impression. I should imagine that Mrs Brewster is not overly pleased with Jimmy's choice in partners."

"Mrs Brewster likes Jimmy very much. She hasn't confided in me at all but she is only ever very formal towards Ms Fortier. I think that is all I can tell you."

"Quite right, too. I'll chat with both of them and find out what's going on there."

"I don't quite understand what it is you do. You're not like the police."

"I'm a private investigator hired by the police. They mainly sift through facts, criminal records, and psychological profiles. I sift through conversations. Once in a while, I'll measure a footprint or examine a fingerprint but the police are so much better organized than I am to do that kind of work."

"Do suspects give themselves away?"

"Hardly ever. What I find is that people's words usually include unintentional limiting factors or directional cues. They don't inadvertently say, 'I did it'. Often, people want me to believe the lies they tell me. It can be anything from a white lie to complete fabrication. One of my jobs is to break through the brittleness of falsehood. Some are tougher than others. You have told me the truth."

For the first time, Marjorie laughed. "I'm glad you said that. I would hate to think you had a bad opinion of me."

"Far from it. You have been very helpful. Look, if you need someone to talk to, not necessarily about the case, just to talk, I'm ready to listen. However, right now, I have others to see and I need to get a lot done today. So, please excuse me. Oh yes, and give my regards to Mrs Brewster."

Chapter 11

Wednesday Morning

*B*rent was sitting at a white-painted wrought-iron table at the far end of the conservatory. This long, triple-glazed room projecting into the gardens was illuminated solely by the bleak December sky. From where he sat, Brent could scan the gardens that lay in their winter dormancy. The hands of many gardeners and designers had transformed a patch of raw earth into a marvel of flowering green life and pleasing vistas. As Brent looked, the winter gardens only suggested these glories that would once again be achieved when the weather was warmer. The strong, symmetrical lines of the well-laid garden could easily be distinguished but the colour and life had long since drained away from the scene. There were now only faded grasses, snow-dusted trees, greys and muted browns under a ragged, dirty white sky that looked cold and dreary - a cheerless day. It was an empty flagpole of a scene with no bright banners flying.

The absurdity was that Brent was in the moist warmth of the conservatory. All he had to do was reach out and touch the deep orange bell-shaped flowers of a Correa Pulchella. In front of the glass wall, a bed of hyacinths was about to blossom. As he looked back to the house he had the long shot of the conservatory's interior and could see a brick floor laid out like parquet - satisfyingly wet with recent watering. On either side were palm trees, azaleas, and groups of poinsettias. From where he sat, the cacti were hidden from view. The air was full of a rich combination of scents but the most notable was lemon. The well-shaped, five-foot-high lemon tree was covered in bright yellow fruit and, there and then, Brent decided he wanted, no, definitely needed, a conservatory of his own with a lemon tree in it. The potted tree alone defeated all the sad effects of winter to be seen outside.

The conservatory project was now burgeoning in Brent's mind. He was happily including orange trees and fig trees in the picture and was beginning to debate where they should be placed when he suddenly remembered Eric. His gardener would need to be consulted and probably wooed to warm up to the idea. He, Brent, would even go as far as giving up the Cosmos he wanted and accept the Rozanne of Eric's choice if only Eric would yield on the placement of the conservatory. The problem was, even Brent could see, the garden was fast becoming crammed with features. Also, Brent well knew that his gardener was highly resistant to new ideas unless they were his own.

From his seat, deliberately selected for the purpose, Brent watched as Merrell Fortier and Jimmy Brewster approached. They soon realized that he was staring at them hard. She was self-assured under his gaze with something like a smile on her face. He, it appeared, was trying to be nonchalant but came off as slightly awkward. She was tall and walked with an easy grace. He was taller but hunched over so they were effectively the same height. Jimmy also hung back a little behind her but it was not clear whether this was due to his manners, to let a woman go first, or to a reluctance to meet Brent.

Brent stood up and gestured towards two chairs he had arranged so that there was quite a gap between the occupants.

"Thank you for meeting me here. I have some difficult questions to ask you both. Please, be seated."

The investigator took out his ring binder and began to write something in it. He held it at an angle against the edge of the table so only he could see what was on the page. He looked up when he had finished but kept the binder in place and pen in hand. He waited before speaking - waited overly long.

The woman was expensively dressed and well-groomed but in a way that made it obvious that she wanted to be noticed. Her tan was too deep and even to be natural and she wore a lot of expensive gold jewellery.

Merrell waited calmly, sitting still in the silence of the conservatory for the questions to come. Jimmy was restless - his jacket suddenly did not seem to fit him properly. It was apparent by his discomfiture that he wanted to get on with the questioning.

"Mr Brewster, did you murder your brother Franklin?" asked Brent flatly.

"What...? No, I didn't!" answered Jimmy.

"You look like you're hiding something," continued Brent. "This is a murder investigation. I naturally assumed you must be the murderer."

"No... no!"

"What Jimmy would like you to know," said Merrell in the breathy voice of a telephone recording giving instructions to a would-be customer, "is that he is so, so upset by his brother's death that he can hardly sleep. He is very sensitive. Can you be a little sensitive, too, please?"

"I'll try. Do you want to call a lawyer, Mr Brewster, or will Ms Fortier speak for you?"

"I don't need a lawyer. I can speak for myself."

"Good. The way I work it out is that both of you could have committed the murder. My chief concern is to find out if either one of you did it alone or if you worked it together. Of course, you might both be innocent."

"I don't believe you're a police officer," said Merrell. "We do not have to answer any of your questions no matter how insulting they might be."

"That's true." Brent nodded. "Let's fix that now." Brent punched a number on his phone. They all waited in silence until the call was picked up. "Hello, Lieutenant Darrow? It's Brent Umber speaking. Please send an officer immediately to the conservatory as Mr Jimmy Brewster is having difficulty answering my questions and I would like an officer present to hear what he has to say… You will…? Thank you." Brent terminated the call. "Someone will be here in a few minutes. Please call your lawyers if you wish to have them present. I will have my questions answered to my satisfaction no matter *who* is or is not present."

Complete silence prevailed in the warmth under the glass with the winter sky overhead. Brent took up his pen and began doing something in his binder. Although Brent did not look up from his work, he could tell that Merrell was signalling to Jimmy to remain quiet by subtle gestures with her eyes and by head movements. Then she spoke, saying,

"Mr Umber, sometimes you catch more flies with honey than with vinegar."

Brent looked up, and replied indifferently, "That's true. As a rule, I don't like killing any creature. However, I find that boric acid is best to deal with cockroaches. Roaches hide in dark places. You have to get at them somehow."

He resumed his work, forestalling any answer. He sensed Merrell was very irritated. Jimmy was on the point of giving an angry rebuke. Merrell stopped him with a quick wave of her hand as though pushing him away.

Detective Alice Bates walked into the conservatory. Brent looked up as she approached but made no further acknowledgement. He closed his binder. Merrell and Jimmy turned round to see who was approaching.

"Good morning. I'm Detective Bates." She pulled up a chair to the table. Once she was settled she took out a notebook and a pen.

"Thank you for sitting in, Detective Bates," said Brent. "Maybe we can get somewhere now."

"Now we're all cozy," said Merrell, smiling, "I think we should have a recording of our conversation."

She pulled up an app on her phone and then set the device down in the middle of the table.

"An excellent idea, Ms Fortier," said Brent. "We will be able to use that in court. What do you say, Mr Brewster? Are you comfortable being recorded and possibly having it used against you?"

"I haven't done anything criminal. So, I'm okay with it." He had composed himself and looked ready enough, better than he had done when he first sat down.

"Good. So, if you have your answers ready, here we go." Brent used his phone to bring up the signed witness statements of both Fortier and Brewster. He systematically went through these, asking questions of each of them by turns. There was a certain rhythm to the process. Brent read a small section, asked if it were true, the answer coming in the affirmative every time. Fortier and Brewster were comfortable with this.

Four turns in, Brent changed tactics. He now asked them to describe something they had stated previously and compared the answer to what was written. Any time there was a small inconsistency he brought them up short. The inconsistencies were invariably minor in nature but the strain was beginning to tell on the couple. Fortier was doing well, controlling herself. Brent, of course, noticed she grit her teeth a couple of times - usually while Brewster was replying. Jimmy Brewster was perspiring. His hands were trembling and he deliberately kept them out of sight. Brent, of course, noticed this. Slowly, Brent was coming to the end of both their statements. With the end in sight, Brewster got control of himself once more. The remaining sections in the statements left to be reviewed were those concerning their going to bed and when they awoke, along with the rest of the household, at the time of Franklin's death.

"I want to go back over something in here. Something doesn't seem right to me. No, it does not look right at all." There was a long silence. Brent broke it by saying,

"Mr Brewster, when you were in the lounge after dinner, why did you not speak to your brother, Franklin? It was the last time you would see him alive." Brent was deliberately being as obnoxious as possible.

"You know we argued earlier. We've been over it again and again."

"So you did. Why didn't you say goodnight to him even as a common courtesy?"

"Look, I told you already. We… had… a… fight."

"That's right, you did. Even though you had a fight, why didn't you speak to him?"

"I didn't want to," said Jimmy in an exasperated tone.

"Why?"

"Look, what is it with you? I was angry… Is that what you want to hear?"

"It's closer… but not good enough. You were up to something. I think you murdered him. I mean, what else should I think? You left the room to go and put thallium in his bottle of rye that stood next to his bed. It was easy enough to do."

"What?"

"You have to stop this," said Merrell. "He didn't kill Franklin."

"Then it must have been you who murdered Franklin."

"You can't talk to us like this!" Merrell became shrill. She turned to Alice. "Don't just sit there like a dummy. Tell him to stop this."

"He's only asking questions," replied Alice.

Brent interjected, "It's likely that you both planned and carried out the poisoning. Other witness reports have it that you both left the room together and two different people made a point of saying you left in a suspicious manner. For me, that makes you both chief suspects."

"We didn't do it!" hissed Merrell. She stood up. "You will pay for this. I have the recording." She glared at him and gripped the phone hard while she shook it at him.

"So you do. I'd forgotten about that. That's all for now. I'll be checking your stories for loopholes. We'll get the evidence we need."

Merrell strode away. Even the way she walked looked angry. Jimmy Brewster followed her out looking very worried.

"You were kind of harsh at the end there," said Alice. "What's it all about?"

"Oh, I don't know. They could have murdered Franklin; they may not have. What I do know is that they have done something that they wish kept quiet. She is far too controlled without being at ease and Jimmy telegraphs his guilt. I need them out of the way as suspects if they didn't do it."

"I don't think you're going to hear the last of this. She has that recording and she'll use it."

"Ms Fortier didn't get the last five minutes. The flash memory on her phone filled up. I saw when the warning light came on."

Alice thought over what he had said. "So you read through their statements to run the time out?"

"That's right. I'm so glad she didn't have a memory upgrade on her phone."

Brent opened up his binder once more to add a few notes to the bottom of the page.

"What's that?" asked Alice. "It's pretty good."

"It's a drawing of that lemon tree behind you. I drew it while I was annoying the Fortier-Brewster combo."

"It's a beautiful tree. Amazing how much fruit is on it."

"Do you like gardening?" asked Brent.

"I think I could get into it but, you know, we live in an apartment so it's just house plants. They look pathetic up against this place."

"What do you grow?"

"I have a few, like, some African violets - they're my babies. I've got a Coleus doing fine. There's a spider plant that's well out of control. It's gone kinda stringy."

"You can plant the spiderettes, while still attached to the mother plant, in separate pots   until they put down roots of their own. Once these are established you cut their stems from the mother plant. If that's too awkward to do, you can cut them off straightaway and root them in water but you have to change the water regularly and only keep the roots covered otherwise they'll rot. Also, you can divide the mother plant into two or three plants."

"How do you do that?"

"Gently pull the tubers into their obvious sections. Use a sharp knife to cut away any dead roots. Then pot them up into smallish pots with a good quality potting soil. I can bring you in a bag if you like. Spider plants make nice gifts for people if you don't want them for yourself."

"That's very good of you, thanks. I'd give them away 'cos I only want the one plant." She looked at her watch. "Oops, gotta get back to the office." Alice stood up. "I wonder what those two are up to."

"Thanks for sitting in." Brent stood up. "They did something… that's obvious. I really don't want to chase it down unless it's connected with the case. It's such a distraction."

"Yeah. I'll run a check on them again. If there's anything there I think it will be on her."

"I'll come with you. I need to take a look at the security camera footage."

Chapter 12

Later Wednesday morning

"*A*re you Brent Umber?" A large man, Steve Aimes, filled the doorway. He was one of those men who appear to be as wide as they are tall.

"Yes. Thanks for coming. Make yourself comfortable in the morning room and I'll be with you in a moment." Brent was seated at the security monitor desk in the command centre. He had been scrolling through the video from the house security cameras.

"Sure."

When he had gone, Brent asked,

"Did you find anything, Alice?"

"Jimmy's clean. For Merrell, shoplifting as a teenager is in her report and nothing since then, although her name's come up in connection with a few different things. The most serious connections were a stolen car ring about ten years ago where nothing could be proved against her and a couple of years back an insurance fraud where the money was never recovered. A guy named Eddie Symes did time for a contents insurance deal. Expensive stuff disappeared from a property owned by Symes. The payout was two hundred and seventy thousand. She was his girlfriend at the time and had been for three years. He died in prison of natural causes."

"What do you think? She got the money?"

"Oh, yeah. Looking at Eddie's record she would have been the brains of the outfit. What are you looking for in the video?"

"I don't know yet. All I'm seeing is rain, snow, and patrol officers. Very few of the family have stepped outside. Oh, what's this? Hello, Merrell. Going for a walk while it's raining?"

"Where? Let me see," said Alice.

She came over to look at the split-screen monitors. Brent scrolled the video back for Alice to see. Merrell, wearing a coat with its hood up, was on screen for less than two seconds. She was exiting through some French windows at the rear of the house.

"Run it forward," said Alice.

Brent did so. Eight and a half minutes elapsed until Merrell returned to the house, entering by the same door. It was on the night after the murder.

"What do you think?" asked Brent. "Did she know the camera was there?"

"Her? Yeah, probably. You go and see your man. I'll check it out."

Alice put on a jacket and left the room to inspect the camera at the back of the house. Brent went to the morning room next door.

"Sorry about that," said Brent as he closed the door to the morning room behind him.

"No problem." Steve Aimes had seated himself at the table. Brent sat down across from him.

"I see that you run your own construction business. I should imagine that keeps you busy."

"Oh, yes. I do custom homes and major renos. There's plenty of work."

"This delay must be causing you concern."

"No, not really. I have two good site managers who are covering for me. We can work out problems over the phone. Having said that, I need to be out of here tomorrow night. I'm seeing a client Friday morning about a new project."

"I wish you success. So, what do you think of this place?"

"This is a beautiful house. It's nice to see the fine workmanship and elegant design elements. It's very different to the work I do. But, to be honest, it's not exactly homey and I wouldn't care to live here. It's a long walk to the breakfast table in the morning."

"That's true. I think a person has to be born in this type of place to get used to servants doing things for them."

"Yeah, that isn't for me. Mind you, Laura doesn't seem to mind either way. She fits in because she grew up here, but she's very happy with our own house."

"That's good to hear." Brent paused. " Now I have to ask a few unpleasant questions."

"I know you do."

"There was a scene after dinner. Jimmy and Franklin had a spat. You were standing right there and may have had a part in it. Can you explain to me what happened?"

"I told the cops all about it. I don't mind telling you… seems most people around here have good things to say about you."

Brent thought of how Merrell and Jimmy would most certainly hold a very different opinion but said nothing.

"I speak my mind," continued Steve, "and I'm focused on business. I figured that Franklin manages a big company and knows what he's doing. Seeing as we're family I didn't see any problem or harm in telling him my ideas about growing the business. Couldn't hurt any and if I came up with a good one it would benefit the whole family. He didn't take it like that. He took it as interference. I couldn't care less what he thinks. What gets me, though, was the way he would never discuss anything. Hey, he could probably have given me pointers I could use in our company. I'd be appreciative of him just trying to be helpful. That's not how he wanted to play it. So, knowing that he didn't want to hear from me, I told him, anyway, what I was thinking just to get under his skin."

"Makes sense," said Brent. "Then this situation was of long-standing?"

"Sure it was. Some years back, while our company was growing, we had some tight situations. Cash flow wasn't great. Laura and I discussed it and we thought that if Franklin could get her a job at Sadler-Creme it would have helped us out. She asked him for a job and was willing to do anything. He turned her down flat. Said there were no openings and made a point of telling her how she had no special skills. Told her that the trust wouldn't permit it. I think he lied about that part. Anyway, the answer was no. Some brother, eh? Wouldn't do anything for his little sister. Course, from then on I disliked him. I didn't murder him, though. He didn't deserve to die like that… no one does. I can't say that I mourn his passing, though Laura's really cut up about it."

"I have heard she was angry with Franklin at the time she learned of his death."

"That's right, she was. I can't make sense of it. Turns out he told her never to speak to him again. Then someone kills him."

"Perhaps it was because she loved him so much when they were children. Then Franklin destroyed that when he spoke to her. She was angry because she could not see their old relationship ever being restored. He removed all hope of restoration. Her last memory of him was an ugly one."

"You reckon? Could be that... it kinda makes sense." Steve moved forward in his chair to rest his arms on the table. "Why did he do that?"

"I have a theory, an incomplete one, but I haven't tested it. My idea is that in some way he was protecting Laura. He wanted her to dislike him. It's a possibility that he knew he was going to die or even be murdered and so he wanted Laura to distance herself from him."

"Aw, that's too weird for me. I don't get it. Glad it's you investigating and not me."

"And I'm glad you build houses and not me. I can't imagine the mess I would make. That reminds me. I have an idea to put in a conservatory at home, just a small one."

"You got permits?"

"No, I'm only in the idea stage."

"Get those first then you'll find out what you can build. You can do it cheaper yourself if you know what you're after. You'd probably find it's best to buy a kit and have it installed. No headaches, see? Randall's does nice, quality work. Pick your design carefully and make sure it blends with the house. You don't want a Victorian-style conservatory on a bungalow, you know what I mean?"

"I do, indeed. Thanks for that."

"You're welcome."

"Now, to my questions," said Brent. "On the night Franklin died, did you notice anything that could possibly be considered as a tampering with Franklin's food or drink?"

"I've thought about that whole night. I can't say I saw anyone do anything in the least suspicious. However, I do remember that I had the feeling something was happening that I wasn't picking up on."

"Hmm, like what, for instance?"

"I don't know. That's what's bothering me."

"Could it be like you would feel if you came into a room, two people were talking about something serious - you could tell by their faces. You heard a little of it but they definitely didn't want you to know what they were talking about."

"Yeah, like that, though not the same as that. I saw Jimmy and Merrell signalling to each other with their eyes. That wasn't it, though. I think it was Evelyn. It was like she knew something but wasn't letting on. If that makes any sense."

"Yes. Impressions like that can be important."

"You don't think it was the old lady? Aw, come on."

"No, I don't. I like her but, as with everyone, I have to investigate every possibility," said Brent.

"I suppose you do… It can't be Evelyn, though. She's a great lady."

"Do you have any idea who could have committed this murder?"

"Yeah, I do but I'm not saying. I don't have evidence. I didn't see anything you would find useful so what is the point in me guessing? It would only cause trouble. I'll keep my mouth shut."

"Fair enough… fair enough." Brent got up from his chair and went over to the window. "There's something else. I don't mean to be rude, but you're running your construction business. Laura is an heiress to a considerable fortune - a huge one. How do you square those two things in your mind?"

"Easy. I'm my own man. I couldn't sit around waiting for someone to die. Besides, it's Evelyn… I hope she lives to be a hundred and ten. No, I want to get on with things - do something - achieve something. It's the right thing to do… for me, anyway."

"How did you get a start in building houses?"

"It was quite late, actually. I started out in an insurance office. Took all the courses, studied nights, and tried hard, really hard, to make a go of it. I was doing okay but I felt like I was going nowhere. I couldn't imagine staying with the same company or even in the same industry for years and years.

I had a moment, right at my desk, when I thought that I should try doing something I like - something I get satisfaction from. It came to mind that what I really wanted to do was build houses. That was it. I've always been handy with tools so I thought 'why not?' I said goodbye to insurance and started in construction the next week.

Hey, you should have seen me with my new safety boots and clean hard-hat at age twenty-seven. I must have looked dopey. Still, I got on and quickly. In a couple of years, I was supervising others and getting good work out of my crews. You gotta watch some of those guys, though. There's a few who like to do half a job for twice the price. It wasn't long after that I was out on my own with a good crew working for me."

"That's very interesting. Making a switch like that could have been difficult. What made you choose insurance in the first place?"

"It was my dad. He'd been an insurance agent since forever. He made good money and wanted me to do the same. I went along with it because it was an easy option. As a teenager, I hadn't sorted my head out yet and it seemed like I had no choice. Plus, he had loads of contacts in the industry. Looked like a no-brainer."

"Then, you'll continue running your construction company even when Laura inherits? And what about your son, Brad?"

"You bet I'll keep it running. You see, I want to leave Brad something to walk into. I don't want him trapped by easy money and he can run the construction company and earn a living. He won't have to go crazy, but I want him to be his own man."

"Oh, I can see that and it makes perfect sense. There's just one problem with it."

"A problem? Like what?"

"Supposing Brad wants to go into insurance?"

"Insurance…? Yeah, I get you. Let me think about that for a moment."

"Certainly." Brent walked to an old oil painting and examined it closely. It was an Edwardian summer scene of bathing machines and bathers on a beach by the sea. A child was sitting on top of a donkey. A boy was running with a kite. In the foreground, an infant girl, bare-footed and wearing a white pinafore over her pink cotton dress, was building a sandcastle while her elegant mother sat in a deck-chair watching her, smiling.

Steve's movement recalled Brent to the present day. He had risen and now both men were standing in front of the picture.

"I think I might have made a mistake with Brad," said Steve.

"We all make mistakes. I know that Brad wants his dad back. You want him to go into the construction industry. He might want to do that sometime. He might not. The dilemmas of being a parent, I suppose."

"Listen, I think I'll talk to him about this. I'll find out where he's at and we'll work through it together. I need to listen to what he has to say."

"That'll do it," said Brent. "He likes pizza. A sports game might be good, too."

"You spoke to him, didn't you? You got past the attitude and the headphones."

"It's my job to talk to people. Usually, you might find this hard to believe but I begin to care about the people I talk to within minutes. Brad's a good boy. He's got a good father. Only it seems that misunderstanding has come between the pair of you. Now you both know what the problem is. Remove it and it will mean you'll only annoy each other half the time instead of all the time."

"Ha, you're right." Steve's face broke into a broad, friendly grin. "It's so easy to forget what it's like to grow up. Thanks, you've done me a very good turn. I owe you one. I really do."

"I'll call it quits if you do something for me."

"Name it."

"Give Karen a message from me. Tell her, 'all clear'."

"That's it? That's too easy! I'll give her the message though I have no idea what it means -and I guess you're not about to tell me."

"That's right. It's been nice talking to you, Steve. I've butted into your family affairs quite enough but there's one thing more. If Brad has no interest in construction you can always try Karen and see what she says."

"You know, that crossed my mind the other day. I *will* see what she says." Steve suddenly looked serious. "Brent, will you please go catch the murderer? The whole family needs to find a way out of this nightmare."

Chapter 13

Wednesday around noon

When Steve Aimes had gone, after giving Brent one of the firmest handshakes he had ever experienced, Brent returned to the office and found Alice there.

"What did you discover?" he asked.

"An empty garden. Besides that, she must have known she was on camera - it's plainly visible from the door."

"Could she have missed it in the dark, I wonder...? No, she's not the type of character to make a mistake like that."

"She probably used her cell phone to see where she was going," said Alice.

"Right, yes, she would. I didn't see that on the tape... maybe she was reaching in her pocket to get it and forgot about the camera. No... no, it makes no sense. She went out for a purpose and would have anticipated the camera."

"So, Brent, are you gonna stand there and tell me we have to search that garden in this weather to find a thallium bottle?"

"I wouldn't be that cruel. Even if we found it, Merrell would have wiped it clean. How would that stand up in court?"

"An interesting fact but her defence would make mincemeat of it. She'd say she went for a walk to clear her head and that would be the end of it."

"Well, then, I'm going to do just that."

Brent was reaching for his jacket when Greg Darrow came into the room. He was obviously annoyed about something and slapped a file folder on a desk.

"What's up?" asked Brent.

Greg turned to him with a scowl on his face to say,

"That butler annoys me. He's clammed right up. If he calls me 'sir' one more time I'll scream at him. Do something useful, Brent. Get him to talk."

"Any hints?"

"He knows something but isn't talking. Family honour and all that kind of thing. We can do without witnesses who think they know best. You found anything?"

"Greg, sit down and take the weight off your feet. Let me get you a cup of coffee and a Danish to go with it."

Greg did sit down.

"What is it?" he said wearily.

"Alice and I have discovered that the Merrell and Jimmy partnership has a very serious credibility problem."

"They're lying? About what?"

"Alice has some background information on Merrell. We both think she's here with an ulterior motive."

"Here ya go," said Alice.

She handed him a paper with her findings on it. Greg read it.

"Where did she go outside?" asked Greg. "She must have seen the camera."

"That's where I was going before you arrived," said Brent.

"How can you search that garden?"

"I'm not. I'm simply going to use my little grey cells in the best tradition. I only hope I have enough of them."

"Whatever," said Greg.

Brent left the room on his mission.

"You sat in on the interview," asked Greg. "What do you think of our boy wonder?"

"Well, I know you like him," replied Alice. "It surprised me how hard he was. He went after Fortier and Brewster and didn't let up on them. Knows some tricks, too. He's good - a team player. Get him in the department."

"He wouldn't come. Likes to be independent. He does that sometimes - comes down hard on people. Most of the time he comes off as trying to be their next best friend."

"Yeah, that's what I figured. I spoke to Evelyn Brewster earlier and she asked if that nice Mr Umber was here today. Would he give her a rough time if he had to?"

"Oh, yes. If he thought she was guilty of something he wouldn't hold back."

Standing outside the back door, Brent looked up at the camera. He smiled and waved before turning away to survey in a more serious manner the 80-foot-long stone terrace. The elevated platform had three sets of steps leading from it - one at either end and one in the exact centre. The broad terrace covered in ancient flagstones extended out from the house to an elegant stone balustrade. This place spoke to Brent of garden parties on summer evenings. The impression was fleeting because the biting wind soon caused him to put up the hood of his thick jacket and thrust his hands in his pockets for warmth. He began to think of that rainy night of the day after the murder when Merrell took a walk. Strictly speaking, it was the day of the murder, being 4:31 a.m. and 11:57 p.m. respectively.

If Merrell was disposing of a thallium bottle why would she wait until after death occurred to do so? She wouldn't, of course. No, she, or Jimmy, would first administer the poison... No, no that's wrong. She, or Jimmy, would make a preparation of the poison first in a liquid form. They would dispose of the thallium bottle at that time… might have been before they arrived at Hill House so the container is not here… It never has been here. They would have put it into a small, squeezy, plastic bottle… like an eye drops bottle or a syringe without a needle or something… Using that, one of them would introduce the poison somewhere into the stream of alcohol Franklin swallowed that day. They would wash out the bottle thing with soap and rinse it thoroughly with water… Now, if they were being really careful, and it was an eye drops bottle, they'd have a second eye drop container and put a trace amount from the new bottle into the old one… to get around forensics. Where is their final report?

Brent walked up to the balustrade to look out over the Italian garden. The steps led to garden paths laid out in grey stone. These three paths constituted the main walks in the garden. At pleasing, regular intervals the paths branched off to form a network of gravel-laid avenues, a grid of opportunities to vary one's daily walk.

Merrell could have used one of several doors but the one she chose to use was in about the middle of the east wing and exited from the drawing-room. It meant she went left or used the central set of steps - that is, if she descended into the garden. He began to search the terrace minutely for anything that would mark her passage in one of the two different directions. The weather had long since obliterated any temporary marks. The wind would have removed any lightweight evidence. The thin scattering of snow and ice across the flags could hide anything that remained. Brent found nothing. He chose the left-hand staircase as being the most likely choice and slowly began his garden walk.

Merrell could have been meeting someone else… someone other than Jimmy. He looked dissatisfied with that thought. He reached the garden path and stared along the length of it.

Eight and a half minutes. She had to know where she was going. She must have been hiding something. Roughly three minutes walk there... and back... six minutes... then a couple of minutes to... bury something? She would have to hold her phone to see what she was doing... could have taken her longer. Would have walked hurriedly... she wouldn't run. That would give a range of about two or three hundred yards... Unless..."

Brent took out his phone and called Greg Darrow.

"Yes, Brent," said Greg when he took the call.

"Does Merrell Fortier smoke?"

"No."

"That's all, thanks." Brent put his phone away.

She might smoke cannabis, thought Brent, as he continued walking. *She'd need shelter to keep out of the weather.*

The central focal point of the garden was a large stone fountain with a circular basin at its foot which stood on the main path. Brent looked for hiding places as he walked down the eastern path of the huge rectangle. He passed statuary and urns of excellent quality. The statues of deer, horses, and lions were of recent date and executed in a smooth, flowing style. These were ranged along and at the base of the twelve-foot-high box hedge which constituted the eastern wall of the garden. Brent carefully examined every one of the installations but found nothing of interest.

He reached halfway along the path where it met at right angles the path that bisected the area in line with the fountain. A tall archway in the eastern hedge led outside. Brent turned and looked about him. He was roughly one hundred and twenty yards from the door in a direct line which, he calculated, would take a good minute or more to cover at a moderately fast pace.

Once through the thick, dark boxwood wall, Brent found himself in a parkland area covering some four acres before it turned into deciduous woodland dotted with a few evergreens. The view was bleak and, in the shade of the hedge, Brent shivered. The vapour of his breath formed a mist in the still, clammy air. Drifted snow mixed with drifted leaves and together they lay untouched by direct light from the grey sky.

Back towards the house could be seen a Victorian-era greenhouse of palatial proportions, surrounded on three sides by extensive flowerbeds. Brent was surprised to see the ornate glass structure, not having noticed it from any window, because it was effectively screened from view by tall hedges and its oblique orientation to the house. Even though it was late morning, Brent could see lights shining within. These drew him like some day-time moth to go closer and explore. Brent resisted the strong impulse to go immediately and investigate the greenhouse. It made no sense to him that Merrell would go to the greenhouse from the door she used - there was better direct access to that area from other exits. He looked the other way, along the outside of the box hedge, where he saw several sheds or huts farther along. There, he hoped, was what he had been looking for - a place for something to be hidden.

"I'm sending you a video." Brent was talking to Greg on the phone.

"What have you found?"

"It's footprints in snow. They're indistinct now but it's a man's winter boot about a size ten or eleven. You can just make out the tread pattern. Must have been made during the night or this morning."

"Go ahead," said Greg.

The video began with a view of the greenhouse. The shot swept along the box hedge, included the entrance to the Italian garden and moved slowly over a large metal shed, locked, where a small tractor might be kept. Next to it, another shed appeared on screen, wooden and locked, probably for small tools and lawnmowers. The sweep of the camera stopped on a third shed, also made of wood. Its door was open. Inside were neatly arranged old bicycles, tennis equipment, and the accumulated bric-a-brac of summer pastimes of many decades. Brent began to move around the side of the last shed. Greg heard the rustle of his clothing. The camera zoomed in on the snow crust where there could be seen the clear but faint outline of a footprint half-filled with tiny granular snowflakes which had drifted into it. Next to the footprint lay extended Brent's small tape measure. He walked slowly and the image of the series of nine prints became a little shaky. The trail led around to the back of the shed. Behind the shed were a confused set of overlapping prints and scuffed-up dead leaves. Someone had stood there, re-positioning their feet several times. A recently fallen litter of dead boxwood leaves, twigs, and small fragments lay on top of the snow. Slowly, the shot travelled up the hedge to a certain spot, about shoulder height, where it stopped. Here there was a small gap to be seen, barely noticeable and only presenting as a dark hole. A freshly snapped twig, still held in place by a string of bark, could be seen on the hole's edge. Brent zoomed in on the thick, forked trunk of a box tree that was barely visible in the hedge's interior. The video ended.

"Got it?" asked Brent.

"Yes. That was amazing. I'll show it at the next department office party."

"Very funny."

"What's your take on it?"

"Merrell brought something out the night after the murder. She stashed it here. Jimmy, or someone else, retrieved it today. I've no idea what it was but it has to be that both of them would be in trouble if it were found."

"Good. Might be drugs or they might have stolen something. I'll go and check everyone's boots. Anything inside that shed - the door was open?"

"I opened it very carefully. There's just a thumb latch and no lock. I couldn't see anything from the door and I didn't go inside. Will you check for prints?"

"Alice will, she's good at that. See you later."

Chapter 14

Wednesday afternoon

"𝓗ello, Mr de Sainte Croix. Mind if I join you?"

"Are you that Umber fellow?" The elderly man looked up when Brent entered the room. His voice was strong and he had a healthy, outdoor complexion. A green crocheted blanket was over his knees.

"I am."

"I suppose I can't stop you. If you're going to ask me questions you may as well sit down."

Brent took a seat in an easy chair. The small, wood-panelled room they were in overlooked part of the garden through large picture windows. Brent had not seen this section of the grounds before. Behind the row of four assorted chairs, all turned to the window were more bookcases. The books here were not an overflow from the main library, this was another library containing fiction for all ages, much of it dating to the first half of the twentieth century. It was the easy reading room with a view over the vegetable patch.

"I think the old Brewster family thought of everything," said Brent. "What a perfect bolt-hole to escape from high-society."

"It's my favourite room in the house," said de Sainte Croix. "Spent many hours here. It's a good place to sit and think."

"You go a long way back with the Brewsters."

"Indeed, I do… over fifty years." The old man continued looking out of the window.

"Do you like gardening?" asked Brent.

"Never took to it… Yachting was my passion."

"Is that so?"

" Too old for it now." Brent could see, at least, he imagined he saw, a faraway look in the old man's blue eyes. Lloyd's look suggested to Brent that the man was reliving once-pleasant memories of open seas and skies with the wind singing through ropes and canvas crackling as it harnessed the air's energy to propel the craft like a loosed arrow through cresting waves. The lack of joy he displayed registered an aching for the past. That freedom Lloyd once had was now lost and, perhaps, the memories of those days taunted the man who could sail no more while he sat staring at a frigid vegetable garden in December.

"I can see why yachting would be attractive," said Brent. "Where did you sail?"

"Huh, where? Oh, many places. The Caribbean, Mediterranean… I've sailed around both Capes."

"Oh, long distances… That must have been challenging."

"Cape Horn was. Sailed there twice and the second time was nearly the end of me."

"You sailed single-handed?"

"No. The wife was with me for most of the time. She was as keen as I was. You should have seen her on our first voyage round the Horn. She loved it… made both of us so alive. But when she died suddenly years later… her heart, you know… I was as miserable as anything so I sailed solo down the coasts of Brazil and Argentina." He paused for a long time. "A storm came up… I'd been through worse, but the sea was surging like a mad thing… I couldn't let the boat go. I couldn't let her sink. It was our sloop… I weathered the storm and went up by Chile and Peru then through the Panama Canal."

Brent allowed the silence that followed to last a little while before speaking again.

"What do you make of what's happened here?"

"Franklin committed suicide. It's as plain as anything. No need to look for a murderer because there isn't one."

"It doesn't seem obvious to me. Why do you think that?"

"No one in the family is capable of it."

"That may be the most astute observation I have heard so far. The problem I have is that Franklin does not fit the profile of a suicide. Then we have facts to face. Franklin gave no indication of his intentions. He left no note. He made no arrangements. Finally, there's no trace of thallium anywhere in the house or among his personal effects. He would not have gone to any great lengths to cover up his own suicide "

"That all may be true. Nevertheless, he killed himself."

"Did he tell you he would take his own life?"

"No, never mentioned it."

"You were the last person to speak to him while he was alive. What did you talk about?"

"His drinking and Sadler-Creme. I told him not to mix the two."

"How did he respond?"

"As one might expect, he told me to mind my own business."

"And?"

"And what?"

"Mr de Sainte Croix, you spoke to him for an extended period of some minutes. You have described a conversation of sixty seconds."

"No, we spoke of Sadler-Creme for a while. I asked him if he was considering any expansion in the business. I heard what Steve Aimes said earlier. His crude suggestion about expansion had some merit."

"How did Franklin respond?"

"Well, he said he'd been considering a few things but didn't want to talk about them just then."

"And what of his drinking?"

"As I said, I brought the subject up and he did not want to speak of that, either."

"Is that all?"

"Mr Umber, you can believe me or not as you wish. I'm a man of my word. I've told you what we discussed."

"Then I will take you at your word. You discussed nothing more than his alcoholism, which went nowhere, and the company, about which Franklin refused to speak."

"That is a fair summary."

In silence, Brent made some notes before taking his leave.

"Thank you for your time, Mr de Sainte Croix. You have told me a great deal."

"Ah, good morning, Mrs Halliday," said Brent.

"Good morning, Mr Umber," she replied.

They had met on the second staircase - she descending - he ascending. Brent had stopped and she, naturally, did so, too.

"Would it be possible to have a few words with you?"

"Yes, it is. I have to go to the kitchen first and ask Cook to do something for tomorrow."

"Of course. We can talk on the way."

They both descended the stairs together. Brent continued, saying,

"I imagine the kitchen staff is feverishly preparing for the funeral reception."

"They are, although Mrs Vance, our cook, is not of a feverish disposition. She rules the kitchen with a rod of iron."

"Ah, I have to interview her later. Will she put me in my place?"

"What is your place?" asked Sophia archly.

"I wish I knew exactly. I would say somewhere between a professional police officer and an opinionated amateur who thinks he knows what he is doing."

"I suspect you know what you are doing."

"Very nice of you to say that. It means I'm putting up a convincing front but the reality is I'm only muddling through."

"I take it the case is proving difficult."

"Most cases do. The only variance is the *degree* of difficulty in obtaining solid evidence."

Brent quickened his step to open the door for Sophia to pass into the kitchen. This was one area the investigator had not yet visited. He was surprised by two features upon entering. The first was the immense size of the room - it was more like a hall with white painted brick walls. The second was how dated everything looked to him. Yes, he saw new refrigerators, a dishwasher, and countertop appliances. Yes, he saw plastic containers, stainless steel cooking utensils, and the like. If these were removed, the kitchen would appear as a nineteen-twenties' set piece. Strange-looking old machinery, such as a tub-like potato peeler on a stand and a wooden butter churn, were littered throughout the space. The ancient sinks were of white porcelain surrounded by a white-tiled and black-trimmed back-splash. Dominating the back wall was a black enamelled range of monstrous proportions that, if converted properly, could once have powered a steamboat. Overhead were two long wooden-railed and ornately metal-framed racks of which Brent could not imagine the original intended use. These were raised or lowered by ropes and pulleys and were presently tied to old iron cleats. Hanging from long lines of hooks fastened to the walls were copper, brass, and stainless-steel pans and utensils of every conceivable size and shape. The whole kitchen shone clean. Of the six people present only two barely looked up to see who had entered. All of them were busy preparing food, cleaning, cooking, or carrying things.

Brent watched from the safety of the door - he had no inclination to intrude upon the busy scene. He saw Sophia Halliday approach Mrs Vance, the formidable-looking cook. Upon her turning around, Brent saw the cook possessed a face flushed with heat from the stove and framed by a shapeless white bonnet-type structure on top of her head and dark curls at her cheeks. As she wiped her hands on her apron, her large forearms suggested she riveted girders or bent horseshoes in her spare time. Mrs Vance, with an impatiently tolerant look on her face, listened and waited for Sophia to finish her request, before nodding an assent. She turned back to her work and Sophia left her to it.

Once the two interlopers were outside, Brent said,

"Let me guess. Mrs Vance cooks like an angel, and I know that to be a fact, she has a heart of gold, but don't go near her when she's busy in the kitchen or she'll tear you limb from limb."

Sophia laughed. "She's not quite as bad as that. She gets focused on what she's doing and doesn't like menu changes."

"Where would you like to chat?" asked Brent.

"We can use the lounge. I doubt anybody is there at the moment."

"I hear you are avoiding the main staircase. I am, too. I find it troubling."

"Every time I pass by I think of the absolute horror of my brother's death."

"May I make a suggestion?" asked Brent.

"A suggestion? Certainly."

"Well, I actually have two suggestions. The first is a simple one. Put a large display of flowers in memory of Franklin on the exact spot. When the flowers have faded, remove them and then use the staircase again as you would do normally."

They walked in silence until they reached the lounge.

"What is your second suggestion?" asked Sophia.

"Completely remodel the hall and staircase."

"Remodel it? That sounds drastic. I can't imagine Mother would ever do that."

They sat down facing each other. Brent continued,

"I suppose Mrs Brewster is using the elevator at present so I don't know how she feels about, well, about the scene of the event. As much as I admire the hall in its present state of elegant proportions it would be a useless feature if it was never used. Hence my ideas - to do something to move past the association with death."

"I can see that… Why do you take such an interest?"

"I don't want the library broken up. It's none of my business, I know." Brent got up and began to walk about as he spoke. "You see, although I could never think of such a place as this as home, it is the Brewster home. I haven't been here for two days yet but already I cannot imagine it belonging to anyone except a Brewster. I fear the place might be sold to cut off the sad memories. There, I said it. I can't apologize for butting in, it's my nature, but I'm sorry if I've been rude."

"I do love this house for many reasons… You are a strange man, Mr Umber," said Sophia.

"Why, because I seem more concerned about the house than finding the murderer?"

"Well, yes. You seem to ask very few questions that bear upon the case."

"The police do that part. To me, in this matter, the house plays an active role just as much as the trust fund document or Sadler-Creme. All these things have helped shape the minds of the people here. Your ideas of house and home are not the same as mine. Franklin, for good or bad, devoted himself to Sadler-Creme. I understand that you have a sense of devotion to this house and its continuance. Homes can have greater, more important souls, as such, than any company has, yet both are also being moulded by the people within them. If you or Mrs Brewster take against this place it will cease to function as a home. In my mind that would mean there was a second victim."

"A symbiotic relationship." Sophia stood up. "I know you suspect me but is there anyone else you think could have murdered Franklin?"

"I know several people who didn't. I know several more who are unlikely to have done so."

"Do you think I murdered him?"

"You could have but I don't think you did. That means I currently rate you as a medium risk. You had the opportunity. You also had motivating factors such as a long-standing grudge against Franklin. But, Sophia, you also have a de-motivating factor. The murder was premeditated. You would not coolly choose this house as a place to murder him. In the garden, possibly; elsewhere, much more likely; but inside your childhood home that you love and will inherit one day, no."

"It is very sobering and unpleasant to hear how one is considered to be a murderer or not."

"Yes. It is intrusive and impersonal, as though your thoughts and feelings don't matter. Worse than that is not being believed which implicitly casts one in the role of liar.

The police get away with it under the guise of routine inquiry or procedures. We all expect them not to believe everything told to them. So, when questioned by the police, we understand they will check our testimony and alibis by seeking corroborating evidence."

"What a dreary time this is. I can't even grieve properly for Franklin. It is as though I had been stunned with a taser last week and have yet to recover."

"It will pass. Do small things and climb your way out of the black hole. Accomplishing a few little tasks puts structure into a messy situation. I sometimes make lists of what I need to do. It is very satisfying to work through a list to completion even when everything is falling to pieces around me. Then there's your daughter, Chloe. She has a good idea. She rewards herself with jewellery when she achieves a goal. You might do something similar."

"Thank you for trying to be helpful. Chloe is funny like that - she bought herself a new ring just at the weekend. However, I feel I still need to wallow in misery a little longer. I cannot shake off the sense of looming disaster that will occur when the murderer is found out."

"The funeral tomorrow will be one marker in your progress to recovering peace of mind. The arrest of the murderer will be another. My wish is to make the latter event a clean and quiet affair."

"Will you be going tomorrow?"

"Yes. I feel I know Franklin quite well. I will go to say goodbye to a troubled friend who hurt others and hurt himself."

"You never met him, though."

"True, but I also get invested in characters in books and, against all the professional etiquette that I'm supposed to abide by, I become attached to the people in the case I'm working on."

Sophia looked at him searchingly for some seconds before saying,

"Have you no questions to ask me?"

"Yes, I do. How is Aurelia's paper coming along?"

Chapter 15

Late Wednesday afternoon

"*U*se that over there." Mrs Vance pointed with her wooden spoon towards an empty metal table where a cutting board lay. "I want four medium turnips in half-inch cubes - do them first and give them to Marcie to get the pot going. That's Marcie over there." The spoon pointed to a young woman in her late teens or early twenties. "Then cut 8lbs of carrots in half-inch cubes, two celeries - diced - quarter-inch, 6lbs of onions - coarse chopped, 8lbs of tomatoes - quartered, and a head of garlic sliced fine. Got that, dear? Or do you want it in metric?"

"No, I think I've just about got it," replied Brent.

"Good. Bowls underneath the table, knives and peelers are in the drawer, there," she stabbed her spoon in another direction, "and, if you're missing anything, ask someone." With that final word, Mrs Vance turned her back on Brent and began once more to stir her sauce gently.

Brent, summarily dismissed, went to gather the vegetables he would wash, peel, and cut as directed. This was the quid pro quo of his own making. Upon entering the lion's den, Brent had seen how busy the staff was. He had approached Mrs Vance and said he needed about ten minutes of everyone's time to ask some questions. The busy cook, without turning around or ceasing to stir, had made a derisive noise with her lips and ignored him. Not to be forestalled by a refusal, Brent had floated the suggestion that, if he worked for an hour to help the kitchen staff, they could then each spare him the ten minutes he needed and the kitchen workload would not suffer as a consequence. He sweetened the pot by saying he had once worked in a restaurant. Brent had half a hope that his suggestion would be waved aside. However, upon hearing his offer, Mrs Vance immediately seized upon it. She set the investigator to work on the vegetable preparation for a beef stew which, Brent felt, was intended to feed an army.

No one took any notice of Brent as he worked at his tasks - at least, he had not seen them taking notice. The young woman, Marcie, received the processed turnips without comment but when Brent returned to his workstation she broke into a broad grin at the idea of the police, as she thought Brent to be, being put to work in the kitchen by Mrs Vance.

When Brent got to the onions he could not help himself - his eyes began to water but he stuck at it as instructed, sniffing all the while. Mrs Vance, who was that type of person who has eyes in the back of her head and knows all that happens, finally turned to watch him in his labours. Something like a smile played about her mouth for a moment as she saw the growing pile of onion sections. It was a difficult expression to interpret and may have been part derision and part approval.

When he had finished and reported to the queen of the kitchen that his labours were complete, she put her rolling pin to one side and came over, wiping her floury hands on her apron, to inspect what he had done. If he had hoped for any praise he did not receive it. Mrs Vance looked quickly over his work and then said, "Give the onions and garlic to

Robin. She's at the small stove. Give everything else to
Marcie. Now, we need 25lbs of potatoes peeled. Put them in
the top of the peeler, crank the handle, and they come out
the bottom into a bowl. Cut them for mash." She was about
to walk away and then added, "Better make that 30lbs. You
and the police will want some if you're staying." She walked
away before Brent could say anything.

After the kitchen had been scrupulously cleaned and
everything put away in its place, the entire kitchen staff sat
down to eat a late lunch in the servants' dining room. The
meal consisted of halibut in a silk-like parsley sauce and
accompanied by peas and croquette potatoes. Marcie left the
table from time to time to keep the stew pot stirred.

"Mrs Vance, you and your staff have my complete
admiration. How you accommodate the eating habits of a
large household, the staff members, and visiting policemen
while preparing for the large gathering tomorrow is nothing
short of miraculous."

"Listen to him," said Mrs Vance, smiling. She was another
person entirely outside of the kitchen. "You'll make us all
blush."

"No, seriously," said Brent. "I am very much impressed
with how all of you get through the work."

"Oh, it's not so much. I think it was three, no, four years
ago when there was a big dinner for forty-five and half of us
were down with 'flu. At the last minute, mind you. I don't
think I ever worked so hard in my life. You were there,
Robin."

"It was terrible, Mr Umber," said Robin, her face showing
the horror she relived in her mind. "All at the last minute
everyone was phoning in sick and there were just the three
of us. The only thing that saved us was it was roast beef. If
they'd wanted something fancy we would have been sunk."

"It's true," said Mrs Vance, nodding agreement, in case Brent might doubt such honest testimony.

"You are heroes, then," said Brent solemnly. "Heroes who rise to the occasion. No matter what is demanded of you, the kitchen shall be triumphant. Let us have a toast, then." Brent stood up at the table and lifted his water glass. All at the table stood up to join in the hilarity. "To the kitchen staff of Hill Hall," said Brent. "There is no finer staff in the land. To the staff!"

"To the staff!" They all clinked glasses and drank. Marcie was laughing out loud, all were smiling, and someone cheered. After they settled down again, Marcie said,

"Your turnips were good."

"I saw those," said Mrs Vance. "In fact, everything was quite acceptable, except the onions. They were a bit on the fine side for a stew. I like them like little transparent flags. They present so nicely when they're like that."

"Those onions were stinging my eyes," said Brent. "I could barely see through the pain and that is my excuse for producing a less than perfect onion piece."

"Oh, get along with you," said Mrs Vance. "You should try French onion soup for sixty. That would give you something to cry about." A couple of the staff nodded in agreement. "Mind you, there are a few tricks to avoid the worst of it - like chilling them first."

"Keep your head back," said Graham, "so the fumes don't hit you as hard."

"Put the onion rings in water as you're slicing them," said Robin.

"I am fast becoming an onion-slicing expert," said Brent. He paused before saying, "Now this also brings tears to my eyes. This awful business. Did any of you see anything or hear anything that makes you think something wasn't quite right?" He scanned their faces quickly and saw no hesitation in their responding head-shakings or murmured words that nothing had been seen.

"I know the police have interviewed all of you separately. Sometimes, a group might arrive at an answer where an individual cannot. The police are looking for anything that can help them."

"They came to us first," said Mrs Vance solemnly, "asking if the food could have been tampered with. 'Not in *my* kitchen,' I told them. 'Not in *my* kitchen.'" She shook her head ruefully at the insulting suggestion.

"I can well believe that. I know first-hand how your kitchen operates. No stranger could have come in and done anything. But just suppose, for a moment, that someone came and asked you to put a special spice into a dish. Would you do that?"

"We would not," said Mrs Vance emphatically. "It's about the quality of what's being added. None of us would take anything from an outsider and add it to the food."

"I see… that makes sense. No outsider could have done anything without your knowledge. What about now? We're all sitting here. Someone could go in and add something to the stew, for example."

The look of shocked disgust on Mrs Vance's face immediately had Brent back-tracking his hypothesis. "Of course, that could *not* have been how it was done the other night. There would have been no way for the poison to reach Mr Brewster without other diners being affected. Unless, of course, he asked for a separate dish." Brent threw the question open to the table at large by looking from face to face. "Did he have a special dish of any kind?"

The universal response was head-shaking or 'no'.

"Then he must have been poisoned through drink… Wait a minute - what about the wait staff? How did they take the food from the kitchen to the small dining room?"

"We loaded the carts and covered trays," said Marcie, "and they took them from the end table and through the door into the dining room."

"Do you think it possible that any of them did something?" Brent quickly polled the table.

"No, I don't think so," said Mrs Vance. "They seemed professional enough. Didn't stand about wasting time and got on with the serving."

"But, Mrs Vance," said Robin, "once they were outside they *could* have done something, couldn't they?"

"I don't know... I suppose they could."

"Not to worry," said Brent. "Robin, I'd like you to show me what you mean exactly." He stood up. "Well, thank you very much for a delightful lunch and some very informative work experience."

"You should get a job here," said Marcie.

"Sshh, Marcie," said Mrs Vance, "don't be rude. He *has* a job. Go and look at the stew otherwise Mr Brent won't have a dinner worth eating tonight."

They said goodbye to each other. Robin accompanied Brent and, although she had suggested a waiter 'did it', she could not demonstrate *how* he 'did it'. The short, empty passageway between the kitchen and dining room did not allow for easy or effective tampering of foodstuffs without a sky-high risk of being seen by someone.

Chapter 16

Early Wednesday evening

*T*he Butler, Henry Jackson, was always on hand when needed to fulfil all ordinary and extraordinary household duties. He would appear in the right place at the exact right moment and do all that resident or guest required or expected. If Mrs Vance ruled the kitchen, Henry Jackson ruled the rest of the house in a firm, fair, and dignified manner. Maids, cleaners, waiting staff, and the handyman would never know when he would approach them quietly and observe their behaviour. Often, from behind a busy person, a voice would come out of nowhere to correct or redirect that person's activities. It was universally held that one could never know just when he would turn up and frighten the life out of a body. Thus, Henry Jackson, Butler, ensured the work of the house ran smoothly.

The reverse was also true. When Jackson's services were not immediately required he vanished like a ghost and could not be found anywhere. Brent was unable to find Jackson until a maid directed him to Jackson's office which was situated very close to the police office. Brent had passed it numerous times and thought it was a cupboard. He approached the door and knocked. It was almost immediately opened quietly and slowly to reveal Jackson in the butler's full regalia. Brent had the distinct impression that Jackson might have been standing right behind the door.

"Good afternoon," said Brent. "May I come in?"

"Of course, Mr Umber." Jackson opened the door wide for Brent to enter. "My office is snug but comfortable."

Jackson spoke the truth. His office was indeed small but it was delightful. It had a rectangular stained glass window the like of which was rarely seen. It was astonishingly beautiful and stopped Brent in his tracks when he saw it. The outside borders were glass rectangles of rose pink and golden yellow. The central glass panel was opaque, uncoloured glass with a painting on it.

The pre-Raphaelite image was of a woman dressed in silver armour, wearing a long, dark green cloak fastened by a thick silver chain. She was holding a sword in her right hand and a golden cup dangled from her left hand so that a blue liquid dripped out on the ground. She stood among corpses of roughly clothed tribal warriors intermingled with those of Roman soldiers. Her complexion was very pale, almost white, but she looked peacefully serene. Her long auburn hair flew out on the breeze except where braids hung at her temples and where a golden circlet held the hair close to her head. A chariot with two white horses stood behind her. The image glowed in the soft grey winter light.

"I had no thought to see anything like this today," said Brent. "Is it by Millais? It certainly looks like it."

"Yes, sir. It is entitled 'Boudicca's Passing'. When he visited America, he stayed at Hill Hall several times as a guest. On one of his visits, some stained glass windows were being installed in the large dining room - you have probably noticed them, sir. There was glass leftover and it was decided to put a small window in here. Mr Millais painted this as a thank you gift. In case you are wondering, sir, at that time, this room was used to store a collection of antique weapons."

"Ha, magnificent. I can't get over its beauty. And you have this marvellous work for your exclusive enjoyment? That is a very, very rare employment benefit."

"It is, sir. Please make yourself comfortable." Jackson indicated one of a pair of chocolate brown leather armchairs. In between them stood a small, mahogany, piecrust-edged occasional table. An old roll-top oak desk, closed, with a matching swivel chair, was against the wall. A small wooden filing cabinet stood next to the desk. The only other piece of furniture crammed into the space was a low bookshelf. The navigable floor space was less than two feet wide and it was covered by a very worn, hand-knotted, Afghan runner only a foot and a half wide that had to be a century old. On the walls were hung ancient sporting prints and street-scene engravings. It was a man's room.

Brent sat in the comfortable armchair.

"Would you prefer I switch on the light, sir? The daylight is fading."

"Oh, please, no. Let me enjoy what I can of your window." Brent was puzzled why Jackson remained standing. Then he realized he was being 'the butler' in his own room.

"Please, Mr Jackson, sit down."

"Thank you, sir." He sat down in the other armchair but he was not relaxed.

"Tell me, how did you get started on becoming a butler?"

"It's a long and rather tedious story, Mr Umber. I used to work in a supermarket until I became an assistant manager. I found that employment unsatisfying in some ways so I sought out a hobby for myself. A local amateur dramatics group was short of a couple of players and when I saw their advertisement I applied. I was accepted and proceeded to play several walk-on parts in their various productions. Even though the parts I played were small I found them most satisfactory. I think it was the spirit of the venture that pleased me the most."

"Chloe Halliday wants a career in the dramatic arts," said Brent. "What do you think of her chances?"

"I think it likely that she will do very well if she receives proper training," answered Jackson.

"Yes, overplays a little… youthful zeal. Sorry, I interrupted you."

"Thank you, sir. As is common, or so I'm given to understand, my private life began to dominate my working life. I switched employment to accommodate my acting - I hesitate to call it a career, but it was certainly becoming that. I was now appearing in some professional productions of a certain type. I was usually cast as a policeman, a detective, a vicar, and, most frequently, a butler."

"Haha! Do I see a connection?"

"You do, indeed, sir. I found the part of playing a butler the most rewarding of them all and, for some reason, I really loved the feeling of being a butler. As a matter of fact, it has been commented by several directors that I was the best butler they could envisage."

"And right they were. What happened next?"

"Well, I thought I would act on my inclination. I took courses to become a butler and in domestic management and hospitality training. I also worked towards an arts degree. I solidified my experience by working at a prestigious hotel. I joined a guild and now converse frequently with my brothers and sisters through a forum."

"Very enterprising. Did you get your degree?"

"I did, sir. The practical training I received was of the very best. Surprisingly, the online courses helped me tremendously."

"You can become a butler online?"

"Only for the academic side of it, as you can appreciate."

"Could you show me? I'm fascinated." Brent looked around the room. "Oh, you don't have a computer."

"But I do, sir." Jackson switched to the swivel chair and opened the roll-top. Everything in the desk was neatly arranged and organized and, sitting where an ink blotter would once have been, was a laptop. Jackson powered up the computer. Very soon, he and Brent, who now stood next to him, were discussing the intricacies of becoming a butler in the modern world.

"I've half an idea to sign up here and now," said Brent.

"Much of the success of being a butler is due to temperament. You have a forthright temperament, if you will excuse me for saying so, sir, which is the opposite of what is required."

Brent looked crestfallen and said, "You are probably right." He sat down in the armchair again.

They were both quiet. The room was growing quite dark as the early evening set in. Boudicca had ceased to shine. Jackson got up and switched on the light. The stained and painted window became ordinary and flat while the room became cozy.

"Your first name is Henry. May I call you by that name?"

"I'd rather you didn't, sir."

"Excellent training but I must talk to Henry Jackson and not the Hill Hall butler. There are things we must discuss that are crucial to the investigation."

"I understand, sir. Please ask your questions."

"Do you want the murderer to be caught?" asked Brent.

For the first time, Jackson hesitated before answering.

"Yes, I do."

"So do I. You possess a unique position in this house. You know much about the guests and family. Butlers keep books on each person's individual requirements and tastes. I'm not asking to see your records. I want you to answer me, man to man, so I can expose the murderer. I know this goes against your code of conduct but, you see, a murder has temporarily invalidated that code for you. I know you wish to shield the family and keep all matters private but you simply cannot do this any longer - not when the eldest son has been so mercilessly killed.

You keep watch over the household. At the dinner table, for example, you would have seen any unusual action by any of the diners. It is your job to notice things. The police are convinced that you *did* notice something. I want you to tell me what it was and, as I tell everyone, I will only use the information if it is absolutely necessary. I have a code of conduct, too, and it is just as entrenched as yours. In this play, I am the relentless investigator and you are Henry Jackson, butler, who has a crisis of conscience but in the end, becomes Harry, the man who saves the day by telling what he knows. We must each play our parts well for the production to be a success."

Henry was agitated. He passed a hand across his forehead then rubbed his eyes. He looked shaky.

"No one has called me Harry in years." He was silent for nearly a minute. "It was a simple thing but I noticed it occur twice. As a rule, diners may look at the serving staff once or twice, usually as they interact with them. After that, they tend not to look at the staff at all because the dinner is before them and each diner is required to play their part as guest. Twice, at different times and for some seconds, I saw Mrs Brewster look directly at one of the hired staff. I could not tell who it was because of the angle I was standing at. It was not a glance. It was a studied look. None of the three servers responded in any way."

Now it was Brent's turn to be quiet. Jackson watched him but could not glean what was passing through the investigator's mind.

"I would say," said Brent at last, "that in this cupboard at the bottom of the bookcase, you keep a bottle of something."

"There is sherry, port and a fine whiskey."

"Very good, Harry. Have a large one of whatever you prefer and I will have a microscopic port, just a teaspoon because I have to work to do. We'll have a token celebration now because you have been extraordinarily helpful. But I shall return when this case is over, and we shall do it properly."

A few minutes after the two men had finished their drinks, the investigator shot out of Jackson's private domain. Immediately, a voice called him to a halt.

"Mr Umber? I would like to have a word with you." Mike Halliday had been crossing the hall and had seen Brent in the passage. He was now walking towards him.

"Ah, Mr Halliday," said Brent pleasantly. "I had hoped to talk to you today to go over a few things."

"That won't be necessary. I have nothing to say to you and I have told the police everything I know. What I *will* say is that you are to stop meddling with my family at once."

Brent noticed that although Halliday was speaking in an even tone, he was repressing something like anger.

"I can do that. I'm not sure how I have meddled exactly but I can ensure that I will distress you no further."

"I'm not distressed," answered Halliday. "If you are a private investigator helping the police then stick to your job."

"It may come as a surprise but that is what I usually do."

"No, it isn't. You should not have given Aurelia help with her paper. It is none of your business."

"You do realize that only last week your brother-in-law lay dead not twenty yards from where we're standing and you are choosing to be upset over a few notes on a term paper?"

"What has a term paper got to do with Franklin's death?" Mike Halliday was becoming more excited and it showed in his voice.

"Nothing and everything. I had to clear your daughter of a possible murder charge. I had to do so in my own way and see for myself that she is innocent."

"My daughter?" Halliday was visibly taken aback by the idea.

"The police hire me to find killers. I do so by first eliminating those who could *not* have committed the crime. Your daughter had a very weak alibi. She could have come to the house without anyone knowing. My interaction with her convinced me she did not have anything to do with the crime. The methods I choose are mine and not those of the police. I'm not changing them because *you* find it upsetting. Now, tell me, why *are* you so upset over such an inconsequential matter?"

As Mike Halliday heard Brent out, his aggression subsided and a thoughtful look came upon his face.

"Um, I thought you were, well, meddling… going off the case. Is that how you work, then?"

"What I do is unorthodox so I am forever forced to explain myself. I need to ask you a few simple questions… three to be precise.

"Then ask them."

"Did you notice anything in Evelyn's behaviour that seemed odd or unusual? It could be the slightest thing."

"No… no, I can't say I did."

"When Lloyd de Sainte Croix was talking to Franklin in the lounge, what do you think they were discussing?"

"I didn't take much notice of them. Come to think of it, I did find it odd that they talked for so long after that scene earlier. Then, Lloyd's like that - very focused and dogmatic. He talks about business, yachting, or anything else, and you think you're having a conversation until you suddenly realize that you are being… oh, it's difficult to say…"

"Told what he wants you to hear."

"That's it… something like that. He's a very good businessman."

"I imagine, when he was younger, he would have made a capable sea captain, barking out orders to a crew who jumped to it immediately."

"Yes, he would have."

"My last question is, what do you think of Merrell Fortier and Jimmy Brewster?"

"They seem oddly matched… completely different personalities. I have little doubt she is after money. Maybe she loves Jimmy, I don't know. I think Jimmy is fascinated by her. She's very sure of herself."

"That's all, Mr Halliday. Those are my questions. Should you think of anything else, anything at all, please let me know what it is. Goodbye."

"Oh, is that it…? Goodbye, Mr Umber."

Having reached the office, Brent sat down and began scanning the witness files on his phone. After a minute he took out a small notebook from his pocket and jotted down some notes.

"Alice." Brent spoke to her at an adjacent desk. "You interviewed the people from Ducal Service Agency. Anything out of the ordinary?"

"One minute," replied Alice, "I gotta get this email off."

Brent began tapping his pen on the notebook as he waited.

"There, it's gone. Ducal Service… no, I don't think so. The guy, Sammy… he was nervous but no more than what's natural for many people when being questioned. Rita was all in. She wanted to know everything about the investigation. Rachel, the younger one, was upset. She got emotional over the deceased… You know, she'd served him veggies and now he was dead kinda thing. Like everyone else in this place, none of them noticed anything."

"Thanks."

Brent made a call on his phone.

"Hello. May I speak to Madeleine Schmidt, please… Thanks… Hello, Ms Schmidt…? My name's Brent Umber. I'm working on the Franklin Brewster case… Yes, it is a terrible business. I urgently need to speak to Sammy, Rita, and Rachel. Where will I find them at present…? Oh… yes, I see. Where are Sammy and Rachel this evening…? Okay, Italian Ambassador's residence." Brent wrote this information down. "Is it a large event…? You're sending eight, I see. Now, Ms Schmidt, as Rita has the night off, do you know where I can find her? It's very important… You don't. Thank you very much for your help. I'll try again tomorrow. Goodbye."

"You got a line on something?" asked Alice.

"Hardly anything worth repeating. I need to talk to these three witnesses anyway. I hope to tie their testimonies in with something I heard today. I'll let you know if anything comes of it."

Brent took his laptop from his bag and began searching. He noticed the time was now 3:27 p.m. The buffet at the Ambassador's residence was due to start at 7:15 p.m. To get there on time meant his driving in rush-hour traffic to the heart of the city, something Brent wanted to avoid.

Having spoken to every person in the house who was present on the night of the murder, and more who were not,

Brent had arrived at the stage where he needed to reflect on what he had heard from them - to block and fill in his mind-painting. Then he would find some direction, some more focus, and begin to close in on the most likely candidates.

He wrote his reports to give Greg. They contained no solid evidence against anyone yet. A member of the Aimes family was one of the least likely to have murdered Franklin. Someone in the Halliday family was a more likely prospect. He thought of Mike Halliday and his irritable display. *Was it real or feigned? Seemed natural enough - meddling with his student daughter's paper - not exactly what a parent wishes to hear but was it enough to make him say he wouldn't answer any questions? Surely, he would have reported it to Greg Darrow before being openly hostile with me.* "You are not off the hook, yet," muttered Brent.

"You say something?" asked Alice.

"No, sorry, I was just thinking out loud. What do you make of Mike Halliday?"

"I questioned him. He's a quiet guy. Pleasant. Defers to his wife in a lot of things. Answered everything straight. I didn't get any warning signs."

"Is he the type of person who is quiet and helpful all the time but if pushed on something will overreact?"

"Yeah, he could be like that. He might blow up."

"If I said Halliday was offended by Franklin to such a degree that he went away, planned a murder, and then waited for a chance to carry it out, could you see that as a possibility?"

"Well, I should think it possible. He's the kind of guy who would avoid people if he didn't like them and yet smile at them to keep up appearances. If he was angry... I think he would be raging rather than nursing a grudge."

"I think I agree with you. Superficially, I believe he would not keep his anger burning very long."

Brent returned to his thoughts. Both Evelyn and Lloyd were problematic for him in different ways. He liked Evelyn, that was one problem. Lloyd was being obstructive, that was another problem. Then there was the third problem. They were both in their mid-eighties and that fact made it nearly impossible to cast either in the role of ruthless murderer.

When he had finished his reports, assigning his likelihood factors, the likelihood of being a murderer, as he thought appropriate, he debated with himself what to do next. Visit the greenhouse, have a chat with Evelyn, or secure some beef stew and mashed potatoes to take away. He had already planned a busy night for himself. Brent was hopeful that he was now on good terms with Mrs Vance and that she would not mind such a request. Yes, he was hopeful. He went to the kitchen first.

Chapter 17

Later Wednesday evening

*T*he old, blue Jeep was stuck in traffic as Brent was trying to make his way to Rita's apartment, having found her address in the police files. He was aiming to arrive at 6:30 on the assumption that this would be when she was most likely to be at home having dinner. If she was not there he would call and arrange a meeting but he really wanted the advantage of a surprise visit.

On the backseat of the vehicle was a container of stew and mashed potato. Mrs Vance had said it was ready to eat but that the stew had really needed a couple of hours more to bring out all the flavour. She had prepared the mashed potatoes herself. Inside the pastry box next to the container were four miniature strawberry pavlovas which, if they tasted as good as they looked, meant Brent was in for a treat. The cook had good-humouredly said that he looked like he needed feeding up.

He stared at the slow-moving line of cars ahead - a long, cheerless row of red lights through a rain-splashed window. Brent wondered about the cook and other women her age that he knew. They tended to mother him. On his birthday, he was sure to receive at least three cakes from women like Mrs Vance, and gifts and cards from ten more - all of them old enough to be his mother or grand-mother and all asking, in their various ways, if he was taking care of himself. Not one of them was a relation of his.

Then, with younger women, it was different. He could make them laugh and they thought he was odd and very funny - hilarious, even. With women his own age it was another story. Unless Brent was on a case, he was shy and reserved. He hoped they might still find him to be somewhat amusing but feared they also would think him slightly silly. While speaking to them he became aware of his nervousness which tended to increase it. The closer he got to a woman he liked the more wretched he became.

Behind that wall of oddly frivolous behaviour and conversation unavoidably lightweight due to his nervousness lay a deep-seated yearning to belong somewhere with someone. Yet he could not commit and he could not remove the barriers he threw up by his own demeanour.   Brent could not open up sufficiently to find that woman he sought because of his past, because of his shame, because he had been a thief.

"Hello, Vane." Brent was calling while parked in front of the Italian Ambassador's Residence.

"Yo, Brent-meister. Wass-up?" Vanessa, who went by the soubriquet Vane, was a former skater girl - a friend of Brent's who worked for the investigator on occasion.

"Are you busy tonight?" Brent noticed that Vane had slipped back into skater-girl mode because of the proximity of her friends. Usually, she was very different these days. Her normal behaviour was now that of a respectful but often cheeky student of computer studies who was quite mature in her ways. She was Brent's sister - not in a legal sense but in a strongly developed relational sense.

"Depends. I've got no papers due imminently so I'm chillin' with friends. What do you want me to do?"

"I need you to make a distraction outside of a house. There are two security guards at the door. You have to get them away from their post so I can slip inside. Think you can do it?"

"Sure. I'll take a couple of buds and we'll make them move."

"I'd like it for nine o'clock - at the Italian Ambassador's house. It's fairly near where you live. Think you can do that?"

"Yeah, I know it. Only, we're over on the east side - there's a jam night tonight. We'll be missing some cool sounds - Ya know what I'm saying?"

"Well… how much?"

"Hold on, I'll find out what Gloria and Caspar think of it… Brent, you're like a brother to me, so I'll go easy. Two hundred, the others wanted a lot more."

"Two hundred! No. I was thinking of a hundred, tops."

"There'll be at least three of us, we have travelling expenses, it's short notice, it's now snowing and we've to break a date to fit you in. Like, what do you expect, man?"

"I expect the youth, the future of the country, to have a better reaction. I think you three are in someone's basement playing video games with nothing doing and completely bored. You're asked to do a task that you wouldn't mind doing for the simple love of it and it will only take you ten minutes' work. One-fifty, take it or leave it."

"Well, I know times are hard for you, Brent. Let me see what the others say." The microphone on Vane's phone was muffled for a few seconds. "Yeah, we're all like really sorry for you. We'll do it."

"Okay, seriously now. There are no drugs where you are at the moment?" asked Brent.

"No, nothing here. I promised you and so I'm clean and it's gonna stay that way."

"How are the classes?"

"Good. I Got 92% on that calculus test I was sweating over."

"That's fantastic. I knew you could do it. So, what are we doing tonight?"

"Ambassador's residence at nine. Three of us, maybe more, get the guards away from the door. You go in and we go away unless you need us to stay or something."

"I don't think I do. I'll transfer the money now. See you later."

"Yep, bye."

The first time Brent had met Vane was two years ago in an alleyway where the skinny, young girl lay dying from a drug overdose. He had sprayed Naloxone into one of her nostrils and she survived her first and last hit of Apache - cocaine laced with Fentanyl. He got her to a hospital. It annoyed him intensely, as he sat with her overnight and she lay sleeping, that Vane should throw her life away needlessly.

Brent, having intervened, could not then let go and accepted the challenge of reforming her life whether she liked it or not. She had been difficult for him to deal with at first. She called him a creep in very colourful terms. Brent called her an idiot. On that shaky basis, they went forward until trust began to build. He helped her to turn her life around. She became good at surveillance, message delivery, and following people - skills that Brent appreciated and used frequently in his line of work.

Rita Wyatt's apartment building was old and well maintained. It had that type of security door where visitors had to use the intercom before being buzzed through by the tenant they were visiting. Brent, having followed someone in, was already inside the building, sitting in an armchair in the tiny lobby. He was reviewing Rita's witness statement for a second time. He found nothing remarkable to make him believe that the waiter was directly involved in Franklin's death.

Sitting for a while, looking out the window, Brent noticed the snowfall, which had been heavy, was now tapering off. Two things were troubling him about the case. The first, and the one he was currently acting upon, was Evelyn's possible recognition of one of the supply staff who served the dinner on the night of Franklin's death. What did that signify, if anything? He hoped to find out tonight and he was doing so in such a way as to keep the police out of the picture, if possible, so that Evelyn would remain untroubled by inferences and accusations. Why, oh why, had she not mentioned she had recognized someone or noticed something? Brent wanted information directly from the staff first to see if it was necessary to the case before handing it to Greg.

The second matter of concern was Jimmy Brewster. He was strapped for cash; that much was obvious from the police reports. He needed money immediately to prop up his business and his lifestyle. Jimmy and Merrell had hidden something in the boxwood hedge. Merrell had gone out in the rain the night after the murder probably to hide an object and Jimmy, as confirmed by Greg's surreptitious examination of his boots, had gone out there this morning probably to retrieve the selfsame article. It had been a package small enough to be undetected when the security camera footage was reviewed. Brent was guessing at the contents of the package but his idea was that Jimmy, prompted by Merrell, had stolen something of value.

Brent, having once been a professional thief, thought he recognized a fellow practitioner in Merrell. That being the case, then the package contained… what? Brent did not know because no property had been reported stolen from Hill Hall. He guessed that the package might contain Evelyn's jewellery. The value of the contents of Hill Hall ran to many millions but most of it was not of a size to be concealed in a hedge or under a jacket. Tonight, Brent would try to find out what was in the package and, if possible, recover it. Of one thing he was fairly certain - it was that Merrell and Jimmy's activities had nothing to do with Franklin's death. Merrell was covering her tracks the wrong way if she had murdered Franklin. And she certainly would have called for lawyers when Brent interviewed them earlier if she and Jimmy had been entirely innocent.

Brent had called Rita Wyatt by phone before knocking on her door. She was in and would see him, although she warned that her apartment was in a mess.

"Hello," said Brent, as Rita opened the door to her one-bedroom apartment. He handed her his card.

"Hi, please come in." Rita was in her early twenties and was wearing sweat pants and a shirt. She possessed a bright, animated face.

"Sorry to barge in on you like this. As I explained, I'm collecting information on a few, specific points." He paused when he saw a mound of clothing piled up on the couch, that, by volume, would be suitable for a family of six.

"It's my laundry night," said Rita, having followed Brent's gaze. "I get it done while I study."

"Good idea," replied Brent. He had the urge to ask what time frame the pile of clothes represented but knew it was none of his business. Surely, it can't be a week, he thought to himself. Instead, he said,

"I promise not to take up too much of your time."

"I don't mind," said Rita. "Let's sit at the table." She waved him towards the dining area. The dining table was littered with books. "Can I get you a tea or a coffee?" she asked when she was halfway to the kettle on the counter.

"No, thank you kindly. Please, don't put yourself to any trouble." Brent sat down and saw a textbook that bore the title, 'Sociological Theory of the Mundane in Western Relationships' and wondered if it contained a chapter on laundry practices. Rita sat down also. She was a fidget.

"Are you getting anywhere with the investigation?" she asked, her eyes alive with excitement.

"Slowly, we are. It is a very difficult case and I need your help."

"Ah, ask me anything you like," she replied enthusiastically. "This is so interesting. I've never been involved in a murder case before."

"Most people would be relieved not to find themselves in your situation."

"Not me. I love the human interactions and the insights it gives me."

"I suppose there is that. Like your textbook, there is a lot of the mundane in any investigation. Once the basic facts and outline are anchored down then it becomes more hypothetical and subjective. I'm at that stage where I need closure on one issue. I think it is immaterial but I have to chase it down. I'm sure you remember the night of the murder vividly."

"I think I have complete recall of everything I did."

"I know it's in your witness statement but can you give me a few instances of what you did do?"

"Sure. We got there early to help with the setup but the butler had arranged for it to be done already. He gave us our instructions and assigned our areas of responsibility. We brought the courses in from the kitchen when they were to be served. Mr Jackson always accompanied us when we entered the room with each course but we served the guests while he looked on. We also served drinks."

"If you had to go back to the kitchen for anything did Jackson go with you?"

"No, he didn't. At least, not with me. He was in the dining room most of the time."

"When a course had been served, where did you stand?"

"The three of us stood in a line near the sideboard."

"I'm a bit hazy on this, how did it work? Did you have sections assigned to you in case a guest wanted something?"

"Yes. Sammy looked after the head of the table. Rachel had the far side, and I had the nearest side. Rachel should have been standing on her side of the table but Mr Jackson didn't want it that way."

"I see. Any particular reason, do you think?"

"He said we would make the room look untidy," she replied, laughing. "I know what he means, though."

"Now, while you're standing in a line how do you comport yourself?"

"Comport? What a lovely old word. We stood like this." Rita jumped up and, in her comfortable clothing, stood erect yet relaxed, with her hands clasped together in front of her. For the first time since Brent had met her she was still. "We watch the table like this." Rita maintained her position and slowly moved her eyes from left to right and back again without unduly moving her head.

"Thank you. That gives me a very clear idea of what you did." Rita sat down again.

"If you can, try and recall if Mrs Evelyn Brewster was trying to attract your attention."

"Oh, no. She spoke to Mr Jackson a couple of times. She said something to Sammy. I remember seeing her do that. It was brief, though, like she was thanking him. I could have missed some interactions while I was busy."

"Yes… I was thinking more of when you were lined up. Did you notice her looking at you or any of you?"

"I can't say I did. I do remember her staring into space once - that's all, I think. As I told you, I had to focus on my section of the table."

"Of course. How were the kitchen staff towards you, Sammy and Rachel?"

"Fine. Usual stress to get everything out on time and not have it go cold. The cook looked a bit of a tyrant, though her cooking was amazing."

"I've spoken to her and in her kitchen, I would agree, she is tyrannical. Away from the kitchen she has a soft side and is a very nice person."

"Is she?" Rita became earnest. "It's funny… you meet someone and that first impression is enough to convince you that the person is like that in all their relational transactions. It is never the case, though."

"Isn't it? Maybe you're right. One last question. Was there anything you noticed, no matter how small or fleeting, that didn't seem right or that stuck out in some way?"

"Let me see… I don't think there was. No. Sorry, I can't be more of a help. You sure you don't want a tea?"

"Very kind of you but no thanks," replied Brent. "I suppose neither Sammy nor Rachel noticed anything or mentioned anything to you."

"No. Sammy's quiet and doesn't talk much but Rachel's acting very weird."

"In what way?"

"She's really upset. I worked with her for the first time at Hill Hall but we've spoken by phone since. I got her number from Sammy. She finds the murder very disturbing. I'm surprised she's working tonight."

"I'm surprised at your not working! I'd have thought you'd like to work at the Ambassador's residence."

"That's a regular gig. I've been there three times. But I can only work one shift a week, max. I have another job and then there's my degree. I don't have time."

"No, I can see that. Thank you for your help, Ms Wyatt." As Brent got up to make his departure, he said, "I can't help asking… Do you take in laundry?"

"Oh, that!" She turned to the pile of clothes and started laughing. "That's my sister's. Her washing machine has broken down and she's trying to get it repaired under warranty. She dropped all that off and she's coming over soon to do it. Mine's already in the dryer."

"I'm so relieved it isn't all yours. Goodnight, and thank you for your help."

"Goodnight, Mr Umber."

After parking his Jeep on a quiet, snow-covered road in a run-down neighbourhood, Brent walked a couple of streets over to an area of mixed use. Most of it was comprised of old commercial buildings with a few newer ones shoe-horned in beside them. The rest was residential of an age and condition that cried out for rehabilitation. He walked along the street until he was midway between the crossroads at either end. He came to a halt before an old, circa 1910 brick building that had heavy steel gratings over the windows and two steel shutters at the front. The larger shutter opened upon a former machine shop that Brent used as a garage for his other vehicles. The smaller of the two was front door-sized. He unlocked the padlock on this shutter and rolled it up to reveal a steel door. Next, he unlocked the two locks on the door and went in. He switched on the light, disarmed one alarm system by use of a keypad, and, by calling out 'Brent's back', put a second system into a restricted monitoring mode.

He closed the steel shutter behind him and bolted it from the inside. He was safe inside his urban pied-à-terre that he now visited at least once a week, although he used to live there exclusively.

The sound of footfalls on the metal staircase against the wall always made a scuffing, echoing, metallic noise when Brent climbed it. He could see his old van and the nondescript daily driver below him. His newer Porsche Macan was at his suburban home where Maria could have access to it to do shopping.

The interior of the building looked bleak under the commercial overhead lights. Nothing much had been done to eradicate the impression of former small-scale industrial use on the ground floor beyond cleaning, painting, and the installation of a rock-climbing wall. There was even an old milling machine shoved right into one corner - a long-forgotten remnant of a long-forgotten business.

When he reached the landing at the top of the stairs, Brent took out a fourth key to unlock yet another steel door. After this had been opened, Brent whispered "lights." A short hallway was instantly revealed, softly illuminated by recessed fixtures in the dropped ceiling. The walls were painted a warm mustard colour and framed pictures hung on both sides making it look like a gallery. The rough-timbered floor had been smoothly refinished while keeping traces of the abuse suffered during its former usage. This level had once been the offices and storage rooms belonging to the machine shop below but it had been converted, by Brent and a couple of professionals, into a luxury, two-bedroom apartment.

The large living room was sparsely furnished and contained few decorative items. It had a modern feel to it overall even though the wooden items of furniture were exquisite period pieces. However, the couch and chairs were

chosen for comfort more than for any other reason. The
uncluttered theme continued in the dining room and both
bedrooms. The kitchen was modern and included stainless
steel counters and tables and cherry red enamelled
appliances.

The first thing Brent did was to put the stew into a
container and microwave it. While that was underway he
went to a closet to take out a grey suit that would be
acceptable to the society found in an Ambassador's reception
rooms. Next, he accessed a desktop computer and reviewed
the security report on his building. The app brought up three
incidents: a burned-out bulb at the back of the building, a cat
walking along the side of the building and a smartly dressed
woman banging on the shutters. Real estate agent, Brent
thought. They visited with some regularity, hoping to buy an
option on the property or get it as a listing. One day, the area
would be redeveloped but little work of that nature had
started as yet.

The stew was good. He put the dishes in the dishwasher
and then attended to himself. While dressing, he could not
quite decide whether to break into Hill Hall and do what he
intended or drive up normally, albeit very late, and talk to
the police officers. On the one hand, he would have to search
in the dark and avoid the police officers. On the other, if he
went in as usual, he could search many places without
raising any alarm.

Mrs Brewster had observed certain proprieties and put
Merrell and Jimmy in separate suites. Brent wished to search
both suites while the occupants were asleep. He felt that
wherever Merrell was so would the jewels be - if jewels were
what had been hidden. He felt compelled to act in this way
because, once the funeral and the reception were over,
Jimmy and Merrell would depart with whatever it was that
they wanted to keep concealed. Once gone, the couple would

be beyond the reach of the law and Brent Umber. If he found out what it was they concealed, he could at least have the chance of proving or disproving any connection they might have with the murder. It was time for him to go. He had made up his mind but he had to deal with Sammy and Rachel first.

The snow had ceased and the street was empty of pedestrians. Only a few cars proceeded carefully along the snow-rutted road. Right on schedule, five hooded, dark clothed figures walked quietly along in a group carrying snowballs in their arms. They stopped outside the gate of the Italian Ambassador's residence. A man, muffled up in his long coat and wearing a winter hat, passed them by and turned in at the gate. The group did not acknowledge him and he ignored them.

He walked down the cleared front path towards the steps at the top of which stood a security guard. The group followed down the same path. As the man mounted the stairs snowballs began flying. They hit the security guard and the door. Five willing arms pelted the officer mercilessly. Dull thumps, from hard-packed snowballs hitting the door, brought a second security guard outside in a hurry. The two guards, shouting hoarsely, began to chase the unruly youths off the property and down the street. The man entered through the open door but not without a snowball hitting him on his shoulder. *I know that was Vane*, Brent thought to himself.

Chapter 18

Wednesday night

*S*everal guests had clustered near the front door because of the commotion outside. Brent quickly hung his coat and hat in a closet and turned to pass through them.

"Excuse me," said Brent politely, as he passed through the knot of people. "It's nothing to worry about. There were some youths outside having a snowball fight."

"Very bad," said a distinguished-looking gentleman to Brent. "They should do that elsewhere," he added.

"I don't know what gets into them," replied Brent. "They need proper employment instead of hanging around in the streets."

"Quite right," said the man.

Brent intercepted a drinks waiter and took a glass of champagne off the tray he carried. He looked about him, glass in hand. It was a large and refined room alive with the murmur of incessant conversation. The hundred or so guests were superbly dressed - men in formal suits of dark greys and blacks, women in elegant, formal dresses. The glint of expensive jewellery and crystal wine glasses, and the attraction of smiling faces and expressive hand gestures presented a dazzling picture. Brent saw that the ambassador was busy talking conversationally to a small group. His wife,

Martina Di Fazio, was talking to another woman nearby to Brent. Martina was wearing a dark, copper-coloured dress that had a dull sheen to it. Brent knew the Ambassador and his wife by sight only because he had looked them up on the internet a couple of hours earlier. Martina had seen Brent come into the room so he approached her and her companion first. They both were looking concerned.

"Good evening, ladies," said Brent, smiling. "Don't worry about the incident outside - it was just some teenagers having a snowball fight. It seems they wanted to include the security guards in their game. I went to see what was happening and the guards had it all under control."

Martina smiled and answered with a very slight Italian accent, "Why would they choose this house?"

"Who can say?" said Brent. "But they have gone now. Your efficient security guards took care of them but not without receiving a few well-aimed shots."

"Well, that is good. One never knows what will happen next. There are so many terrible things going on in the world."

"That is very true. I'm glad it did not disturb his excellency."

"Oh, once he is talking the roof could fall in and he would not notice." She and the other woman both laughed.

"Conversation is the currency of diplomacy," said Brent. He noticed that a security guard was at the doorway - probably scanning the room for him. It prompted him to say, "That reminds me of something I wanted to ask you. As important as the post of Ambassador is in this country, if you could choose anywhere in the world for you and your husband to be posted, where would it be, seeing that the winter is often so dreary here?"

"I don't know. I have never thought about it. Where would *you* go, Claudia?"

"Me, I would choose the Caribbean as a post," said Claudia.

"Okay, that sounds good. Mind you, somewhere in North Africa would be nice," said Martina.

"I suppose that would put you closer to home," said Brent.

"Yes, but that is not a problem. It is not the distance, it is finding the time to get away from the duties."

"Factoring that in," said Brent, "then the best situation would be to have a split post between Australia in our wintertime and Spain in the summer, for example."

The women laughed. Brent noticed the security guard had left.

"But!" said Claudia, earnestly. "Who would get the other side of those posts?"

"Yes, that is a problem. I know, the newest ambassador would get it… or someone who had fallen out of favour."

"It could never happen," said Martina, shaking her head. "Being an ambassador is about building long-term relationships. You can't do that in six months."

"Yes, there is that," said Brent. "Look, I don't wish to detain you, ladies. I'm sure you both have other guests to meet." Brent formally addressed them, "Mesdames, it has been a pleasure talking with you." He shook each lady by the hand and left them to find Sammy and Rachel.

Sammy was a small, wiry man with quick, efficient actions when he worked. While motionless, the waiter stood as though in a trance. Brent approached him while he was in the latter condition.

"Mr Sammy Katz, my name is Brent Umber. I'm an investigator. I need to ask you a few questions about the night of the Brewster murder."

"Ah, I'm working. Can't we talk tomorrow? I'm, like, really busy right now."

"Mr Katz, the guests have been fed and watered and you are essentially doing nothing that another team member couldn't cover."

"Like I said, I can talk to you tomorrow."

"That's fine. I'll just call a squad car and have you arrested. I'll ask them to process you slowly and carefully so you might get away by about eight in the morning after I've questioned you for an hour."

"You can't arrest me. I haven't done anything."

"Obstruction of justice would be a start. I'm sure something else can be found if the police look hard enough."

"But this is an embassy, like foreign soil, the police…"

"Residence. It is a residence, not an embassy. That one won't work."

"I've got nothing to say."

"What will your employers think?"

Sammy was sullen and looked away. Brent saw him clench his jaw muscles.

"I know you're hiding something. Tell me what it is."

Sammy's eyes flickered but he remained stubbornly aloof.

"Pride is very strange. It makes a person do and say absurd things, often harmful things."

"Who's proud?" Sammy glared at Brent.

"It isn't me so it must be you, seeing as we're the only two people standing here. I'll make it easy, Sammy. You're covering for someone. At Hill Hall, you were put on the spot and agreed to keep quiet over some issue. Now you're taking the heat and so pride, mixed with misplaced loyalty, is making you angry. You're determined to keep your promise but you don't like it at all."

"If you're so clever you don't need me to answer your questions."

"You should change tactics, my friend, even if you don't want to co-operate. It would make life a lot more pleasant for you. However, I accept your challenge. I know a lot about that evening. Your movements and conversations are well documented. Apart from a few brief exchanges between you and Jackson, the butler, and then some of the kitchen staff, you did not converse at length with any of the guests or other household staff. That means you are covering for either Rita or Rachel. Having already spoken with Ms Wyatt, I am confident in saying that you are not covering for her. That leaves Rachel, only Rachel. I'll talk to her once I've finished with you."

The waiter suddenly smiled sheepishly. "Yeah, you just about nailed it."

"You could be in a lot of trouble over this," said Brent who did not accept the man's admission as anything but camouflage. "You'll answer my questions and then I'll see what I can do about your having made a false statement."

"Huh, I guess I don't have a choice."

"None. First, think carefully, did you notice any unusual actions by the diners?"

"No. The old lady made a kind of nasty comment to the guy who died. The rest of the time they seemed like a normal bunch."

"And afterwards?"

"There was a row… not a big deal but there was tension in the room afterwards."

"Did you see anyone do anything to the food or drink at any time?"

"No. That's what I said in my statement."

"Did Mrs Evelyn Brewster stare at you or any of the staff?"

"Yeah, probably three or four times. But it wasn't at me. I looked after the head of the table and I kept thinking she was wanting something while we stood in line but it wasn't that."

"What was it?"

"She was looking at… Rachel."

"Why was she looking at Rachel?"

"That's what I can't tell you. And I'm not going to. You ask her and you'll soon find out."

"Okay, Sammy. That's all I wanted to ask. I'll let the omissions in your witness statement slide for now. You keep your secret. I have a good idea what it is."

Brent left Sammy to hunt down Rachel.

Rachel Cummings, serving drinks from a tray to a small group of guests, looked bright and pleasant. She was twenty years old and intent upon her work at the white linen-draped drinks table when Brent approached her.

"Can I help you, sir?" she asked when Brent came and stood before her.

"Thank you, I don't actually want a drink. My name is Brent Umber and I'm investigating the Brewster case. Can we talk somewhere privately?"

The look on Rachel's face changed in an instant from one of polite attentiveness to one of mild shock.

"Uh, I don't know…" she said in some confusion.

"I can wait," said Brent, "while you get someone to cover your station. I only want to sort out a few things in my mind and I need your help to do so."

"Yes, I see… Um, please, I'll just be a moment."

Rachel attracted the attention of another staff member. When he came over she whispered something to him. The waiter walked behind the table and took over Rachel's place. Brent and Rachel left the room together. She had a little of the air of one walking to her execution.

In a quiet side passage, away from the reception rooms and kitchens, they stood together. Brent looked affable. Rachel looked worried.

"I can't stay long. I'll get in trouble with my supervisor," she said.

"I think I ought to have spoken to your supervisor first."

A woman appeared at the end of the passage near the kitchens.

"Rachel, is everything all right?" It was the supervisor. She appeared as if summoned at the mention of her office and looked as though she thought everything was not as it should be.

"Please join us," said Brent, taking a step towards her. "My name's Umber and I'm an investigator for the police. It's concerning last Thursday night."

"Oh, you're one of them," said the unimpressed woman.

"Yes. I need Rachel to answer a few quick questions and then I'll be on my way. I'm very sorry to disturb your professional arrangements like this but I literally need only five minutes. You can stand with us and listen if you like."

"Ah, no, that'll be fine. I have to watch the rooms."

"I see. What is your name, by the way?" asked Brent.

"Josie Phillips."

"Well, Josie, thank you for being so understanding in this matter. Blame all the inconvenience on me."

"It's no trouble," said Josie. She smiled and left the passageway.

Brent turned to Rachel once more. The young woman's face had blanched and showed the strain.

"Rachel, listen to me carefully. You are not in trouble but I need to hear all of the truth from you. Last week you did something and it is being covered up. What did you do?"

Rachel looked miserable. "I… I can't…"

"Okay. Do you know Mrs Evelyn Brewster?"

"No."

"Why was she staring at you?"

"She wasn't. I don't remember that."

"If that's true, then someone took your place last week. I think it was Chloe Halliday. How well do you know Chloe?"

"Know Chloe? I don't understand what you mean."

"Then answer me this. What jewellery was Mrs Brewster wearing that night?"

Rachel looked down at the carpet. Brent stared at the top of her head of dark hair. Where her hair parted in the centre he could see a small scar. He immediately imagined her as a small child, falling off a swing, or something similar, and getting a gash in her scalp. Then he saw Rachel, with blood in her hair and a trickle of red running down her cheek, crying out and running home. He suddenly felt very sorry for the woman standing before him in the passage of the Ambassador's residence.

"I want to be your friend," said Brent gently. "I'll keep everything you say a secret and make sure no harm comes to you. Please, tell me all that you can. I will be talking to Chloe about this. I have to know the truth."

Rachel looked up at Brent. She was close to tears.

"You seem to know most of it. I don't know how you found out."

"Take your time and tell me what happened."

Rachel took a deep breath. "Very well," she said. "Chloe and I were in the same drama class last year. We're really good friends… I don't know about her or whether she feels the same but I would say she's one of my best friends. Anyway, the reason I went to drama class was that I needed an easy course credit. Acting isn't my thing but with Chloe, it's her passion. One of the things they teach is for the

students to act out a different persona in a real setting."
Rachel paused.

"Like acting as though one were a doctor or a lawyer?"
asked Brent.

"Yeah, like that. The teacher said we should get the work
experience and act the part out as though we were a different
person entirely… It was kind of open-ended as to how we
did it. So, I've finished with drama but Chloe is working at it
like crazy. When she heard that I was going to be working at
Hill Hall she came up with the idea of switching places. She
would be me, acting out the role of a waiter. The kick she got
out of it was that she was going to make herself up to look
different. Only Mrs Brewster knew of her plan."

"That makes sense," said Brent. "She must have played
her part very well because no one else noticed that it was
her."

"She's really good. I saw her when she played Goneril in
King Lear and I hated her… and she's my best friend."

"Whoa! Can you get me a ticket for her next production?"
asked Brent.

"Ha… Yes, I can try."

"Now, because the murder happened that night, for some
reason both of you decided to keep quiet about Chloe's
substitution."

"Pretty much that's it…. Mr Umber, I have been feeling
really bad about all of this. I haven't been sleeping well. I'm
so worried about getting into trouble."

"I imagine you would be. Did she say why she wanted to
keep it quiet?"

"Well, part of the reason was so that I didn't lose my job.
Sammy knew… I think Chloe gave him fifty to keep quiet
about it."

"What other reasons were there?"

"Well, that the police would think Chloe killed her uncle."

"Was Chloe frightened about that?"

"At first, she had a meltdown. Then she pulled herself together. We talked it through and decided that we would just pretend it was me at the dinner."

"What about Mrs Brewster?"

"Oh, she's a sweetheart. She said she would back Chloe in whatever she did and would not say anything about Chloe being there that night."

"Is that so?"

Brent thought about the bond that these three women had and how they had deliberately avoided the questions the police had asked. He found their devotion to each other admirable in one sense and intensely stupid in another.

"I promised not to keep you too long from your duties. Thank you for answering my questions… You've been a great help."

"What will you do now?" asked Rachel.

"I need to talk to Chloe at some point but there's something else I have to do first. I want to reassure you that no trouble shall follow on from this revelation. You do understand that misleading the police can have serious consequences?"

"I do. I've been feeling just awful about it."

"I can see that you have. Don't worry anymore."

"Thank you so much. I didn't know the police would be so understanding. Goodnight."

"Goodnight, Rachel," said Brent.

He watched her walk away. He asked himself how it was that decent, intelligent people could make such bad decisions. He left shortly afterwards, bidding goodnight to the security guards, who now seemed in good humour.

Outside, the air was sharply colder and he was happy to find his Jeep to get out of the chill breeze. He started the engine and, feeling the coldness in the driving seat, let out the clutch. He was heading for his apartment first to get changed and then on to Hill Hall. The vehicle traversed the snow-covered roads easily. The sky overhead had cleared and stars shone cold and brilliant like diamonds. Brent thought that very apt for the mission he would be soon undertaking.

Chapter 19

Later Wednesday night

*I*t was far easier for Brent Umber to walk into Hill Hall than to break into it. That is what he had chosen to do for simple expediency and to save time. Had he decided to break in, he would not have arrived in his easily recognizable Jeep, of course, but would have used another vehicle and parked it some distance away. Then he would have crossed the snowy open ground in boots he would later discard. Knowing where the security camera blind spots were on the building, Brent would have taken advantage of them and easily scaled the outside to one of the upper floors - he did not mind which one. There he would force open a window. He preferred using a glass cutter and suction pad to remove the cut out section - he hated making a mess. Once inside, he would remove his boots and walk slowly and quietly - controlling his breathing - listening for sounds. He would wait often and guide himself by a tiny flashlight with a narrow beam. If he heard voices he would wait patiently, for hours if necessary, until all threat of discovery had passed. When his way was clear again he would move to find what he was looking for.

Instead of such painstaking effort, Brent had driven up in his Jeep at 11:00 p.m., said hello to the police officer outside in the car, and rung the bell at the front door. Jackson the butler, arrayed in a burgundy red silk dressing-gown, admitted Brent while listening to his profuse apologies at the lateness of the hour and the necessities of work. Jackson preserved his professional mien while Brent spoke.

A tour of the house revealed to Brent that the disparate members of the family were very much alone in their grief, remembrance, or distraction. Mike and Sofia had retired for the night. Steve and Laura were in the process of doing the same - Laura always seemed to remember at the last moment that she had numerous things to do before going to bed and would rather get them done than lie awake thinking about them. This turned her getting ready for bed into a protracted affair. The Aimes and Halliday children were not present in the house. Lloyd was an early riser and, correspondingly, was early to bed. Evelyn was in her suite in bed with the light on. Marjorie was in her bed in her room with the light off. That left Merrell and Jimmy to be accounted for. Jimmy was downstairs watching television and seemed likely to continue doing so for some time. Merrell was in her room. She was listening to music with headphones on and was singing along with it. Brent believed it was going to be a long night.

In the temporary office, Brent caught up on his reports. He was leaving out of them large chunks of sensitive material so that when Greg read them he would not be prompted to ask problematic questions bearing upon those things Brent had promised not to divulge.

Midnight came and Brent raided the refrigerator. He made himself a cheese and tomato sandwich, poured himself a glass of milk, and took three chocolate biscuits from a packet. The kitchen seemed just a big, hollow, unattractive room when empty of its staff. He ate there anyway and washed and dried the things he had used.

By 12:30 a.m. everyone had gone upstairs for the night, except Jimmy, who was still watching a show, and the police officer, dozing in a chair in the hall. Merrell was now in bed with a lamp on. All other bedrooms were in darkness.

Brent cautiously and quietly opened Jimmy's bedroom door and then, in the same manner, shut it behind him. In about seven minutes he had searched the room thoroughly. The investigator, who was now well beyond the bounds of his police-given mandate, looked in the toilet tank, under the bed, between box-spring and mattress, in light fixtures, under rugs, and deftly went through every drawer and cupboard to find nothing. Jimmy's personal effects, bags, and clothes were similarly searched with the same result. Brent closed the door quietly and returned quickly to the office. The only discovery he had made was that Jimmy had to be either a hypochondriac or a very sick man. The bathroom cabinet looked like a well-stocked dispensary.

Brent found a likely-looking couch in the living room, sat on it, took off his shoes, put his feet up, and shut his eyes. It had been a while since he had employed his old talents. In some ways, he wished he had never been a criminal. He had stopped now for good. Yet he still could not quite let go of his old habits nor quell the impulse to utilize his peculiar skills, with this very night proving these points. He enjoyed the challenge, the risk, and the pure subversive nature of it all.

He remembered when he had started his career in crime - falling in with the wrong crowd, as they say. The trouble with that, as Brent well knew, was that he became the 'wrong crowd'. As an eighteen-year-old, he had burgled houses and stolen cars. That made him no different to Merrell - as far as he could see. What changed things for Brent was when he showed a real aptitude for picking locks and defeating alarm systems. This got him noticed in the right, criminal quarters. He was soon working with a team and targeting high-end residences and commercial operations. He was glad that career change had come along when it did. He had recently stolen from a house - the burglary had been successful. Once away from the scene and looking at the old lady's jewels in his hand, Brent suffered a crisis of conscience. He saw them as her treasured possessions that would mean far more to her than their insured value could ever compensate for. Brent went back to the woman, when the police were absent, and returned her jewels. He paid her five hundred dollars by way of saying sorry and they spoke at length. She made him a cup of tea.

When he was fairly embarked upon his criminal career, Brent began saving for his future and, although what he put aside was mostly illegal gains, he did work regular jobs, too.

After several years, he decided that he needed to regularize his position and worked towards that end. Brent got himself educated, bought the old machine shop to convert into an apartment, and took to building wealth through his stock portfolio.

With investments, he found he possessed an occasional yet uncanny ability for spotting undervalued companies. One such coup had netted him three million. He now had a net worth of ten million, all made legitimately except for the relatively small amount of start-up capital. And that, decided Brent, was a very good cover beneath which he could reintegrate himself into normal society.

Brent did not need to work again but he could not stand inactivity for more than a few hours or days at a stretch. More recently, well after his criminal career had ended, Brent had acquired a suburban home with a large garden.

The house renovations were complete but the massive garden at the back was only part-way through being transformed from an unloved lawn into a show-piece garden. Brent had help on this project from an experienced gardener named Eric.

Some years prior to the acquisition of his suburban house, and while Brent's life of crime was still in progress from his apartment, something occurred that forced him to re-evaluate everything.

The final chapter in the history of Brent's criminal activities was enacted when he became involved in a certain high-value robbery. He was not the organizer of this escapade and only received a relatively small share for his specific services. Bob Rowan, Brent's best friend, had planned the job with another man named Arnie Black who was associated with a criminal gang of a violent disposition. The strength of this association was not apparent until after the job had been completed. Violence was something that both Brent and Bob abhorred.

On this particular job, Brent only had to get the two men inside a warehouse by disarming the alarm system and then leave separately after having acted as a lookout. Black's major responsibility was to take care of a night watchman which in the plans that had been discussed amounted to him tying up the guard before the alarm could be raised. Bob Rowan was to help load and then drive away a truck full of expensive computer parts for later disposal. However, Arnie Black tried to kill the security guard and only Bob Rowan's intervention prevented the disaster. This caused bad blood between Black and Rowan.

The job was completed. Arnie Black had badly beaten the security guard. Brent decided he was quitting crime for good.

The gang with which Arnie Black was affiliated was run by a man named Danny Gould. For some reason, and Brent never did find out why, Gould had Brent's friend Bob Rowan killed by a contract killer. Brent was horrified and sickened by this senseless murder of his friend.

From then on, Brent worked hard at bringing home the murder to Gould, Black, and the contract killer whose name was Percy Smith. He talked to dozens of people in careful ways so as not to draw attention to himself. He built up a picture of what had happened. Brent could draw everything out step by step as though he had been present. However, he was left with two insurmountable difficulties. None of the evidence he accumulated would stand up in court and the witnesses he had interviewed would not openly go against Gould and his gang. Another bitter vexation was that he had never found out why it was Bob was executed - that knowledge, it seemed, was exclusive to Gould and Black.

From this ugly, harrowing experience, Brent discovered he had a talent for investigation. Unable to do anything for his dead friend he decided he might be able to help others. He took the right courses, got a certificate, and so became a private investigator.

In the beginning, Brent threw himself into and was busy with that occupation but, recently, he had worked fewer private cases, especially since he had been drawn into Greg Darrow's world to help out in police investigations. These cases were so immersing an experience for Brent that his routine investigative work became uninteresting to him.

After a couple of investigations where Brent had given material help, the police department began to employ him on a 'when needed' basis. They realized that Brent could get people to talk and had a flair for it. Brent, while thriving in murder investigations, also had a faint but insistent hope that Gould and Black would cross his path on some other issue. It was a one in a thousand chance or it could be the very next case he was called in on. Brent did not know Gould personally, and Black may or may not have forgotten him. Brent would take that chance, if it ever came, for his friend's sake. He still wanted justice for Bob Rowan's murder.

Chapter 20

Very early Thursday morning

*I*t was now just before 2:00 a.m. and Brent trod carefully and noiselessly along the hall. Jimmy was asleep in his own room - he had made sure of that fact. Outside of Merrell's room, he paused to listen and put on a pair of surgical gloves. The whole house was quiet and no sound came from within the room. Brent inserted two pick-locks into the keyhole very slowly. The lock would only take a few seconds to open but to do it without making a sound, any sound, took a lot longer. One false move might wake the sleeping occupant.

There came the faintest 'click' within the lock as Brent succeeded in unlocking it. He depressed the handle and waited, his ear close to the panel of the door. Thirty seconds passed and he heard nothing. This was now the most dangerous part for him because even the dim light from the hallway might wake the sleeper. He opened the door silently, slowly, and then fluidly moved inside. He shut the door to, without allowing the bolt back into its recess in the frame. He let go of the handle and crouched down to wait again.

The room was dark, save for a tiny crack of light beneath the bottom of the door, starlight barely showing where the sheer curtains were, and a weak gleam emitted by illuminated numbers on the digital display of an alarm clock.

There were three windows with their thick curtains drawn back. Brent hopefully took this to mean that Merrell was a heavy sleeper. He waited just beyond the end of the bed for his eyesight to adjust and to listen. In the silence, he heard the regular, untroubled, slow breathing of the sleeper. Had she been quiet, holding her breath, Brent would have known she was awake and listening. As he stood there, he discovered that Merrell liked vanilla scented candles.

Brent crouched low and moved slowly to the bathroom. The door was partially open but he had to open it wider to get in. He hoped it would not squeak. It did not squeak and for that he heartily thanked the attentive Jackson. Once inside, he closed the door and switched on his pencil-like flashlight. The metal cabinet had a magnetic closer and, try as he might to avoid making any sound, when he opened the mirrored door it made a small, hard noise. He waited again, motionless, until he was sure that the sleeper had not been disturbed. He then searched the cabinet without any result. To lift the toilet tank lid would make too loud a noise, as would putting it back. He decided against that action - the risk being too great. He looked into the vent and light fixture, in the trash bin, and searched a small linen cupboard without success. He switched off the flashlight and waited for his eyes to adjust once more to the dark before returning to the bedroom.

The dressing room area was in an alcove with its own window. Brent painstakingly went through a dressing table, chest of drawers, closet, and a small glass cabinet of Limoges miniatures. He examined her travelling bags. Next, he went to look under the bed. He lay on the floor with his head under the valance. His flashlight revealed nothing. He was about to get up when Merrell stirred. He waited as she turned over in bed and, in the silence that followed, Brent strained to hear sounds of wakefulness. Her breathing returned to the rhythm of one who was sleeping well.

There were two matching bedside tables with drawers. One contained a Bible, some potpourri, and several lace handkerchiefs. These things Brent found by touch and smell alone because he could not risk a light. On the side that Merrell was sleeping, the nightstand was obviously the one she used. As she slept she faced Brent. Cautiously, he searched the top by touch. A plastic medicine container, a novel, and a pair of reading glasses was all he found. Opening the drawer was agonizing as it made a tiny rubbing noise that he could do nothing to prevent. He slowly slid it open and found a long jewellery case inside. On top of it was a small revolver. Brent removed both silently. He searched the rest of the drawer, left it open and went into the bathroom. Anticipating his search was about to bear fruit he shut the door to, put the revolver in his pocket and began to examine the contents of the case. It contained Merrell's personal jewellery - some costume pieces and some valuable ones - including a very pretty and expensive jade pendant that Brent thought of taking with him for his trouble. However, he remembered he was now a reformed character and put it back. In disappointment, he proceeded to return the case and pistol to the drawer.

Sitting on the floor at the end of the bed, Brent racked his brains to think of a hiding place he had overlooked. Then he considered Merrell and tried to think as a thief would do who was stealing something, wanted it close by them at all times, and yet have it safe from the police. Under the pillow was what he thought first. There was nothing for it - he had to try.

One of the pillows was easily searched. Merrell rested her head on the other pillow. Brent could not remember having done anything like this before. From her side of the bed,

Brent carefully slid his hand underneath her pillow. Almost immediately, he touched her arm and he recoiled in shock with his heart thumping. Fortunately for him, the contact had not woken her. Considering the situation, Brent contented himself with lightly running his hand around the free edges of the smooth pillow. He found nothing and decided he should leave.

As he was about to make his way to the door a thought struck him. He could not remember where he had learned of the trick, probably in a story as a child, but he had thought it was a good one although he saw no personal use for it. It required fishing line. A bag was tied at one end and then hung out of a window with the valuables inside of it. A small knot with a loop was on the other end. To put a finger in the loop and close the window over the line was easy to do. When the window was closed all that showed was a nearly invisible piece of fishing line and a small knot holding it securely in place. In case of a raid or other threat, the person concealing the valuables would merely open the window an inch allowing the bag and valuables to fall to the ground outside. Later, these could be retrieved at leisure.

At the second window he searched by touch, Brent found what he was looking for. It was just a knot of line with no loop showing. Clever Merrell, thought Brent. We must have read the same story.

He dared not open the window because of the noise it would make. It would be the one noise this particular sleeper would be most attuned to hearing and could have her out of bed in an instant. Brent took off a glove and grasped the knot with his fingernails. He then pushed gently upwards on the frame relieving the pressure on the line. The line was now free and Brent pulled it in a foot or so before letting the window grip the line again. Whatever was on the other end weighed several pounds. Using a small knife he cut off the knot. Brent pushed on the frame once more and, with satisfying rapidity, felt the line disappear from his hand. He then left the bedroom as quietly as he had come.

Chapter 21

Thursday morning

*I*n the morning, thin, hazy clouds came in on the wind and the temperatures rose. Yellow filtered sunshine started to melt the snow and the air became balmy and soft. Winter had not yet officially started and it already felt as though Spring was arriving because of the sudden rise in temperature.

Brent had returned to his suburban home and caught a few hours sleep. He was now sitting at the breakfast table in the kitchen. Monty, the ginger cat who occupied the same premises but did not necessarily acknowledge Brent's ownership over him, was eating his breakfast by the back door.

In front of Brent on the table was spread out a glittering array of jewels. Each individual piece was in a plastic evidence bag to preserve any prints and DNA to be found on them. Evelyn's jewellery was a sight to behold. Much of it was old and all of it in its way was fabulous. Brent estimated the nine pieces at well over three million at wholesale prices. The collection consisted of a Burmese ruby necklace, emerald earrings and matching necklace, a near-flawless diamond ring of at least twelve carats weight - as far as Brent could tell, a pearl choker, a long pearl necklace, a sapphire ring, a diamond and gold bracelet, a glorious garnet necklace fit for a monarch to wear, and a massive and exquisitely cut pink beryl brooch.

So as not to leave any prints, Brent wore a pair of blue nitrile gloves to handle the valuable pieces. While he held and carefully examined each piece through several jeweller's loupes of different magnification, thoughts of his past came to mind. His former occupation in which he used skills to bypass security systems had led him to concentrate his activities on where the greatest and most portable stores of value were to be found. Naturally, this steered him to target jewellery stores.

There were ways around the various alarm systems commonly installed in a jewellery store. For Brent, getting in was easy enough, particularly if the entry could be achieved by going through an adjacent, unsecured business in a mall and then through the partition wall. Jamming wi-fi signals or cutting power to the store took care of all but the most sophisticated systems. Line security systems, which are the most secure type, proved to be highly problematic for him at first. The work-around Brent developed was to employ the use of hackers to get him into the target store's alarm system account. From there he simply switched the alarm system off from outside the building, picked the door lock and walked in. He would bring along a safe-cracker as an accomplice if a safe needed to be opened.

He missed the excitement of those times but he now hated the harm he had caused and the worry he had given to so many innocent people. If he could turn the clock back he would. There was no way for him to do this. He had to live with his now sensitized conscience.

His inspection of this ruby necklace brought to mind a recent incident where a woman had been wearing a magnificent ruby ring of exceptional value. He had quickly become enamoured of her and, almost before he knew what he was doing, he had blurted out to her that he had once been a thief. She had not recoiled in horror when he told her a little about his criminal past. Even though nothing much had come of the encounter in the end and they had both moved on from it, that woman's acceptance of him despite his past had done much to boost Brent's hope that one day he would find his soul-mate and be able to call her his own.

Brent stared at the rich red rubies and became slightly hypnotized by them. He would return the necklace but, while looking into their cloudless warm depths, he was struck by how fragile or how strong a thought could be. Eight years ago, he would have only considered the monetary value of what he now held in his hand. Today, he considered the value of the person who wore them. He liked Evelyn. She was rich and acclimatized to possessing wealth. If she had no wealth he would still like her - Evelyn was the strong Matriarch. All of the Brewster family were moons rotating around her planet. In a way, the children, spouses, and grandchildren drew some strength and certainty from her as they lay trapped within their orbits. Chloe and Steve Aimes loved her. Robert Halliday wanted respect and love from her. Jimmy Brewster wanted her financial help. The others... Brent could not decide where they stood exactly but they all seemed close. Lloyd, earlier, and Marjorie, later, were also satellites drawn into Evelyn's gravitational pull. The exception was Franklin who had seemed to travel an eccentric path in relation to his mother's static, central position.

Brent considered that although Franklin had been said to have distanced himself from Evelyn, he had, nevertheless, made recent efforts to be important and useful to her. Evelyn said he had gone away but there Franklin still was. Was Franklin a hypocrite, a sycophant, a man seeking yet more financial advantage and pride of place by fawning over his mother? Or, had he felt a wretched loneliness in moving away from the moral rectitude of Brewster family life and then latterly had sought to replicate a species of the love he had once known by a pretence of love and affection? Was it real, feigned, or feigned in the hope it would become real? Whatever it was and whatever Evelyn might say, Franklin had still been circling close to his mother.

He slid the necklace back into its bag - a little tumbling river of deep red and gold flowing smoothly from his hands. Once inside the plastic bag, the necklace, without the warmth of a touch, or clear light, or the careful attention of an onlooker, was robbed of all its splendour and may as well have been cheap costume jewellery.

The idea that Brent had, while he sipped coffee and the cat crunched biscuits, was to confront Merrell and Jimmy with their crime and return the jewels to Evelyn without her knowing she had ever been robbed. Today was Franklin Brewster's funeral and how Brent would fit everything in was proving to be a conundrum to him.

"What shall I do, Monty?" asked Brent of the cat, who ignored him. "I absolutely have to be at the funeral but that's also the best time to put the jewels back. Mind you, I don't know where they go exactly and I don't even know if this is all of them. That jade piece that Merrell has is of the same quality as this lot." He looked at the cat. "You're not helping me much. Sleep, eat and disappear outside... that's all you do. We should swap places for the day... Would you like some milk?"

Brent carefully wrapped all the jewels and put them into a small box and the box into a backpack. He left the breakfast things in the sink because Maria, his housekeeper, got annoyed with him if there was nothing for her to do. Maria was Brent's housekeeper - at least, that was the nearest job title that fitted her duties.

Maria lived a few blocks away and came in a few days a week and often more than that. She and Brent had taken to eating Sunday dinner together - they both appreciated the company. Her husband had died several years ago after a protracted illness that had left Maria in financial difficulties. So bad was it at one point that if she did not sell her house quickly and pay off the mortgage she was going to lose it and she had said to Brent at the time, "I don't know what I will do." Brent quickly came to like Maria and contracted her services as his housekeeper to help her out. It helped him out, too, because Maria almost immediately became like an aunt or mother towards him. Shortly after she became his housekeeper, he paid off her mortgage.

Maria was devoted to Brent but they had one problem in their otherwise mutually agreeable relationship. She would keep asking him when he was going to get married and settle down. Maria showed Brent photos or spoke often about her numerous marriageable nieces and cousins with no equivocation as to her intent.

"Christine would make a very good wife," she had said. "Brent, Lisa has just broken up with her boyfriend… You should call her… She's very lonely, like you." Maria had urged Brent about Lisa to the point where he had little choice but to take lonely Lisa on a dinner date.

They had both got along fine on the date but Lisa was far from being lonely - she was a party girl. They left it at one date and had not spoken since because they really had so little in common. Brent, however, got social media notifications on Lisa's life and wondered when she would tire of telling the world how she was out with a few friends having a great time. The accompanying photographs were of a very different nature to the demure examples Maria had waived in his face from time to time accompanied by remarks such as: "Lisa is always saying nice things about you."

Chapter 22

Thursday afternoon

"Where are we at?" asked Greg Darrow. He was sitting in the office at Hill Hall and dressed a little smarter than usual. He had dispensed with the police patrols about the house because of the funeral and because there seemed no real threat to justify their continued presence.

"I can't say with any certainty yet," replied Brent. "There are three of them that stand out more than the rest and another two who are likely candidates. I'm hoping for great things at the funeral today. There are four from the cast of characters that I hope definitively to exclude."

"Give me something to work on, Brent. I've got my boss breathing down my neck. He wants a result to get his boss off his back."

"Then there's the media," said Alice. "Did you see what the People's Press said today? 'Police investigation stalled with a killer right under their nose.'"

"That's bad but the Daily Crier was worse," said Greg. "'Police on winter vacation at Hill House - scene of a murder.' That's us they're talking about."

"I didn't see those," said Brent. "The tasteless example I saw was, 'Franklin Brewster's funeral today - police along for the ride.'"

"Well, we can't take much more of that stuff," said Greg. "It will have consequences before long - career consequences."

"That's the truth," said Alice who was dressed formally in black which really suited her.

"Okay. If I wasn't in the picture, who would either of you pinch?" asked Brent.

"Jimmy Brewster, for the obvious reasons," said Greg.

"Sophia Halliday," said Alice.

"Got evidence beyond what you've already shown me?"

"I choose Sophia because she seems more calculating and more passionate than the rest of them. As to evidence… a case could be made but she wouldn't get convicted. The only new item that I've seen was the report that she went into Sadler-Creme last year and had a blazing row with the deceased. A lot of bad feeling there."

"That's interesting. I already knew that Sophia has something to tell me about her feud with her brother but I can't hurry her to do it. Greg, do you have anything on Jimmy?"

"Nothing new. Jimmy Brewster might have been put up to murdering Franklin by Fortier. There's something about those two that I can't put my finger on and it makes me suspicious. Her criminal record's against her and makes her a likely prospect."

"Thanks. All I can say is that I hope to move forward significantly on the case after today. Oh, yes. There's something I've been meaning to ask. Who is running the company now?"

Alice replied, "Galbraith, the lawyer, and Shickleman, the accountant, have divided the decision-making duties between them. A guy named Knight, he's the production manager, he's been stepped up temporarily to take over the work that the trustee managers don't understand. They've moved quickly because there's a big defence contract about to be signed with a value of five hundred and thirty million. Brewster was the guy who landed the deal."

"Really?" said Brent. "Then that might explain Franklin's indifference to outside help. Surely, Lloyd knew about this deal?"

"He did. The trustees were kept in the loop the whole way along."

"I don't know," said Brent, frowning. "This information seems like it should make a huge difference but I don't know how to fit it in."

"The whole case is like that," said Greg. "There's no clear path anywhere."

"Cheer up, Greg. A break comes sooner or later in every case."

"I hope it happens before I'm demoted," replied Greg.

The funeral service was held in a large, red-brick church that could not quite stylistically decide between being revived Baroque or revived Gothic. It seemed a little too much of both on the outside while inside it was like a relatively featureless white-washed cavern with pictorial stained glass windows that puzzled the viewers rather than illuminated them. The oak pews were wide and comfortable enough as long as the sermon was short. After a few hymns and prayers, Franklin Brewster received a shortish eulogy from the well-intentioned Minister who, avoiding the issue of murder entirely, managed to elevate Franklin a little way towards sainthood. The packed building received his words in respectful solemnity.

Brent had been surprised by two things. The first and most obvious was the size of the turn-out. Certainly, there was a sizeable contingent of company employees present but that did not account for the church being at its capacity with nearly eight hundred people present.

The second surprise was when Laura and Sophia rose to say some words about their brother. It was not what they said, it was that they looked so small and defenceless in the big church that caused Brent to want to put a brotherly arm around each of them and share in the sorrow they were expressing. Sophia was crying before she spoke. Laura cried when she had finished. The only other person to speak was Lloyd. He said some amusing things, in his clipped, emphatic way, that had the audience laughing over some childhood mishaps and other insights into Franklin's life.

The coffin was raised and taken away by the pallbearers. Then the service was over. The people moved slowly and politely towards the exit. Some would head to the graveyard and some would go back to their everyday lives.

Outside, Greg said, "That was nicely done."

"Ah, sorry? Yes, yes it was." Brent was watching the bereaved family like a hawk. Evelyn and Chloe were evidently avoiding each other. Jimmy and Merrell had separated themselves from everyone else. Laura was animatedly talking among a large group of women which included Aurelia Halliday. Sophia was talking with a woman who was accompanied by three small children. Steve Aimes was talking to the funeral director. Mike Halliday had disappeared. Lloyd could be seen talking to a reporter. Evelyn was receiving many well-wishers while Marjorie stood by her side. Chloe was standing with Rachel. They knew Brent had been watching them from time to time and both looked very awkward. Robert Halliday seemed bored and was with a woman who looked equally bored. Brad Aimes, former recluse, smiled and waved to Brent, and drifted from group to group not yet knowing where to fit in but trying anyway. Karen Aimes was smiling and laughing along with several cousins who came in all ages and sizes.

There was no opportunity for Brent to talk to anyone. He needed a private setting with no distractions and a time when it would be fitting to speak of the things he had to address. He saw Merrell looking at him while Jimmy was in conversation with some distant relatives. He approached her as she moved away from Jimmy. They spoke in low tones so as not to be overheard.

"Well, what will you do? You can't pin it on me now," she said coolly.

"There are three letters in the alphabet you should consider."

"Oh, and what would those be?"

"DNA - you will have worn several items and left traces of yourself. Not much is needed for a conviction."

"Yes… They were too beautiful for me to resist."

"By the way, was that all of them? Because, if not, I must have the other items returned before you and I cut a deal."

"What about Jimmy?"

"He doesn't look like a deal-maker to me. You'll be leaving him shortly, I should imagine."

"Maybe, I haven't decided yet."

"What have you got?"

"There was one jade pendant I had to have. I'll give it to you back at the house."

"Good. Play the game and you can walk."

"You're a funny sort of cop."

"You could say that. I'm after a murderer and not jewel thieves. I would wager that Jimmy does not know that you took as much as you did."

"He is a sweetie and I do like him. He only wanted to take his mother's diamond ring and have a copy made so that he could pawn the original. Then he would return it when in funds."

"He would return it?"

"Allow me to return it, then, if you want to be precise. I should never work with an amateur."

"We'll chat later," said Brent.

He left her because Jimmy was in the process of saying goodbye to his relatives. Brent understood that Jimmy believed it was just the diamond ring that had been taken. Merrell had forgotten to mention the other jewels to Jimmy and how she had kept them hidden outside her window all the time. It had to be that Jimmy panicked and Merrell, to keep her accomplice quiet, had hidden only the ring outside in the box hedge for him to fetch later when he had calmed down.

"Are you avoiding me, Mr Umber?" asked Evelyn politely. The family was beginning to get into the cars which would lead the procession. The old lady had seen Brent and, holding everyone up, had gone over to speak to him. She was beautifully dressed in black, even to her smart black hat and becoming veil. Her silvery-white, neatly coiffed hair framing her pallid face, barely warmed by the cosmetics she used, was in stark contrast to her attire. Her eyes were tinged pink. She and Brent gently shook hands.

"Not in the slightest, Mrs Brewster. I had hoped to see you after the funeral and pay my respects then."

"You don't strike me as a diffident man. I would have had you travel in the car with me and you tell what you have found out, only there isn't the room, I'm afraid."

"Then, let me say what I would have told you in the car, only in a brief summary. I have gotten to know Franklin and I miss him in some strange way. I have yet to identify the person who killed him. I'm working all the time - even now -

to narrow the field to that one person. When I know who it is I will tell you just as soon as I can and that, I believe, will be within a few days. I'm sorry if that does not bring you the relief you need."

"What if you are mistaken in your… selection?" asked Evelyn. She looked very serious.

"I won't be mistaken. I will know who it is."

"The family is very shaken by all of this. Some of them have behaved foolishly or without thinking of consequences. Don't take their foolishness to mean they are hiding guilty motives, will you?"

"No, I promise not to do that, Mrs Brewster." Brent wondered what *her* motive was in saying what she had just said.

"Thank you. I knew you would understand. I hope I will see you later." Evelyn smiled conventionally and then returned to her waiting car. When she had turned away, her face was paler still.

Chapter 23

Later Thursday afternoon

*B*rent got in the back of the unmarked police car. Greg and Alice occupied the front seats. The talk was desultory between them and so it gave Brent time to consider what Evelyn was trying to do. He guessed she was shielding Chloe and had given her word to keep secret her granddaughter's substitution for Rachel. She did not want to break her promise.

He was wondering if Evelyn thought Chloe had killed Franklin. Would she go that far to protect a guilty granddaughter? If that was Evelyn's belief, then she must have cause to consider remaining silent. Could it mean that she believed Franklin, in some way, deserved to die?

Brent considered Franklin once more, focusing on the more recent, degraded version of the man. He had assaulted a woman several years earlier - the details of that had not yet been investigated thoroughly by the police. Brewster had paid her hush money. The woman in that affair or assault was beyond reach, being on holiday in Brazil and not returning until next week. She was yet to be questioned by the police. Now there was something else, another similar incident, perhaps. How did Evelyn come to learn of any of these things? Would she attribute Franklin's bad behaviour to his alcoholism? If that was not bad enough, there were Franklin's ambitious and greedy nature, his pride, the divisions he caused in the family, his self-serving attitude towards Evelyn. To what did she attribute all those things?

No, Franklin was in no sense a likeable person but was he such a debased character that his own mother thought him worthy of being murdered and would protect the identity of Chloe, whom she thought might have carried out the deed? Would she do the deed herself?

"Positively Shakespearean," said Brent out loud.

"What's Shakespearean?" asked Alice from the front, while Greg drove the car.

"I was thinking about Evelyn," answered Brent. "If she killed her son it would be material for a tragedy."

"Yeah, it would," said Alice. "I was thinking something like that. I mean, with Evelyn in her eighties and the deceased sixty, how much of the maternal instinct remains?"

"That's a good point," said Brent. "I can see that there would be attitudes and behaviours continuing from when the children were growing up but probably not the protective passion of a mother for her young child."

"Brewster was all but estranged from the family," said Greg.

"He was," said Brent, "but even the black sheep of the family is still one of the family. He may have been hated but he was still son or brother to them all."

"You feel sorry for him, don't you?" asked Alice.

"I do. I think he was a lonely man. I think it likely he was guilty of more than we know about - guilty in the sense of moral failings and harming others. Yet, for all that, the picture I conjure up in my mind is of a once-proud knight fallen from grace in broken and bloodstained armour on a windswept, barren hillside with enemies all around. There is no heraldic device on his shield, his horse has gone, and he has just killed his servants because they wished to retreat. He awaits his certain destruction when his enemies, the people he has angered, charge him. I see this scene in over-painted stained glass, the companion piece to 'Boudicca's passing' in the butler's office."

There was silence for a while until Greg broke it by saying,

"See what I mean, Alice? Sometimes it's hard to understand what he's talking about."

"He's using metaphors to describe Franklin, I suppose," replied Alice. "Here, Brent, what's this Boudicca thing?"

"You haven't seen it? Ask Jackson to show it to you. It's a strange and beautiful work by a famous artist named Millais and it's worth a fortune. What madness to have it tucked away in a former over-sized cupboard."

"I'll do that. So, are you saying that Brewster was proud, lonely, and dedicated to his cause?"

"That's about it. A bad, selfish cause, by the way. I think he became deranged because of it."

"Yeah, I'd go along with that. Funny, though, we get to know so much about the other people in a case and are always looking for motives that it becomes easy to miss who the person who died really is... or was. That holds true for the suspects, too, actually."

"We have the facts in front of us," said Greg quizzically.

"I know," said Alice, "but we look for patterns and reasons for them to do something."

"Right, that's our job," said Greg.

"Sure, but we don't look at the whole person. If it's the victim or the perp, we build up details around the case. We don't build up details around who they are."

"Is that what you do, Brent?" asked Greg.

"Ah, come on. I've only told you a hundred times," said Brent.

"Yes, you have but you've never laid it out like that before," replied Greg.

"As of right now," said Alice, "who's in and who's out of the picture?"

"Yes. I'd like to hear this," said Greg.

"You're putting me on the spot. This is my current estimation and it is subject to change, but here goes. Out are the Aimes family, Merrell Fortier, and, I expect, Jimmy Brewster... I'll know that for certain very soon, I hope. From the Halliday family, both Sophia and Mike are definitely in. Evelyn is in. Lloyd is in. Another person who I cannot name is probably out. Robert and Aurelia are out. Chloe Halliday is probably out. Marjorie Bellingham is probably out."

"Who's the mystery person?" asked Greg.

"I'm not saying. Nearly all shall be revealed in time."

"What about Laura Aimes?" asked Alice.

"Franklin himself excludes her," replied Brent. "He insulted her badly on the night of his death and it was too late for Laura to give him poison because of the insult. I can find no discernible reason for her wanting to kill him before that moment. The same goes for Steve Aimes as well. The trigger to motivate either of them to kill Franklin would have been the insult but they would have needed to bring thallium to the house in advance of the trigger. They would have had to know what was coming and that's impossible."

"I'm glad to see my choice, Sophia, still has a shot," said Alice.

"It seems my boy, Jimmy, is going to be out of the running," said Greg with a laugh. "Mind telling me why?"

"His mind was occupied with a few things and I'll have to leave it at that."

They drove on and began to talk of other matters.

"I've got that potting soil and a few other bits and pieces for you in my car," said Brent.

"Have you?" replied Alice. "Thanks, that's very sweet."

"Has he got you gardening or something?" asked Greg.

"No, my spider plant needs an overhaul and Brent gave me some tips."

"Brent, my lawn's dying off in one area. What do I do?" asked Greg.

"Tell me about it. Is it shaded?"

"Yes, it is. There's a dwarf cedar tree that's supposed to grow to no more than eight feet tall that's shot up to about sixteen feet and it's got very bushy as well."

"You have to move or remove the tree."

"But it's a dwarf. It's only been in for four years."

"It's not a dwarf anymore. If you don't want to move it you could put in a flowerbed with plants that tolerate shade, like hostas, lobelia, coleus, or a nice hydrangea. Then prune the tree to keep it contained."

"What, you're asking me to do real gardening? Maggie puts in a few bulbs and has a couple of hanging baskets and stuff. I just mow the lawn. I'd like to keep it that way."

"You're missing out, Greg. If you insist on passing by such an opportunity to mess around with plants, the tree will have to come out or you'll have a bigger patch of dead lawn."

"That cedar was expensive. Why didn't it stop at eight feet like it was supposed to?"

"There you've got me. Go back to the nursery you bought it from and complain. Arrest them for something if they don't give you a refund."

"Yeah, right. I've never heard that one before. Here's the cemetery."

Grief visited and became visible at the graveside. The men of the family looked mildly distraught or helped the women, who all seemed to give way at the same time.

Evelyn was the most composed and resorted to pressing a handkerchief to her mouth while visibly shaken. Sophia was crying openly as were Aurelia, Karen, and Mrs Vance, the cook. Laura Aimes wailed, "No! Oh, no," and required Steve's physical support. Several others shed tears among the crowd. Chloe cried, too, but, Brent determined, it was not of the same quality. He surmised that she cried at the sight of the others crying and not because of any independent feelings for Franklin. However, he was not fully convinced by his estimate of her emotions.

Hill Hall was alive with people relieved to have their duty behind them. The reception was underway and the large dining room was full - nearly to capacity. It was a strange, awkward atmosphere, as it can be at such events. The relaxation from the restraint of being solemn and quiet for an extended period had, on the visitors at least, the effect of making them want to laugh or talk over ordinary things. The majority of people there simply wanted to move past the funeral and get on with life.

Stray catches of conversation revealed that many friends and acquaintances were talking of things unrelated to Franklin Brewster or the Brewster family's grief. One man forgot himself entirely when he guffawed out loud. He did not notice that his action denoted that the world was moving on while the family was only beginning to come to grips with its loss. Brent wanted to take the drink from the man's hand and pour it over his head. For him to do that would be worse than the offence so he contented himself with finding Merrell to conclude the business he had with her.

"Here it is," said Merrell. "I'm sorry to see it go. That jade is just my colour." They were talking in the library which was empty apart from themselves. Brent received the blue velvet bag from Merrell and checked to make sure it was the exquisite jade pendent he was receiving.

"I'm sure you are," replied Brent. "How did you get hold of Evelyn's jewellery?" He put the bag in his pocket.

"I went to her suite and Evelyn was in her bathroom. Marjorie had gone to her room for the night. Jimmy watched outside to make sure Marjorie didn't come back.

She has more stuff than the things I took. Those pieces were in an old locked box. It was so easy to pick and take what I wanted. Any thief would have taken the whole box and just, pfwhhhit, gone with it."

"Where is the box now?"

"Still in the bottom drawer of an armoire in her sitting room. Like, what are you going to do? Sneak them back or tell her?"

"I don't wish her any more trouble than she already has. I'll see what I can do."

"Good. That's good. I had no idea that Franklin was going to die on the very night I take the jewels. Talk about unlucky."

"For you or Franklin?"

"Yeah, well, Franklin wasn't all he seemed to be. He got me on my own once and was pressuring me to dump Jimmy and hook up with him. He's like my dad's age so forget it and I told him so."

"Did you? That's interesting about Franklin. He seems to have had a real problem that way."

"Whatever. You know, I can't make you out at all. Why are you giving me a break like this?"

"The police employ me on murder cases to help them find the culprit. I uncover many interesting things while I'm investigating. It doesn't usually include a major jewellery robbery, though. What you do outside of the case doesn't concern me except in so far as it holds up the murder inquiry."

"I get it. Lucky for me it was you and not that detective with the sour face. Ah, well, nearly got away with it."

"I'll talk to Jimmy next. As far as I'm concerned you're cleared from being a suspect. I hope Jimmy will be, too."

"C'mon, tell me. You must have an idea by now. Who do you think did it?"

"Whether I know or not, I'm not about to tell you."

"I think it's probably Sophia. She dislikes me but that isn't why I think it's her. She's had a feud with her brother for so long. Maybe she snapped… you know, had enough of him."

"That sounds a reasonable theory. Any proof?"

"Like I said, she's hated Franklin for years. It looked to me like that grudge was as fresh as the day it started. Anyway, are you going to tell Jimmy what I did?"

"Would you mind?"

"I don't know. I'd like it if you didn't because it makes everything kind of awkward for me. We came down in his car and I'd have to get a taxi back. What's a poor girl like me gonna do?"

"I don't think I'll tell him. That's a matter between the two of you. His knowing or not makes no difference to the murder investigation."

"You know, you're a nice guy. I really should punch you in the face for ruining my chances," Merrell got up and kissed Brent on the cheek, "but I don't hold grudges," she said, as she began to walk to the door. "They're not worth it."

Chapter 24

Later Thursday afternoon

"*M*r Brewster, you and Ms Fortier stole your mother's diamond ring and it's most fortunate for you that the robbery and the murder haven't been put into the same file." Brent was in the library with Jimmy.

"I know… I know that. I must have been mad. Merrell said it would be easy… and it was. I told her that mother rarely wears her best jewels. She brings out her diamond ring two or three times a year. I thought it would be okay seeing as she had just worn it that night. You have to understand, I just needed to raise a little bit of money until things improved. I was going to return it."

"At what time did Ms Fortier steal the ring?"

"It was after Mother went to bed. Bellingham had already seen to her and had then gone to her own room for the night. Merrell sneaked into Mother's sitting room and brought the case out to me. She picked the lock with a hairpin so easily and took out the diamond ring. She couldn't resist trying it on and then she handed it to me to look after. After that, she took the case back and returned it to the armoire. She did it all so well."

"Okay. Why is your mother so lax about the security of her valuables?" asked Brent.

"I suppose it seems stupid. It is stupid. Even the box they're in is some old antique monstrosity that's probably worth something. I really have no idea… Her habit, I suppose."

"What do you suggest I do with the ring?" asked Brent.

"Give it back to her. Look, I'll come with you and explain everything. I do wish we hadn't done this."

"What did you do when, having just stolen the ring, you learned of Franklin's death?"

"Ah, I panicked… I went to pieces. It was only Merrell who stopped me from going immediately to confess to Mother or the police."

"Why didn't you return the ring to your mother, then?"

"Merrell said that it was now too difficult. The police were everywhere and people were awake at odd hours. I had this idea, to hide the ring outside in the garden. I persuaded Merrell to go… I couldn't manage even that, I was so nervous. I told her of a place behind a shed. She's so brave… She went and hid it while I stayed behind like a coward. You know when you interviewed us, I was sure you were on to our game. Then I calmed down when I realized you couldn't be. Of course, you were here about the murder. You were pretty brutal to us, you know."

Brent was silent and only glanced at Jimmy Brewster. He was astonished at the man's naïveté. It was not so much that Merrell had so easily manipulated and deceived him but that Brent could not comprehend how the man did not realize he was also a possible suspect in a murder investigation. Even when Brent had pushed him so hard during that first interview, it had still not penetrated Jimmy's mind that he could be considered a possible assassin.

"What do you make of Franklin's death?"

"I don't know what to think. I can't say I'm grief-stricken but… I miss him. I guess I do. I'm finding it hard to sort out my feelings about Franklin and about what happened.... He must have poisoned himself. Franklin was a selfish idiot most of the time but I don't think anyone would want to kill him.... What are you going to do now?"

"I will return the ring and you just forget all about it. Thank you, Mr Brewster. I think that will be all for now."

"You mean you're not going to say anything to Mother?"

"Do you want me to?" asked Brent.

"I don't know... Ah, no. I prefer she never knows."

"Then I won't ever tell her. Let's get this straight, though. I'm keeping quiet about the theft of her ring for her sake and not so much for yours. I'll tell you this much, Jimmy, what you did will be on your conscience for a long time to come. We none of us fully escape the consequences of our actions."

"I'm sure I'm ashamed of myself, right now."

"That's only because you've been caught. Had I not found out about the theft you might have got away with it. You never would have returned the ring - of that I'm sure. That's not what I'm talking about.

Let's say you had got away with pawning the ring and then returning it later. Even if you had done that, which I doubt very much, you still would have been left with your conscience. Even now, you will never look at your mother in quite the same way. You have betrayed her trust and you can only make amends for it and not wipe it out - unless your mother wipes it out."

"Well... I don't quite understand what you're saying... It's over as far as I'm concerned as long as you do what you say and return the ring. I'll never do anything like it again. That I promise you."

"Maybe it will work for you. You might be right and I'm wrong. Forget what I said. Goodbye."

Brent got up and left the room quickly, allowing Jimmy only enough time to call a hurried goodbye after him.

"Chloe. My dear, dear Chloe, what a wicked web of deceit you have woven." Chloe was the third person in a row to enter the library to meet with Brent. He had left the room temporarily and had returned after Jimmy had gone.

Family and guests alike were giving the library a wide berth as the thought of an unsolved murder case in the house began to sink in. Some guests left as a consequence, some doggedly remained, hopeful of witnessing something interesting.

"I know I should have told you," said Chloe. "You have to believe me, it was all completely innocent. I didn't want Rachel to get in trouble and lose her job."

"So, to protect Rachel, the three of you, including your grandmother, decide to give misleading statements to the police. What were you all thinking of?"

"I know it looks bad. You can't imagine the agony I've been through."

"Yes, I can. To tell the truth, I don't think your agonies are nearly severe enough. I have a good mind to tell Lieutenant Darrow the whole, pitiful story of you being here the night of the murder."

"I suppose you have to."

"I should do. At some point, I may well *have* to. For now, let's see what happens. First of all, I want the names of the two people having the conversation you walked in upon the day of the family tour of Sadler-Creme."

"Oh, I can't. Please don't make me." She looked wretched.

"One of them I'm sure about."

"You can't know. How can you possibly know?"

"One of them was Evelyn and I strongly suspect the other of being Lloyd. It couldn't have been either of your parents. So, it must have been Evelyn and Lloyd who were having a conversation about Franklin. You told me you overheard one of them saying, 'We shall have to remove him' and you have jumped to conclusions based on recent events. Much more likely is that some distressing information had come to light and they were discussing his *removal as manager* of Sadler-Creme. That's what I believe it might be.

The likelihood of two people urgently and openly discussing a murder in a semi-public place is absurd. A hurried and reactionary conversation about a Sadler-Creme-related problem being reported by one person to the other is quite plausible."

"I don't know exactly what they were talking about... Maybe you're right. Yes, it must have been something like that. Please, believe me - it wasn't Nana who killed Uncle Frank. I know it wasn't her."

"There's a massive difference between knowing something and believing something. Chloe, I do not want your Nana to be the murderer almost as much as you. However, I have a task to perform and I will complete it. If you have some proof, even scraps of conversation, the smallest something that can demonstrate that it wasn't Mrs Brewster, please tell me what it is. This is no time for games of any description. Do you understand what I'm saying?"

"Yes, I understand.... After I interrupted their conversation, Nana knew it had sounded bad because she had been angry. She told me on the way home that there were going to be some changes at the company but they would take place in the new year. She said that something disgusting had happened and steps had to be taken. Nana wanted me to forget about it. At the time I never connected what she said to Uncle Frank.

When Uncle Frank died I couldn't help it... It all came together. I thought Nana had killed him." Chloe began to cry and, this time, it seemed to Brent as though it was probably unfeigned. She did not seem inclined to continue with her statement so Brent prompted her by asking,

"Since the October tour, has anything occurred to make you believe that Nana could be guilty or that she must be innocent?"

"No, nothing I can think of." She shook her head emphatically. "I could never believe she had done it."

"What about since Franklin's death?"

"That's just it, she was fine… well, you know what I mean. She was just the same as ever towards me. She agreed not to talk about my being at the dinner. But now, just in the last couple of days, she seems to have changed completely. She won't speak to me and I don't know why."

"Is she cold towards you? Or angry? Indifferent? Dismissive?"

"I went to speak to her in her suite and she put me off. Said she was tired. Then she sent Marjorie to tell me that it would be best for me to leave the house while the investigation was ongoing so I didn't get involved. I tried calling her. First, she took the call and she said she couldn't speak because she was busy with something. After that, only Marjorie ever answered and always with some excuse why Nana wouldn't speak to me."

"Evelyn's never behaved like that to you before?"

"No, never. She always made time for me."

"Hmm, it could be the strain of it all. Is that possible?"

"I don't know. I doubt it."

"Perhaps Evelyn is fearful of what must follow on from the investigation and is just trying to keep you out of the way of it all."

"You think so? I hope you're right."

Brent got up from his chair at the desk and walked about the room. He was wondering whether he should bring up his unfounded assumption that Evelyn believed Chloe had murdered Franklin. How would the young woman react? If it was a simple misunderstanding on Evelyn's part, then it could all be cleared up quickly and their relationship restored with smiles and apologies all round as they admitted how silly they had both been. That was one outcome.

But what if Evelyn were right and Chloe was indeed the murderer. The outcome would then be that Brent was on the brink of destroying her life. He hesitated to proceed. The Halliday family would be forever stricken with grief and suffer grey years of misery. The rest of the family would suffer, too. Then there was Evelyn. However much longer she had to live would be marred by this horrible knowledge that would come up in her mind continuously. There again, how would Chloe immediately react? Dismiss the suggestion as foolishness, be puzzled, or become like a cornered animal?

Concluding, finally, that the first possible outcome was about ninety per cent likely and the second only ten, he made a decision.

"What do you think of this as an idea?" Brent came and leaned against the edge of the polished table next to Chloe. "Just suppose, for a moment, that your Nana got it into her head that you killed Franklin. How do you think she would behave towards you?"

"She can't believe that! It's impossible… Why would she?"

"These are strange circumstances we find ourselves in. They produce strange thoughts in people. It is possible. How would she behave?"

"I'm not sure. It's too horrible to think about."

"The idea that she mistrusts you is not a nice one. That she could believe you capable of such a crime is offensive. But think about it. Haven't you given her cause to think that way? You substituted for Rachel… a harmless game. Evelyn probably found that game amusing. Then everything changed.

Next, the only thing she knows is that you're trying to conceal the substitution. Out of her love for you, she agrees to the idiocy. Now, Chloe, think about this. Your Nana knows someone killed Franklin. The thought gnaws at her when she's alone. Add to those gnawing thoughts the fact that she's already keeping something from the police... She's involved in a cover-up. It wouldn't take long for her to think she is providing you with an alibi for a lot more than just for Rachel's sake. At some point, she probably imagined that you had an ulterior motive..."

"Oh, don't... My poor Nana... I didn't do anything." Chloe became moved beyond speech. Her shoulders shook and she sobbed freely.

"I'll be right back," said Brent. He left to find a napkin for Chloe's tears. Within a minute he returned with a neatly folded square of linen.

"Here you are." He handed the napkin to her.

"I'm sorry. I must look a mess."

"Yes, you do. That's fine, though, and nothing to worry about now."

"Do *you* think I killed Uncle Frank?"

"Oh no, I don't think so at all. I maybe should have used a different approach to come to that conclusion but, as it stands, you're in the clear. Sorry, I can't give you a completely unqualified answer but please don't worry about it anymore."

"Why didn't you say that first?"

"Because I didn't know for sure until just now."

"What...? You mean because I cried?"

"Not exactly.... It wasn't that alone. I have seen many people cry throughout the cases I've worked on. One or two of them have been guilty of vile things. It was not that you cried, it was how you cried and what you cried about."

"I'm so sorry for causing all this trouble…. I don't know what you must think of me."

"Everyone makes mistakes. False statements to the police can be construed as obstruction of justice. Your little escapade could have got you a few months in prison if the police had a mind to press charges. Imagine you, Rachel, and Evelyn behind bars. Have you learned your lesson, do you think?"

"Oh, yeah…. I feel so stupid. I can't believe I put Rachel through all of this just to save myself… What does that make me?"

"Very selfish and a pain in the neck."

"That's telling it like it is…. What happens now?"

"Tell Rachel she is off the hook because she is worried sick about it. You do not breathe a word of any of this to another living soul and that includes your Nana. I want to hear you promise me you will keep your mouth closed. Mention your false statements to anyone and all three of you will be in jeopardy and then there's nothing I can do about it."

"I absolutely swear I won't say a word. I'll stay away from Nana until this is all over."

"Make sure you do it. I have to see Evelyn but that might be difficult today. I'll probably see her tomorrow. You have to leave it to me to sort out this situation. Okay?"

"Okay. And thank you…. Thank goodness it was you who found out. You're so kind."

"And probably a little stupid. Off you go and stay out of trouble. Goodnight."

"Goodnight, Brent."

Chloe left the library. Brent had Evelyn's jewels with him, ready for their return to the armoire. He was unable to get them back just yet because, although some of the mourners were starting to take their leave, many of the distant family connections had taken to walking about upstairs to look over the house or go to their bedrooms. Besides that, Brent had observed Marjorie going upstairs twice, presumably to Evelyn's suite or her own room. The last thing Brent wanted was to be discovered while returning the jewellery. He was now feeling tired, having missed much sleep the night before. Also, he was faced with another late night - one including a reverse burglary, on top of interviewing some of the more difficult suspects such as Lloyd and Mike Halliday. Then there was also Sophia and Evelyn. If he could get the interviews with those two out of the way as well, Brent felt he might be getting somewhere.

There was plenty of food left on the tables. The investigator helped himself at the buffet. Surveying the fifty or so occupants of the large dining room, Brent saw that they were all in groups of twos, threes, or fours, talking quietly. All talking. What are they all talking about? Don't they know that one of them has been killed and one of them is a murderer? He wanted to draw their attention to this fact. He wanted to shout it at them. Even self-possessed Evelyn, the perfect, sorrowing hostess, was now smiling as she spoke to someone. The mask of convention was in evidence everywhere in the room. Brent thought to find Laura.

Chapter 25

Thursday evening

"*H*ello," said Brent, when he found Laura in the office once more, sitting in her father's chair. "Can I disturb you for a few minutes? I want to find someone who's grieving." He had brought two glasses of wine.

"Then join the club," said Laura. "There only seems to be the two of us. Some of them make me sick… talking about dress designers and food."

"If Franklin were here, Franklin the good, that is, what would he say about it?"

"Well, I don't know. At one time he would have called them out. Yes, he would have got all righteous, and pompous, and told them what he thought about their stupid new restaurants."

"Would he? This is for you." He handed her a glass of wine.

"I don't normally drink very much," said Laura.

"Out the window with convention, say I. Here's to Franklin… May he have found rest at last."

"Yes, to Franklin, my dear brother."

"Did you know he landed a huge government contract?" asked Brent. "He must have been an excellent negotiator."

"I did hear a little about that business. I think he must have been very good at his job. He was always so precise about things."

"Was he? In what way?"

"His room was always tidy. He knew where everything was at any time."

"I've come to be like that and I find it very hard work," said Brent, "but when I was a teenager my room was an unholy mess."

"I don't think I was as bad as that. I like pretty things and I seem to collect far too much. I can't seem to throw anything out."

"Delete the prettiness and I'm very much the same now. I'm a bit of a hoarder. I have a storage locker full of… Now that's funny, I can't quite remember what's in there. An old air-conditioner, a bed-frame… oh you don't want to hear about that… To Franklin's neatness and precision!" They clinked glasses.

"He used to get mad if the maid put something away in the wrong place." Laura smiled.

"Orderliness is a wonderful attribute and, to run a complicated business like Sadler-Creme, Franklin must have had it spadefuls." Brent raised his glass again. "To the orderliness of Franklin's sock drawer, from which small beginnings he became a captain of industry!"

"You cheer me up no end." She clinked glasses with him.

"I'm rather silly at the moment but it is only a reaction to the stifling atmosphere of high society in grief. What should have happened was that we had an Irish wake. Then we could do these toasts properly with whiskey and get plastered. Nobody would mind us one bit and Franklin would look down and say that we were doing it right."

"Do you believe that? Do you think people exist after death?"

"I most certainly do. I think the good Lord has arranged it so that the intellectuals wake up and realize what idiots they have been, and the idiots wake up and realize they had some wisdom after all but didn't know how they came by it. Death is the great leveller - and the life after, that is the great beginning."

"Do you have any proof of that because I don't have any faith at the moment?"

"None. But I'm happy to believe it's true. Should I die before you do, I will send a message telling you how wonderful life is on the other side and how Franklin is doing."

"Oh, that's too silly for words."

"Silly it may be but I promise to try, anyhow."

"But Franklin did something wicked, you know. There have been several women he's treated badly. I think that gets him barred."

"Maybe, then, he will deservedly get barred from some things but not everything. The full reward is to receive everything going, punishment is to miss out on some of it, and the full punishment is not to wake up. I'm sure we have to make some choices there as much as we do here, otherwise what would be the purpose of our existence?"

"Does there have to be a purpose?"

"Yes, of course. The fact that we can ask such an existential question and consider it perhaps the most important question to be answered, puts it beyond doubt, as far as I'm concerned. We can put purpose into our lives or we can drain purpose out of it but we all either make sure we have some purpose present or realize our sad lack of it. Whoops, I'm in danger of getting off-topic and talking about things I know nothing about. So, I say, to the memory of good brother Franklin, who loved his sister Laura with a perfect love!"

They raised their glasses once more.

Having laid to rest and then memorialised the former Franklin, the youth and young man who seemed to Brent to have been kind and considerate, it was now necessary for the investigator to deal with the undead spectre of the latter Franklin. This spirit that still walked was the abusive, proud, greedy, selfish man which his family knew him to have become. The public was unaware of the dead man's private nature with its moral failings - the attendance at the funeral service attested to this. Brent went looking for Lloyd and, when he found him, insisted they speak in the library at once.

"I find it unseemly that you are conducting investigations on this day, of all days," said Lloyd, throwing down the gauntlet. He declined Brent's offer of a chair.

"Unseemly... that's a good word. I find *your* behaviour unseemly and ungentlemanly. That you would knowingly and willingly withhold information in a murder investigation is totally reprehensible. All consideration of manners aside, what is it you think you're accomplishing here?"

"I don't like your approach. Pussy-footing around. Scaring all the women out of their wits while you pretend there's a murderer on the loose. Making yourself out to be important when you're not. Just a jumped up sneak who probably makes a living from divorce cases."

Brent found him to be quite magnificent. Lloyd's back was ram-rod straight and, despite his eighty-six years, the old man kept his anger coherent and controlled.

"I've never worked a divorce case in my life so you'll have to trot out some other diatribe. Don't you realize you're at fault? I'm only talking to you now because you were far from forthright with me when we spoke earlier. I'm calling you on it. Lloyd, you lied to me."

"I did no such thing."

"You lied when you said that what you were telling me was all that was spoken about with Franklin on the night he died."

"Umber, you won't believe me and I don't care to put you right. I am not in the habit of repeating myself."

"You withheld vital information when you did not tell me that you were going to have Franklin removed as manager of Sadler-Creme."

"Who told you that!?" The old man was visibly affected by Brent's statement.

"Please sit down," said Brent in a softer tone. Lloyd did sit down.

"Who told you?"

"No one, specifically… everyone, in part. It wasn't Evelyn if that's what's bothering you."

"Then you must know of that awful business." He shook his head. "Bad business," he said slowly and looked away. "There have been several other incidents in the past but they were all dealt with quietly. I only wanted to keep this latest enormity quiet… to protect the family and preserve the company's reputation."

"I understand. Please, tell me what you and Franklin discussed."

Lloyd now moved his head in quick little nods as thoughts about the evening began to coalesce in his mind and he started to address Brent's question.

"We had spoken by telephone several times about the matter. Franklin always vehemently denied any wrongdoing. I put it to him that there was no smoke without fire. He said that he would welcome his day in court if it came to it. Well,

I didn't like that. I said, at the next opportunity we must talk face to face and settle this matter completely.

Our schedules did not coincide until last week. When we spoke, I told him plainly that if he insisted upon going to court rather than settling out of court he would be doing so on the understanding that he would no longer be an employee of the company. He was quite pigheaded about staying on and seeing it through. I pointed out to him that, even when the government contract was signed, there were clauses in it that could permit the government to back out because of the way the company was being run. If it became known that the chief negotiator had abused a woman and was still running things, well, I'm sure you understand the probable consequences."

"How did your conversation end?"

"I suppose he softened. Said he would think about what I had said. Then he committed suicide. Plain as anything."

"Yes, I can see that he might do that. The 'only way out' type of thing."

"Exactly, my point. Exactly." Several times Lloyd tapped the table quite hard with the tip of his index finger as though he was nailing something down.

"Was there anything else?" asked Brent.

"Nothing to speak of… no." Lloyd now drummed his fingers on the table several times. "Look, Umber, apologies for my behaviour. I thought I was doing the right thing by keeping quiet. Please disregard anything I have said out of bad temper."

"Well, likewise for me. It's all very trying for everyone and makes us ragged around the edges. I'm very sorry that Franklin turned out the way he did. He sounded like a nice young fellow."

"Yes, he was. That's the pity of it all. Evelyn feels it very badly."

"Oh, by the way, were the other trustees aware of Franklin's crime?"

"They are as of this week. Had to be told, you see. Somebody at the company told me about the situation and so I acted immediately without consulting the others. If I had thought Franklin were innocent of the charge I would have backed him… outside of the company, you appreciate. Trouble was, I believed the woman. I spoke to her, you know."

"Of course I don't know because this is the first I've heard of it. What did she say?" Brent quashed the surprise he felt.

"I promised her I would not give anything away to anyone because of her upcoming suit. She knew me by sight. I remember we met once. I suppose she trusted me. She told me several convincing things that had the ring of truth in them. These demonstrated that she had been systematically victimized. Most certainly she was a victim. I've been very disgusted with Franklin's behaviour."

"What will she do now?"

"The company needs to make a proper settlement so that the poor woman is not put through any more distress."

"She might still feel she needs to tell her story publicly to find closure."

"That's possible and entirely her business. We won't drag the matter through the courts, that I do know."

"Thank you. I won't detain you any longer. If you do think of anything else, please let me know."

"There won't be. That's the end of it."

The two men stood up and shook hands. Brent watched Lloyd leave the room.

In the library, Brent applied himself to bringing his notes up to date in the ring-binder that lay in front of him on the table. He reviewed thought after captured thought set down in his peculiar style. Ideas were beginning to resolve themselves into definite patterns and the patterns were becoming coherent in forming a whole disposition of all that was the Brewster family in relation to Franklin's death. He had only a few gaps to plug and then he would know. He might not yet know within any degree of certainty that could, for example, be reported to Greg Darrow, but he did have the right path in front of him to follow up to its conclusion. He looked up when Mike Halliday entered the room. It was now after 5:00 p.m.

"Have you come to see me?" asked Brent.

"Ah, yes I have. It's a… it's difficult, you see." He came up to the table in a hesitating, awkward way and, with a hand on the back of a chair, said,

"May I sit down?"

"Yes, please do," Brent looked at him for a moment, then smiled, saying, "How can I help you?"

"Um, I was rude to you before and, er, I shouldn't have been. You were only doing your job."

"Forget about that. I offend lots of people. I'm essentially an annoying, meddling type of person when I'm on a case - I have to be to get anywhere."

"Do you? I mean… thanks." Mike Halliday did not seem inclined to say more. The pause lengthened.

"I should imagine," said Brent, "that you've seen something and it's bothering you. You think it's probably nothing, but still feel you must speak to someone."

"That's it. You asked me to tell you if I noticed anything so, here I am."

"And?"

"Oh, yes. It's Marjorie Bellingham. She's acting very strangely."

"In what way?"

"Personally, I like the woman. She's always pleasant and helpful but today she's been downright strange."

"It would help if you could tell me in what way she is afflicted with strangeness."

"Right, I'm not used to this type of thing. Well, this afternoon, since we returned from the funeral, she keeps disappearing from the room and then reappearing when, usually, she's with Evelyn the whole time. Always stands near her, you see."

"It could be that she has errands to run for Evelyn."

"That's what I thought at first. Once I started noticing Marjorie's odd behaviour I kept an eye on her. She goes out of the room for five or ten minutes. Comes back in for ten minutes. Then goes out again. What do you think she's doing?"

"I don't know. I'll ask her."

"Ask her? Yes, I suppose you could. I didn't think of that."

"Is there anything else?"

"Yes, there is. At the funeral today, I noticed a man who looked very suspicious. I followed him."

There was a long pause until it suddenly occurred to Brent that Mike Halliday had taken upon himself the role of amateur sleuth and was now making his report.

"Very good," said Brent. "What did you find out about this man?"

"I saw him arrive. Here's the plate number of his car with the make and model. I even got the VIN number. This man was following Jimmy. I saw you talking to Merrell and he came up and spoke to Jimmy just after that and handed a paper to him. Jimmy said something in return and had an unpleasant look on his face. Now, then - what was that about?" Mike raised his eyebrows about as high as they would go.

"Very, very interesting. I'll have to find out."

"That's all I have for the moment. As soon as I get more I'll let you know."

"Well, thank you. This information might prove very useful."

"Oh, good. Well, I'll get back to it." Mike left the room with a pleased expression on his face.

Almost as soon as he had left, Greg Darrow came into the library.

"Halliday looks happy and you've chosen a nice office for yourself. I only came in to say I'm going back to the department to tidy up a few things. I'm exhausted and I've had enough of funerals for one day. Do you know that I've been at this case straight without a break since we were called in?"

"So, an early night to recharge the batteries?" asked Brent.

Greg nodded. "You in here again tomorrow?"

"Yes, I will be. Do you know, Mike Halliday is detective material? He's getting into the spirit of detection and might ask you for a job. Even worse, he might ask *me* to take him on."

"Ha, bless him. What did he say?"

"Two things and I have to follow up on them. Marjorie Bellingham is acting strangely which could easily be explained by an upset stomach. A suspicious gentleman approached Jimmy Brewster after the funeral and handed him a document. He was probably serving a writ. Mike even got the VIN on the vehicle."

"Maybe I should talk to him. He sounds more enthusiastic than some people in my department."

"Perhaps they don't sleep well."

"Sleep is a luxury for detectives. Any closer?"

"Yes, a lot closer but I've still a few things to do. Jimmy Brewster's out of the picture. I'll tell you everything tomorrow. One of us should get some rest and I don't like to worry you so near to your bedtime. You'll get frown lines and bags under your eyes."

"I have those already, if you hadn't noticed. We'll be out of here tomorrow," said Greg. "We can't keep the suspects for any good reason and all of them will go."

"And when they do, the murderer goes with them. Anything new come in?"

"Huh," Greg yawned. "Sorry. We got a lot done but no new leads that are useful. All dead ends. It's been a fact-checking kind of day. We really should have had a break by now."

"It'll happen. I feel sure we're close."

"Brent, if you need me for anything tonight, call me. I want to get this one done. The department's about at capacity with casework. One more homicide and we're sunk. It'll be all-nighters for everyone forever."

"How does Maggie put up with it?"

"She's pretty good about the hours I work as long as it's not all the time. Anyway, I'm gone. See you tomorrow."

"Goodnight, Greg."

Chapter 26

Thursday night

*M*arjorie walked up the main staircase. All the guests had gone and there only remained family relatives and a sprinkling of close friends - about forty in all, including the Brewsters. When she reached the top stair, Brent put his foot on the first stair to follow her. He walked up quickly and stood at the end of the gallery to watch what she was doing. Marjorie was systematically working her way along the west wing hall. She tried all the doors to see if they were locked and, if they were not, she first knocked, then waited, before opening the door to give a cursory look inside. She found most of the room and cupboard doors locked - those that were not she locked with a master-key. As she reached the end, Brent went back a few paces to the head of the stairs. Waiting some seconds he then walked forward.

"Hello, Marjorie," he asked innocently as they nearly collided. "Looking for someone?"

"Oh, Mr Umber, hello. No, I'm only checking that everything is secure up here."

"I see. Couldn't one of the staff be doing that for you?"

"I suppose I *am* one of the staff. I don't mind though, it gives me some exercise."

"Have I interrupted you? We can do the East Wing together if you like."

"It's no trouble… 'though I wouldn't mind having someone to talk to. I've found today very exhausting and I don't seem to have done anything…. Mind you, I've been up and down the stairs ten times. That's probably it."

Brent gestured towards the opposite hallway and they began to walk. As they came to each door, Marjorie made sure it was locked.

"Why is it necessary to check the doors?"

"Well, some of the family are careless about keeping them locked. They forget. You see, apparently, there was an incident before my time. It was a large family get-together and during the afternoon someone went into two of the bedrooms and helped themselves to a few items."

"Oh, that's awkward. What happened?" asked Brent.

"It definitely had to be a relation, probably one of the children or so I've been led to believe. A chair was broken and some things were taken - mostly trifling except for the gold watch that disappeared. It belonged to a cousin called Mary who happened to be in the bath when it was stolen. She died last year. Mrs Brewster compensated her for the loss at the time but, apparently, the incident caused ill-feeling on Mary's side."

"Then that made Mrs Brewster determined that such a thing should never happen again. I wonder who it was? They must have been here today and so, precautions had to be taken."

"Yes. Despite that cautionary tale, Mrs Brewster still keeps her very valuable jewellery in her room when it should be kept at the bank or, at least, in a safe. That worries me more than many other things."

"Ah," said Brent, "it would do." He felt a little uncomfortable because the jewels of which they were speaking were in his pockets at that very moment and they suddenly felt heavier than they should do. "Mrs Brewster is wearing very simple jewellery today."

"Well, she would never wear anything showy at a funeral. In fact, she rarely wears her best jewellery. Once in a while, she likes to take them out just to see them. She says there's a treasured memory attached to each piece."

They came to the end of the east wing and began to work their way back.

"And what about you? Are you still bearing up okay?"

"I am. I wish it was all over. I'd like the house to return to normal… I don't think it ever will."

"Life goes through phases. The times, good or bad, come and go. Eventually, I believe a semblance of normality will return to this place. It will have a different flavour to it, though."

"I expect you're right." Marjorie paused while trying a door handle. "If you don't mind my asking, have you a suspect in mind? I know you can't say who it is if you do."

"No, I would not be able to tell you… You're probably wondering where you stand in the scheme of things. I can only say that you are a very pleasant person and nothing I've discovered has made me change that opinion."

"Ah…. Thank you for telling me that. I can't deny that it's a horrible strain. I know I'm innocent but I somehow feel guilty. I keep thinking I must look suspicious and that thought keeps me on edge."

"When I started, everyone was tinged with the colour of suspicion. Some in the household had a deeper hue and, the staff, for example, had a lighter hue. By a process of elimination there now remain three candidates so saturated that I have difficulty distinguishing between them."

"Oh, dear me. What would be the colour of suspicion?"

"It's a sort of radioactive violet - very unattractive-looking and toxic."

"Yes, I think I can see that. Envy is green, sadness blue, and anger is red. That type of violet is a suitable choice for suspicion of a person, a person whose guilt or innocence is questionable.

It was the same with the children here today - if it was a child who stole Mary's watch. Of course, if it were, he or she would probably be an adult by now. All children look innocent but one of them had to have done it so they all got suspected. Now that old misdeed affects the children here today."

"Yes, they all get penalized," said Brent. "For the bad behaviour of one or two, none of the children can now run in and out of the rooms of this glorious place and discover the interesting treasures it contains."

"That's right. We've taken away their delight in exploring a strange house."

"Here we are. Your tour of duty is over without incident. When will the next inspection be?" asked Brent.

"I do the rounds twice an hour at least. Though I think it's likely Mrs Brewster will go to bed early and so this will probably be my last inspection…. There were some children up here earlier. I had to send them downstairs again. Obviously, they were getting bored with the reception."

"I was guilty of that myself," said Brent. "I think I would prefer a little more open weeping and wailing than there has been. I'm not sure bottling up grief is always the best way of dealing with it. In my opinion, one person publicly beside themselves and dissolving in tears would make everyone else feel much better. Also, when the wailing mourners have finished and cried all the needful tears, they might be able to take off their grief like a garment and return to sanity."

"We're not expected to behave that way. Certainly not in this house. I think the colour of grief must be grey if it's any colour at all."

"Well said. A long, enduring grey. I wonder, have you seen Sophia about anywhere?"

"Last time I saw her she was in the conservatory with her cousin, Barbara."

"I'll see if I can have a few words with her, then. Thanks."

Brent entered the close warmth of the conservatory. The two women were alone and comfortably seated together in attitudes of ease on the rattan settee. They both looked up. Sophia did not seem particularly pleased to see Brent. Cousin Barbara appeared to know who he was already. She was about the same age as Sophia and of the same class.

"Hello," said Barbara. "Have you come to give us the third degree?"

"I have, actually. I need some information that only Sophia can supply. I'm going to be unforgivably rude and butt in where I'm not wanted. Personally speaking, I do not mind if you stay, Cousin Barbara. Sophia might, though."

"Call me Barb. Soph, do you want me to go?" asked Barbara.

"He's here to talk about Gillian," said Sophia coldly.

"Oh, really!" Barbara turned to Brent. "Does that have to be raked up again?"

"I'm afraid it does," said Brent. "You see, Sophia has not told me anything about Gillian. I know that Franklin injured Sophia's friend in some way. I could guess what happened and draw my conclusions but I might be wrong. I'd rather have the whole story and any consequences that arose from it so I can fit everything in properly to the overall scheme of things."

"You see," said Sophia, while staring hard at Brent, "this nice man is looking for motives for Franklin's murder. Gillian is my motive. If he thinks it's worth his while he'll try to make me out to be a killer."

"Wow," said Barbara. "I'm not going even if you tell me to."

Brent pulled up an armchair close to the settee and sat down in it.

"You know, I'm envious of you two ladies. You have first names that can be affectionately shortened. That makes things very cozy. I'm saddled with the short name of Brent. That means people have no means of showing extra friendliness towards me."

"You remind me of a snake," said Sophia. "It's all fascinating talk before you strike."

"That is exactly the effect I'm striving for at present. Usually, I hope to cheer people up. I'm only after the guilty parties and what they think of me doesn't matter. If you're innocent, Sophia, and I'm telling this to you straight because you stand in jeopardy at this moment, my superficial talk is, at worst, an irritant. If you are guilty, then I will not care what you think of me. Would you have it any other way?"

"I don't have much of a choice, do I?" said Sophia. "No, I suppose not…. Is it just a show or can you really be trusted?"

"You cannot know that someone is trustworthy until you extend trust to them. As I told you before, I will not say a word of what you tell me to anyone else unless it is necessary to apprehend the murderer. The worst I will do is this: if the information is not used, and I'm put on the spot by Lieutenant Darrow, I will tell him that years ago, Franklin caused trouble for a family friend but that the story has no bearing on the case. I promise not to say any more than that."

"There you go, Soph. That seems okay to me," said Barbara.

"I swore to Gillian that I would keep the matter private. Barb only knows because she was here when it happened."

"Ah, I see. This is important. Where will I find Gillian?"

"You were close to her today. She's buried in the cemetery."

"Oh, no. I'm so sorry to hear that." Brent went quiet. Then he said, "Was her death in any way connected to the incident?"

"Yes and no," said Barbara, when Sophia seemed disinclined to answer. She went no further but said, "Tell him and get it over and done with. Unless you want me to tell him?"

"No, I'll do it. It might look bad in his report if you speak for me."

She sat up on the settee and faced Brent directly.

"Barb and I have birthdays a week apart. We were seventeen and Gillian was sixteen. We were all of us young and relatively naïve for our age. We were products of our social circle and not like girls are today. Barb and Gilly came to stay here for the week. Franklin was twenty-two at the time. He was here, also. Not to relive the whole event, it soon became apparent that Gilly had become infatuated with Franklin. He could be very nice, you know, but most of it was superficial. We had a party on a Friday night - about twenty of us, boys and girls. An obvious story played out although it wasn't obvious at the time. Franklin deliberately got Gillian drunk and seduced her. Perhaps he was drunk himself. None of us seemed to have any idea what was happening. This is a big house and they disappeared somewhere. Barb and I looked for Gilly because we missed her at the party. We were so stupid. Some of the bedrooms were locked.

I suppose we would all have forgotten about it if Franklin had stayed and been kind to Gillian. He didn't. He cleared out first thing in the morning and left her without saying a word. He never spoke to her again. Barb and I have talked about this often. Another girl would probably have gotten over it with some regrets and moved on. Gillian didn't. That he had left without talking to her became her nightmare. She cried that day.

Shortly after that, she started taking drugs, drinking, and just making a mess of everything she did. It wasn't long before she wouldn't have anything to do with us. Gilly died fifteen years ago.

When she lay dying in a hospital bed at the age of forty, she looked like a frail, old woman. All her organs were shutting down. She was forty and she'd lived a miserable life. That's the story and its consequences. That's what my brother did to our friend and never did he do anything about it even though I told him often enough."

"That's very ugly and very sad," said Brent. "Did you murder Franklin?"

"No."

"I think I might have felt like murdering him," said Brent. "I don't mean that flippantly. I agree with you. He should never have treated Gillian like that in the first place and he had years to put matters right."

"I wanted to kill him sometimes because it made me so angry," said Barbara. "He was callous and selfish and she was such a lovely girl." Barbara began to sniff and took out a tissue from her purse.

"You asked me if I murdered Franklin," said Sophia. "My answer was untrue. I've murdered him hundreds of times in my heart. We used to have terrible rows. He always acted as though he were blameless and that what had happened didn't matter. He even laughed sometimes. I told him he had ruined Gilly's life and that he was responsible. He never spoke to her. Not even once." Sophia was angry and she spoke sharply.

"Now someone *has* killed him," said Brent. "Lloyd is convinced it was suicide."

"Not Franklin. He thought too much of himself to ever do that," said Sophia derisively.

"Who else knew of what Franklin did?"

At this question, Sophia went very quiet. Barbara said,

"We didn't tell anybody. Not for a long time. I think you told Evelyn about it three years or so afterwards, didn't you, Soph? You see, she was puzzled by the arguments that broke out every time Soph and her brother met. So she asked questions."

"How did Evelyn react when she was told?" asked Brent.

Both women tried to answer together. Barbara let Sophia explain.

"She was very saddened and upset but not unduly surprised. At that time, she was having her own set of difficulties with Franklin. He was no longer a son to her in anything but name. Mother was pretty good about it… at least she tried to make up for it all. She went to see Gilly who had to be nineteen or twenty at the time… I don't quite remember.

It was too late. Gilly had become a very hard person to deal with. She took the position that Mother had somehow betrayed her by allowing the party in the first place. All the help Mother offered her she refused. She offered her rehab, to pay for her to go to university, and support her while she was there. The only thing that Gillian asked for was some cash. She got it but we all know where that went."

"Then Gillian must have left home," said Brent.

"Yes. Her drug addiction got her into all kinds of trouble… with the police and the wrong people. She was angry with the world and she didn't care that she was destroying herself."

"Was anyone else in the know?"

"Only Mike, Jimmy, and Barbara's husband, Dennis. We kept it from Laura. None of the staff knew back then… At least, I don't think they knew. The staff here now weren't present at the time."

"What about your dad? He was alive in those days. Surely, he could have intervened."

"Father was so old school and unapproachable. He wouldn't have listened to any disparagement of his son. He worshipped Franklin and put all his hope into his precious firstborn. There was no point in talking to him. Anyway, he was already quite sickly by this time and was out of it really as far as being able to do anything was concerned. He never knew about Franklin's behaviour as it would only have disturbed him. Mother insisted we never mention it to him."

"Oh, dear me, this story is just so awful," said Brent, "and so unnecessary. I'm very sorry to have brought it all up again… I wish… Huh, it doesn't matter what I wish… Think of this, if you can bear with me for a moment. Supposing Gillian, the one who had never met Franklin, were to come into this room right now. What would she say to both of you?"

"I've no idea," said Barbara.

"It's very hard to imagine… hard for me to imagine," said Sophia.

"What do you have in mind?" asked Barbara.

"I believe young Gillian would pull up a chair, sit down, and have a heart to heart discussion with both of you. She would start by saying that it is all over now. It is behind all of us and that it's time to lay those old memories to rest. I'm sure of that. Next, she would put her arms around both of you and thank you for holding her memory so dear and for keeping faith with her for so long.

This part is trickier. She might then go on to say that Franklin has gone now and there is no one to be angry with anymore. That he never paid for his abuse of her is true but matters have moved beyond that time and it is a different day entirely. Finally, I believe she would say, live your lives in peace and do not trouble yourselves any longer with the past. One way for you to do that is to realize that Franklin died an unhappy, unfulfilled man who had made some seriously bad choices. In a sense, those choices of his caught up with him and killed him. If forgiveness is possible… forgive him as far as you are able.

Now, this is me speaking and not Gillian. I think both of you should go and talk to Evelyn about it so that you all get closure over the various bits and pieces that still cause you pain."

They all sat quietly after Brent's speech.

"I can't quite do any of that yet," said Sophia. "Not until the murderer is identified. Afterwards… perhaps I can. Something does need to be done… The thought uppermost in my mind at present is where does our telling you this story leave me?"

"I'm sorry to say it leaves you in roughly the same position. I sincerely want you to be innocent in the matter of Franklin's death. It is only by my prying into things that do not concern me that I eventually learn the truth. You still have the same motives but, and this is important, you have been candid and I appreciate your candour. It means that, more than ever, I want to bring the investigation to a successful conclusion. I'm getting closer to the truth of it all. But I feel there is a resistant inner circle of events and motives that I haven't broken into yet. The police have a similar problem. They can find no hard evidence. However, we'll all get there in the end.

I can give you this comfort, as slight as it is. Barbara, being present as a witness to your testimony, proves that you have not in any way tried to manipulate the story to suit your own purposes. For that, and for the story itself, I thank both of you. I'm so sorry to be as intrusive as this. I can only plead that it had to be done. Sophia, I will keep my word and mention this to no one. Goodnight, ladies."

After Brent had gone, Barbara said,

"Do you think he's married? I didn't see a wedding ring."

"I'm not sure. For some reason, I don't think he is. He's very intense, though," said Sophia.

"That could be because of the case."

"Yes, maybe. He might go into a depression when he's not working."

"He might… I was thinking, you know who would suit him, like perfectly?"

"You mean someone we know? Who?"

"Freda's daughter, Samantha."

"Samantha. Yes, I can see them together. She's twenty-eight, isn't she?"

"Twenty-nine last August. She's smart and very patient. She could put up with depression once in a while from him."

"If she could put up with that former husband of hers and all the lying he did, this one would be no problem. I think she must be a saint… But he's very honest…Seems to be, anyway. Did I do wrong to tell him?"

"I don't think so. It is time to let go of it all. He'd have had me telling him the story straight away. He looks you right in the eye and explains everything carefully. Like there's no hidden agenda."

"He is quite the charmer. He's got Mother, Laura, and Chloe eating out of his hand. Steve likes him. He's even taking Karen and a couple of her friends on a date. He got Aurelia settled on writing an essay in the middle of all this uproar… And! Get this. Mrs Vance thinks he's some kind of marvel because he did some work for her in the kitchen."

"Mrs Vance? Really? Now you mention it, I saw him talking to Brad earlier and Brad was actually replying and smiling… Is he some kind of magician…? I almost wish he had to interview me but don't let Dennis know I said that."

Sophia smiled. "It would be nice if Samantha did meet someone like him."

"What do you say?" asked Barbara excitedly. "Shall we set up a blind date? We could pressure him and he'd probably say yes just to be nice."

"Barb! What are you thinking of? I'm a murder suspect and Franklin was buried today."

"Oh, yes. I forgot."

Chapter 27

Later Thursday night

"Why, it's Mr Brent. Are you hungry, dear?" Mrs Vance smiled when she saw him walking towards her in the kitchen. She and her staff had done battle in the kitchen for two whole days and had achieved a stunning victory. The last of the cleaning up of the buffet dishes was in progress. A light supper had been prepared and was ready to be heated and served as soon as it was called for by however many wanted it.

"I think I've helped myself to more than my fair share. Your cooking is marvellous. Some of those little cakes were like airy puffs of flavour. How do you do it?" He said this as he was walking towards her.

"Part of it is having the knack," she said, as she wiped her hands on her apron which she did often. "Part of it is practice. Once you've got hold of a good recipe it's a matter of judging the quantities properly and knowing how your oven runs. Have you ever done any baking?"

Brent came up to her. "I made this jam doughnut type of thing when I was on a camping trip once and it was vile."

"You should never admit defeat," said Mrs Vance. "If it doesn't turn out well then correct your mistakes and try again. I've baked bread over an open campfire and it came out very nicely. Had a slight smokiness to it that's only to be expected."

"Don't tell me you take an oven and pans with you when you go camping?"

"Oh no, don't be silly. You make the dough and then wrap it around a nice clean stick. You know, with the bark peeled off. My husband whittled the sticks and got a nice fire going while I prepared the food. That brings back some memories, that does. Newly-weds we were and couldn't afford a hotel so we made do and had the time of our lives camping. It was nice weather, too."

"That sounds lovely. I think I might have to try again. I've never made bread."

"A lot of people don't know how to anymore. That, or they don't have the time. My mother taught me and she was a very good cook. Nothing overly fancy you understand but everything always turned out perfectly. Except for her soufflés, of course. She always had trouble with those."

"Well, excluding the troublesome soufflés, it sounds like you had a very sound basis on which to build."

"That's true. I enjoy cooking. It's always a challenge. Like today, for example. We had plenty of time to get everything done and so we did. Then, all sorts of fussy eaters came to the reception. Not that I blame them, it's just hard to accommodate on short notice. We were ready for the vegetarians, that's a given, and then the Israelites and the Halals were covered off because they asked ahead of time. But out of the blue, we got two Celiacs, two Diabetics, and…" she suddenly turned and bellowed loudly, "Mar-cie! How many Vegans was it today?"

"Seven, Mrs Vance," called back Marcie, "and a couple of them weren't happy after they were fed. Said they thought there was animal protein in the ratatouille or something."

"Seven Vegans, I ask you. Makes it difficult to plan ahead, it does. Then, to top it all, some fellow, as thin as a rake, came in here asking for a fat bomb."

"How inconsiderate of him. What did you do.?"

"I threw him out. I said to him that this wasn't a restaurant and, if he hadn't noticed, there had been a funeral not two hours earlier. Fat bomb, indeed. Cheeky beggar. There was plenty of food for him to chose from. Wasn't like he would starve."

"Well, I didn't starve. You have my wholehearted thanks for your superb efforts and marvellous dishes."

"That's very nice of you to say. It's not many as will take the time to be polite." Mrs Vance raised her voice, not quite as loudly as before, and called over her shoulder, "Did you hear that, Marcie?"

"I did, Mrs Vance. You're ever so nice," called Marcie to Brent. She then giggled to herself.

Brent smiled and said, "I wish I could stay here longer but I have work to do and I'm probably holding you up."

"Not a bit of it but we understand. Good night, Mr Brent." Mrs Vance turned back to the work she was doing. As Brent left the room he could hear her singing to herself.

"Mr Umber, could you spare me a moment of your time?" asked Jackson. He had discovered Brent sitting in the lounge by himself. It was a little after nine and the investigator was sleepy, sitting in an armchair but still thinking, thinking. All the guests - the mourners - had gone. A few additional relatives were staying overnight because of the distances they had travelled to attend the funeral.

"Of course. Please, take a seat," said Brent.

"Thank you, I will. Technically, I'm off duty at present. Should somebody come in I shall resume my duties."

"That's the same situation with me. Once the investigation begins, I'm on duty no matter where I am or who I'm with. Even when the case ends, I can't let go. Haunted by memories and finding I always could have been better at my job."

"It is not quite the same with me but then my duties do not include such periods of excitement as you experience. For myself, I am a butler all the time. While on holiday, I am the butler on holiday. My mind keeps reverting to the requirements of the household and whether everything is as it should be."

"What you really should be praying for," said Brent, "is that everything falls to pieces in your absence. So much so that when you return, the universal response is, 'Jackson, thank goodness you've come back to us. We're giving you a raise.'"

Brent saw one of Jackson's rare smiles. He thought the butler looked to be such a thoroughly nice person.

"That is something to consider," he replied.

"Do you have a question?" asked Brent.

"I do. I cannot help but be curious. The information I gave you - did it come to anything?"

"Yes, it did. Thank you for telling me and I know it was difficult for you to do. The result was that it cleared one person completely of all suspicion."

"Ah, that is most gratifying to hear. Very gratifying. I see I was mistaken in being silent."

"That was only your butler's etiquette overriding all other considerations."

"Thank you, sir. I won't trouble you further. Good night."

"Good night, Mr Jackson."

Chapter 28

Thursday to early Friday morning

*A*round ten o'clock, Brent wandered back to the office. The house was much quieter. A few people he did not recognize were talking in a sitting room area. They looked at him as he passed them by. Brent nodded but said nothing.

"Alice. You're still here."

"Do you know how much paperwork there is? It doesn't do itself."

"Greg went hours ago."

"Yeah, well, he put in his time over the weekend. I don't think he slept for forty-eight hours and hasn't had much since."

"I don't know how you do it. I suppose the overtime pay helps to compensate."

"It does. But you should see the tax that comes off it. Now, *there's* a real robbery."

"To corrupt thoroughly an over-used saying for your situation, there's nothing more certain in life than murder and taxes."

"That's true. It's really, really odd, though. Overall, the homicide rate is dropping. Sure, some years are worse than others but the average is declining. The thing that gets me is that the workload keeps increasing. It's true we've had a few cuts in the department but it's the amount of paperwork we have to process. It means we work as hard, and I'd say harder, than detectives did in the past, never mind the decreasing caseload. It's weird."

"I suppose somebody reads everything you write?"

"Oh, sure. But sometimes it feels like I have a desk job with a little bit of detection thrown in to keep it meaningful. You know what I'm saying?"

"I do. Reports are just about the last thing I ever want to do. Yet, once I get started on them, I find it helps me resolve issues. I think it's having to put my thoughts down, knowing they're going to get reviewed, that keeps me from flying off in all directions."

"Yeah. So, I've nearly finished here and I'll go soon. I've been assigned another case as well as this one. I start the new one tomorrow, bright and early."

"Oh, then I won't be seeing you again?"

"'Fraid not."

"That is really sad. I've enjoyed our working together."

"Yes? Well, me, too. It's been very interesting."

"Do we shake hands or hug?"

"Aw, Brent. I'm a hugger."

Midnight came and the house was dark. The hallways were dimly lit for safety by subdued sconce lights but, other than those, no reception rooms were occupied or illuminated. Brent climbed the stairs slowly and quietly with the purpose of returning the twice-stolen jewels to their rightful owner.

Evelyn's suite consisted of four rooms in all. She had a large bedroom, ensuite bathroom, a dressing room and an adjoining sitting room. Of the two hallway entrance doors to her suite, one led into the bedroom and the other into the sitting room. Her dressing room and private bathroom could be accessed from either bedroom or sitting room but not from the hall. On several occasions, Brent had talked briefly to Evelyn in her delightful sitting room which was so pleasant with its grey watered silk wallpaper, thick Aubusson rug, and elegantly delicate French furniture. He intended to enter from the hall into this sitting room to gain access to the armoire in the dressing room.

Passing Marjorie's bedroom, Brent noticed there was no light on. Next, came Evelyn's suite. There was a light showing beneath the door of her sitting room and no light from her bedroom. No sound was to be heard. He was puzzled. The investigator had been sure that Evelyn was asleep in bed but now he was not certain because of the light in her sitting room. He had a choice to make between waiting to see if the light was switched off or to climb outside and look through the window. The latter was possible to do now, entry into the room was not - in case he alarmed Evelyn. The inevitable noise that would be produced with screens being removed and sashes raised put accessing the room via the window out of the question. Brent would go outside merely to observe if Evelyn was awake or asleep in a chair so that he could choose which door to enter through.

In choosing to climb along the ledges and stonework, Brent looked for a suitable window through which to exit. All the bedrooms were occupied in that wing and it was only at the very end of the hall that Brent was able to find such a window. He prepared himself by doing some push-ups and then stretches - particularly for his hands. Once through, he would be on the side of the building and would have to traverse a corner. He opened the window carefully and removed the screen, placing it behind a cabinet. When he had climbed onto the frame, he closed the curtains behind him so the open window could not be seen and the tell-tale cold, December draught kept out or, at least, minimized.

Now he was in semi-darkness with an exterior light below him and he had to feel his way slowly along the narrow ledge.

Brent clung tightly to the cold brickwork and gritty stone. He shuffled his way along the narrow four-inch ledge and left the relative safety of being able to grip the stonework around the window. The tips of his fingers now found only a tenuous hold in slight crevices or depressions in the mortar of the brickwork. At the corner, Brent was more secure again because of the stonework there but now he had to step carefully over two, separate security cameras, each mounted to survey a different side of the house. If he was recorded at all, he would only appear as a black shape in the night.

He came to the window he wanted. The two heavy curtains were drawn but not completely across and left a thin vertical panel with soft, warm light filtering through translucent lace sheers. Although Brent's view was restricted, as he crouched on the ledge he could see enough of the room to convince him that neither Evelyn nor Marjorie was present. He made his way back with straining, cold hands that would not be able to grip the meagre finger-holds for much longer. He could have climbed down but then he would be seen on camera and would also have to wake the sleeping butler to get back into the house.

Once more safely in the hallway, Brent took out the tools of his trade and applied them to the locked door. It was always a satisfying moment for him when he defeated a lock. Opening the door cautiously and quietly, Brent went inside. It was so completely a lady's room. Beautiful by day, possessing a fresh alertness that suggested a practical attitude towards household affairs being conducted in a refined and tasteful atmosphere; beautiful by night, having a cozy and peaceful ambience created by the warm glow of the lamp picking out such things as dull red velvet cushions.

He first checked on Evelyn. He found her asleep in bed. He then set about returning the jewels to their place of keeping. Without fear of interruption or alarm, Brent began to open the long drawer at the foot of the old armoire holding his thin flashlight in his mouth.

The drawer proved noisy to open. So bad was it, Brent seriously considered trying the repatriation of the jewellery at some other time. He imagined that Evelyn, having been disturbed, would suddenly surprise him by switching on the light and exclaim, "Mr Umber, what are you doing in my boudoir?"

He tried once again by lifting the awkwardly long drawer off its runners and inching it slowly outwards. This method was quieter. He could now see the box. Far from being the valuable monstrosity of Jimmy Brewster's reckoning, it was a large, gaudy affair, of some forty years in age but artificially made to look much older. It had a few paste jewels, copper studs and paintings of cherubs on its exterior. The colour scheme was good but the painting was awful. He had seen this type of box before in a flea market. He wondered what story lay behind this oddity that looked out of place in Evelyn's elegant rooms.

The drawer was open sufficiently now for him to lift the case clear of it. He quickly undid the cheap lock and opened the lid which was held in place by red-dyed strings. The interior held a sectioned tray. Merrell had left a few pieces of lesser value behind. The diamond ring's small box soon had its treasure restored to it. Brent could only guess where everything else went as he emptied his pockets and put all the jewellery back into the various compartments. As he was putting the emeralds into the bottom of the box, he noticed quite a difference between the interior's floor and the bottom of the box. He started looking for the way to open the secret drawer he assumed must be there.

It took nearly a minute before he found the catch concealed beneath one of the copper studs right at the base. When he depressed it firmly, the drawer of a hidden compartment shot out awkwardly, jostling the few contents it contained. He pulled the drawer out to its full extent. There lay an old, unopened pack of cigarettes, along with a few handwritten notes and postcards. The item that next caught his eye was a glass vial with a plastic screw-in stopper. Handwritten on a sticky label applied to the outside of the glass were the words - 'Thallium - Poison'.

"Hello, Greg. It's Brent. Sorry to wake you. I'm in the office at Hill Hall."

"Yes. Okay. It's one a.m. This better be good."

"I have in an evidence bag before me an empty glass tube that states it once contained thallium."

"What! I'm coming over. It'll take me forty-five minutes. Where did you find it?"

"Difficult for me to say at the moment."

"I'm on my way." The phone went dead - Greg had hung up.

Chapter 29

Friday morning

*I*n silence, Brent stared at the evidence he had found. It was just a lucky break for him - all because of Merrell's theft. His discovery had not solved anything. He was vaguely dissatisfied and could not decide in what way exactly. Evelyn - what had she done? Had she destroyed her own son? It was now entirely possible for her to have done so. While he was looking at the thin glass tube within the plastic, he noticed how a tiny droplet of moisture had made the bag stick to the glass below the stopper. He found that curious.

Brent began to think of Lloyd and his blunt assertion that Franklin had committed suicide. He thought of Chloe and her 'poor Nana' declaration. He thought of Franklin, who had pitched himself down the stairs while in the throes of thallium poisoning; Sadler-Creme needing a new manager; Lloyd, again, wanting to sink the sloop after his wife died but failing because the sailor and loving husband in him wouldn't let him. Now he thought of Evelyn, the pleasant woman who had dearly loved her son and had seen him grow into a monster of sorts. Then, Evelyn, once more, not talking to Chloe, distancing herself. Why? Finally, Franklin, deliberately insulting Laura, perhaps to protect her… because he was once her good brother.

Too much love, too many foolish cover-ups and misunderstandings, talks of suicide, and Franklin on the stairs. Now, a stupid droplet on the outside of the glass requiring explanation.

He sat still, picked up the plastic bag and, without thinking of anything at all, details began to click into place. He exclaimed to himself softly, "So *that* is what happened!" He sat for a few seconds more, then he hurriedly shoved the evidence bag into his pocket and ran out of the office as fast as he could. He took the stairs of the grand staircase three at a time.

He arrived at Evelyn's bedroom door which was locked. Brent fumbled with his pick-locks adding seconds to the process of unlocking the door. He burst in and switched on the light.

"Evelyn! Evelyn! Wake up! He shook her by the shoulder and, getting no response, called the emergency services.

"My name's Brent Umber. I'm an investigator working with the police at Hill Hall. Send an ambulance here immediately for a poisoning case." He answered the few questions the operator asked him and told her the police were already en route. He ended by saying, "It's thallium poisoning. Tell the medics to bring Prussian blue. Make sure they understand that… Prussian blue. Thank you."

He turned back to Evelyn. She was still. He lifted her eyelids. The pupils of her eyes were like dots and did not respond to the light being shone in them. He left the unconscious woman to go and hammer on Marjorie Bellingham's door. When Brent returned to Evelyn, he noticed that mild twitches and tremors were beginning to afflict her. He was in an agony of indecision. He did not know whether to try to wake Evelyn, and so increase her metabolic rate, or leave her unconscious, hoping the deadly process slowed sufficiently to keep her alive until help arrived. He began to look spent and careworn.

Greg arrived some minutes after the paramedics had. He was surprised to find Hill Hall partially awake and an ambulance outside. He went in through the unlocked front door. A sickly looking but fully dressed Jimmy Brewster met the detective in the hall.

"It's Mother," he blurted out. "She's been poisoned."

"Has she? That's who the ambulance is for, then?"

"Yes. Your man called them in."

"Did he? Where is everyone now?"

"Upstairs. She's very bad."

"Right," said Greg Darrow. "Sorry to hear that." He went upstairs to Mrs Brewster's suite.

In the bedroom, the paramedics had just transferred Evelyn to the stretcher and were in the process of securing her to it. Brent was ineffectually and anxiously hovering about, trying not to be in the way and be by Evelyn's side at the same time. Marjorie was on the far side of the bed. Laura and Sophia were standing out of the medics' way near the door. Mike Halliday, Robert Halliday, and Steve Aimes were in the dressing room, crowded around the doorway looking in. As soon as the wheeled stretcher was in motion, they followed or preceded it by exiting into the hall through the sitting-room door. It was clear that some of those present were intending to follow the ambulance by car to the hospital. Sophia was going in the ambulance with her mother.

Greg walked beside the stretcher while it was in motion and showed his ID to one of the medics. They were heading for the staircase because the elevator was too small.

"What's happening?"

"The poisoning is quite advanced," replied the paramedic. "She's gone into toxic shock. Another hour and we'd have been too late. We gave her what treatment we could to keep her quiet and to counteract the poison."

"Thanks," said Greg. The medics had arrived at the top of the staircase and Greg left them to the work of taking the stretcher downstairs. He saw that Jackson, partially obscured by the massive chandelier, was standing by the front door, holding it open. Greg made a phone call to bring in uniformed officers.

Greg found Brent sitting on the bed in Evelyn's now empty room with his elbows on his knees and both hands covering his nose and mouth, as though praying. He stared straight ahead and only moved his eyes when he saw Greg.

The detective picked up a delicate-looking chair and placed it in front of Brent. The chair looked as though it should collapse under his weight. It held.

"What happened? Attempted murder or suicide?"

Brent took his hands away from his face. "Suicide," he said flatly. "Oh, yes… these are yours."

He took from his pocket the glass tube contained in the bag and handed it to Greg. Then he handed over a separate bag that contained a note signed by Evelyn Brewster. It read, 'I killed my son, Franklin.'

"You should find Evelyn's fingerprints on the tube. Also, there's a water glass in that drawer in a bag. I think that's how she took it."

"And you found the poison where?" asked Greg.

"Evelyn had it."

"So, she really killed Franklin Brewster?" Greg Darrow, hardened detective though he was, could scarcely believe this latest turn of events.

"No," replied Brent.

"What do you mean, no? Who did, then?"

"I have one person in mind. As far as I am concerned the picture of Franklin's death is complete."

"Do you mind telling me who?"

"It's only conjecture on my part at present, though I'm quite certain about it. It was Lloyd."

"Lloyd? What makes you think it was Lloyd? You must have a lot more to tell me than you've put in your reports so far."

"I can tell you much more of what happened later, although I can never tell you all. But right now we need to talk to Lloyd. Would you mind if I spoke to him alone first?"

"Yes, I think I *would* mind. I have a job to do and I can't tell you how irritating you are sometimes. I give you as much latitude as I can when I can."

"It's true, you do. I really don't know how you put up with me. Could we see him together, then? I've got an idea he might be in the mood for a confession."

"I'll go along with that," said Greg. "Where is he now? Did he go to the hospital?"

"I should imagine so," said Brent.

"Are you okay?" asked Greg, after a few moments.

"No, I'm not. I've been too slow and muddled in my thinking. It may have cost Evelyn her life. If she dies… If she dies, Greg, I'll give up this detective work and leave it to the professionals. I'm not cut out for it."

"You might be right. I think you're wrong. I've had moments like this that you're going through. I've made mistakes - too many of them. One of them saw a murderer walk free because I hadn't got enough evidence. It was all circumstantial and the case was dismissed. Guess what? That guy killed someone else and I got handed the new case. He was found guilty and it was an easy conviction but there was a man unnecessarily dead because I had overlooked a lead and thought it was… well, it doesn't matter now what I thought it was. Beat yourself up if it makes you feel better but don't do it forever. Promise me that."

"Would my promise stop me from thinking the thoughts I have?"

"No, it wouldn't. Let's get the case closed. I'll drive you to the hospital and we'll see what happens. She might pull through."

"Think so? She didn't look good. The paramedics didn't say anything about her condition. I watched them and I fear the worst."

"Come on. Sitting here doesn't change a thing. I hope Mrs Brewster survives for her sake as well as yours. If she doesn't… there's still a lot to be done and you didn't *make* her take the thallium."

Chapter 30

In the night and Friday morning

*T*he large hospital's emergency department, a busy place at all times, was a hive of activity when Greg and Brent walked in at two-thirty in the morning. About forty people sat in the rows of blue plastic-backed seats which were bolted to metal beams. Another dozen stood about. Patients, who had long given up on patience, waited resignedly. A uniformed officer was standing next to a seated man whose head was swathed in a bandage through which blood had seeped. Another man was sprawled in a chair, unconscious or asleep. The livid marks on his swollen face showed he'd been in a brawl. A woman, presumably a mother, was comforting a little boy who pressed hard against her looking frightened. Brent wondered how long they had been sitting there. In the back row, with empty seats on either side, an old man coughed loudly - excessively so, it seemed. The dismal hospital lighting and the early hour made the place look bleak and the people were bathed in its bleakness.

In one corner of the waiting room, the Brewster clan had staked out its territory. They had claimed five seats but only two were presently occupied by Jimmy and Merrell. They guarded the coats and bags of others. Brent was both surprised and a little heartened because Merrell was taking an interest in someone other than herself. At least, that was the construction he put upon her presence in the waiting room.

Greg's credentials had their effect upon the hospital staff he encountered. Directions were immediately given by the nurse at the triage desk which guided the two men to where Evelyn was to be found. They walked along the corridor to the elevator and went to the third floor.

Outside of Evelyn's room were Steve Aimes and Mike Halliday, sitting silently in chairs. Steve Aimes stood up when Greg and Brent approached.

"What's the latest?" asked Greg, as they met. Mike stood up and joined the group.

"We don't know much," said Steve Aimes. "No one's really spoken to us yet and the Doctor looks tense. You know what I mean? They've got her on some kind of dialysis machine."

"Haemoperfusion, the nurse said," said Mike Halliday. "She's just been hooked up to it."

"I'm sure it takes time," said Greg. "We can only wait, right?"

"Is she awake?" asked Brent.

"No," replied Steve. "They sedated her to keep her heart rate down."

"At least I did something right," said Brent. "I tried waking her up at first but stopped as soon as I realized that her wakefulness would make the poison act faster."

"That is what we've all been wondering, Brent," said Mike. "How did you know she had taken poison?"

"We won't go into that now," said Greg in a tone that shut the topic down completely. "I'm sure that all your questions will be answered eventually. What is the doctor's name?"

"Rinalda Zapatero," answered Steve.

Greg went into the critical care room. A nurse greeted him with a hostile stare which softened when she saw the ID he showed her. Behind her, standing by the bed, another nurse was looking fixedly at the flow rate display of the dialysis machine, while the white-coated doctor used her stethoscope to check on Evelyn's breathing. Greg waited for an opportune moment to speak to her.

The three women, Marjorie, Laura, and Sophia, returned from the farther end of the corridor after getting drinks from a vending machine to find the four men outside of Evelyn's room. Each woman bore the look of the life-draining worry worn by family and friends in hospital corridors when a loved one is stricken and they are powerless to help. Laura seemed as though she would speak to Brent but changed her mind. She sat down in a chair and Steve sat beside her. She looked brittle, as though a slight shock would break her.

By way of explanation, Marjorie said, "I'm just going downstairs to tell Jimmy and Merrell where we are." No one responded and she left.

Sophia looked directly at Brent for some moments before asking him, "How did you know?"

"It was by luck alone. I'm very sorry, Sophia. I should have seen this earlier."

"Did my mother kill Franklin?" she asked.

"No. As was already explained, nothing more can be said at this time."

"At least you have given us that relief." She turned away.

In the silence that followed, Brent asked, "Has anyone seen Mr de Sainte Croix?"

"He was here just before you arrived," said Mike.

"He went that way," said Steve. He pointed beyond the elevators.

Chapter 31

Friday before dawn

*G*reg and Brent walked together along the corridor to find Lloyd.

"The Doctor says it's too early to tell," said Greg. "She has a chance of pulling through. Her age is against her, though."

"A chance… keeps me hoping." Brent sounded lethargic and disinterested.

"She said that over the next twenty-four hours there will be an improvement if there's going to be one at all. They don't like to commit, do they?"

Brent did not answer.

"She also said that whoever called for the ambulance insisted on the one antidote that the paramedics could use and would be effective. Prussian blue… where did you hear of that?"

"Oh, I read up on it. It absorbs the thallium and eliminates it from the system."

"Well, good on you. If there's a chance for the old lady to survive you gave it to her. Dr Zapatero said thallium poisoning can present in a wide range of symptoms and is difficult to diagnose because it occurs so rarely."

"The dose Evelyn took is probably high enough that it would kill her before any symptoms would begin to show. She's comatose."

"Ah, I see. They're doing everything they can."

They found Lloyd sitting in a waiting area of six chairs outside a doctor's office that was closed.

"Mr de Sainte Croix," said Greg, "we need for you to explain what happened at Hill Hall. We want the whole story. Mr Umber will speak to you while I take notes. Anything I write down may be used as evidence against you. I'm bringing no charges at present but you must understand that I am led to believe you are complicit in Franklin Brewster's demise."

The old man no longer had any wind in his sails. He looked very pale and tired. He seemed to overlook Greg's presence and spoke to Brent directly. "I'll tell you everything. I'll sign a statement, too, if you want me to. I never meant for Evie to get hurt. I don't understand what's happened."

Brent shook off his lethargy sufficiently to begin the interview. Greg took out a notebook and pen.

"When your wife died," said Brent, "you thought to ease your pain by going down with your sloop, scuttling it off Cape Horn. Is that correct?"

"Yes. I found it hard to go on. I felt awful. But as I told you before, when it came to it, I couldn't bring myself to do it. It was against all my instincts of self-preservation - both as a man and a sailor. I got over it. Time is a great healer… a confounded slow one… but a great healer, nevertheless."

"Did that experience make you sympathetic towards people committing suicide?"

"Naturally it would. I had always thought suicides were weak-minded people. When I went through my grief at the loss of my wife, I began to despair. I've never considered myself weak-minded and yet there I was, wishing to end it all. Therefore, I tried to do it in what I thought was a fitting way."

"So you thought it would have been fitting had you gone down with your boat? However, you found that the mechanisms in our minds often run counter to our thoughts, plans, and wishes."

"That's right. That's what I discovered."

"Did Evelyn talk of suicide with you?"

"Oh, yes. When George, her husband, died she was helping out in the Sadler-Creme offices until everything was sorted out. That's where she got the thallium. Showed it me, she did. Said there was enough in the glass tube to kill three people. I recall her telling me how she wanted to die, too. I had been through that experience with my wife's passing so I knew what she was going through. I told her, 'You think you want to die but you don't, really. It's better to live and keep the memories alive than to die and have them extinguished forever.' That seemed to register with her. I believe it got her thinking. Some people say suicides are selfish. I suppose they are really. But tell me, what do you do when life is so awful, you and your thoughts are so dark, that you can't take it anymore?"

"Change your life and find some light," said Brent.

"Huh. I suppose that's true. Sounds easy but the doing is so difficult."

"How did Evelyn respond to what you said to her?" asked Brent.

"It's a funny thing. She said she liked to keep the poison by her and just knowing that she had it made her forget about suicide. It was something like that and I never did quite understand it. What I do remember was her saying that thallium was colourless, tasteless, and painless. So, I said to her, that it sounded like one of the easier ways to die and it made sense for her to have it."

Brent and Greg exchanged glances. They both knew that thallium was colourless, tasteless, and odourless, and also very painful.

"Do you know why Evelyn took the thallium?"

"I don't know. I think the obvious reason is Franklin's suicide. And that is why I feel so bad about it all. I should have seen there might be consequences. I never thought of it for a moment. It just never crossed my mind."

"So, can you tell me, please, how Franklin died?" asked Brent.

"Yes. I knew Franklin had to leave the company. It was no longer possible for him to stay on with his behaviour towards women. Evie and I discussed the matter as soon as we started to hear the rumours. She totally agreed with me - and she had yet to hear all the details of the latest incident."

"Was that in October?"

"Yes, that's right. At the time of the annual meeting in the company's office. I felt I had her backing on the matter and that's all I wanted. That's why… I explained it to you… That's why I telephoned Franklin and told him he had to go. He said he wouldn't. But the writing was on the wall and he knew it.

At the beginning of last week, I remembered that Evelyn kept the poison in her jewellery box. I wondered if she still had it. I didn't like to ask while she was having surgery and all that, so I planned to look when I was next up at the house which would be two days later."

"Did Evelyn ever show you where she kept the poison?"

"No, but she told me. I knew of the box and where she kept it. I bought it for her as a gift. It was a bit of a gag. I got it in Italy years ago when I was sailing around the Med. Great big fake jewels on the lid. I thought she might like it. Surprised when she actually took me up on my suggestion of keeping her valuable jewels in it. I've never understood why some people are obsessed with expensive jewels but there you are. Some can't live without them."

"Where did she keep the box?"

"In the armoire in her dressing room. She kept the thallium hidden in a secret drawer. I remember when I showed her how it worked. Her face lit up like a child's."

"That was where you found the thallium? When would that have been?"

"It was the day she came out of the hospital. I was the only guest in the house at the time. The staff was busy. I went and got the thallium."

"Can you tell me in detail what you did?"

"Well, I knew I needed to have it with me to give to Franklin in case he wanted it. I carry a flask with me… a habit of my yachting days. I poured out most of the rum so that there was about a double left in the flask. I poured only half the contents of the glass tube into the flask and shook it vigorously to mix it. Then, I refilled the glass tube with water from Evie's bathroom, wiped the tube clean, and put it back into her box."

"Why did you go to such lengths?"

"Oh, you know, to keep Evie out of it if there were any awkward questions being asked."

"And the fingerprints?"

"Yes, that. Blame that on the cinema. It's what you're supposed to do, I think, isn't it?"

"It's what you did. How did Franklin come to drink the poisoned draught?"

"We were in the lounge talking and I told him that he was out of Sadler-Creme. He said he could not imagine how he would be able to live without working for the company. He said he was very depressed. I knew he would take it like that. So, I said, 'Franklin, in this flask is something that will cure all your problems'. He asked me what was in it. I told him it was thallium and that it had no taste and was painless. 'Painless?' he asked me. 'Of course, it is', I said. I poured out a cap-full and offered it to him. 'The honourable way out,' he said. 'Exactly', I replied. He hesitated, looked me in the eye, then he took the beaker-cap and knocked it back. 'I haven't had rum in a long time,' he said. 'There's some more,' I said. He asked for it, I gave it to him in the beaker. He drank and handed it back to me. Then we shook hands and said goodnight. I stayed for a jigger of something myself and he went upstairs to bed. Later, I washed out my flask."

"How did you feel about what he had done?"

"I believe he atoned for everything the only way he could."

Brent asked no more questions. He got up and walked away.

"Is there anything more you would like to add?" asked Greg.

"I don't think there is… no."

"Then I'd like to just firm up a few times and dates with you now so I can have the statement ready for your signature later in the morning."

"That will be fine. Whenever it's ready, I'll sign it. I only hope Evie recovers."

Chapter 32

Friday to Sunday

*T*he sun rose again and warmed everything it touched. The population of the emergency department had diminished and changed in character. There were now more seniors present, accompanied by a friend or relative. The corridors and rooms of the hospital were now alive with daytime activity - patients walking slowly and staff walking hurriedly. On the third floor, the group outside Evelyn's room had decreased in number. Marjorie, Sophia, and Brent were the only ones present. Marjorie was reading an ebook. Sophia looked at her phone from time to time. Brent sat with his eyes closed but was not asleep.

A little after ten in the morning, Dr Zapatero came to Sophia and asked her to walk with her a little way so they could talk privately. Brent opened his eyes and Marjorie put down her tablet. They both watched Sophia and the doctor discussing Evelyn. After a few minutes, the doctor walked away purposefully and Sophia returned to the others.

"She said there's been a change. Mother is responding to the dialysis. The levels of thallium have dropped significantly. She's still sedated and the doctor says she'll allow that to wear off to see if Evelyn will wake up. She's more optimistic but she says that it's still too early yet."

"That's something," said Brent.

"Can we go in and see her?" asked Marjorie.

"In a few minutes. A nurse is tidying up and she'll let us know when."

By two in the afternoon others had come to relieve those of the morning watch. Brent had gone home to sleep after Evelyn had awakened. He had kissed her on her forehead and then whispered in her ear, "Chloe is innocent of everything." After he had gone, a massive bouquet of flowers had been delivered with a note attached that read, "To Evelyn - From a very relieved Secret Admirer."

Two days later and it was Sunday morning. Brent, having written and delivered all his obligatory reports to Greg's official satisfaction but which fell far short of answering all that detective's numerous questions, went to see Evelyn. When he arrived, he found Chloe sitting on her Nana's bed. Both of them were smiling as though they had not a care in the world and both of them visibly lit up when he came into the room.

"Mr Umber!" said Chloe, as she scrambled off the bed to give Brent an exuberant hug. "Thank you, thank you. I can never, ever, ever thank you enough."

Brent smiled. "Oh, I'm not entirely deserving of all this warm affection."

"What do you mean?" said Chloe pulling back with a frown on her face. "You saved Nana's life."

"If I did, although I think the hospital staff and paramedics played the biggest part in that, it was only because by the skin of my teeth I awoke from the stupor of my idiocy. I was nearly too late. Now, how is my lady doing?"

"Better than a foolish old woman should be," replied Evelyn. She looked frail, hooked up to the dialysis machine. She was wearing a turban and although there was a look of exhaustion on her face, her eyes were bright.

"Yes, you have been foolish. As to old, oh, I don't know. I was thinking of asking you to marry me."

Evelyn smiled. "It was you who sent those flowers, wasn't it?"

"Guilty, as charged."

"I have a lot to thank you for besides the beautiful flowers. You have saved my wretched life and my silly family."

"That's all too, too much. Please… no more," said Brent, becoming embarrassed. "Your turban is very becoming. I take it there's been a side-effect."

"Nana's hair is coming out in clumps," said Chloe.

"And I have this itchy, very prickly, burning sensation in my feet," said Evelyn.

"Have they given you anything for those conditions?"

"There's nothing to be done for her hair until the poison has been eliminated from her system," said Chloe.

"They put some cream on my legs and feet but it hasn't made any difference," said Evelyn.

"I'm sure these things will get better."

"But my hair? I don't see how that is possible."

"I think your hair will grow back," said Brent. "In the meantime, you could dress up that turban. How about a huge ruby or sapphire pinned in the centre?"

At the mention of jewels, Evelyn became quiet.

"I think, for everyday wear, you could have different colours and materials," said Chloe. "Silky textures, heavy cotton weave… and patterns." Chloe faltered to a stop. She could see Evelyn and Brent looking at each other.

"Are you well enough to speak?" asked Brent of Evelyn. The old lady nodded. Brent continued, now addressing

Chloe, "This is very rude of me to ask but I need to talk to Nana for a little while. Twenty minutes should be enough time."

"Yes, Chloe. Mr Umber needs some things explained and I would prefer to speak to him alone."

"Oh, I see. I can find something to do." She smiled a little crookedly, turned, and left the room.

When Chloe had gone, Evelyn said, "Don't mind her. She always likes to be at the centre of things."

"I can appreciate that. Now, where shall we begin?"

"I don't know. I, also, have some questions. The first that you must answer before I say anything is - did you say something to Robert?"

"Robert… Has he been to see you?"

"Yes… He's very much changed… He explained something to me and I now realize I have been misjudging him for a long time. It all goes back to that wretched trust... I can see by your face that you had a hand in it. He must have explained what happened to him and you told him to talk to me. Am I right?"

"It seemed to be a logical solution to me."

"Yes… I wish it had happened sooner… So much time wasted in stupidity. I hadn't the imagination to see that a sixteen-year-old would be affected by the sudden knowledge of a large inheritance in such a life-altering way. I was too accustomed to it all."

"Then make up for lost time," said Brent. "Like all of us, he wants someone to love him for who he is and not for what he does or doesn't achieve."

"Hmm, you're being very profound… Do you want to ask your questions now? You should do so before Chloe comes back."

"Of course. Let's start way back. In roundabout ways, I have learned that Lloyd was once very sweet on you. That you refused his wooing at some moment in time is apparent, yet he has remained a friend of yours and the family all these many years. What can you tell me about that early episode?"

"I don't see how that helps you but since you have asked, I will tell you. I had finished my education and my father knew Lloyd's father through a business connection. It was a summer weekend and my parents were hosting a modest garden party. Not on the scale it would have been done at Hill Hall. My origins are quite humble. So, Lloyd's family was invited to the party. He came and we got talking. I liked him. He was pleasant, courteous and alarmingly frank. I think, for him, he had fallen in love with me."

"Love at first sight, eh?" Brent smiled.

"Almost. He followed me about the party the whole afternoon so that I couldn't escape him even if I wanted to. Not that I minded, particularly. He was trying to convince me to come out on his sailboat." Evelyn smiled to herself. "It was only a dinghy, although he was already planning to get a sloop. The way he spoke of sailing and boats one instantly knew that any future marriage priorities with Lloyd would be:- sailing first and second, and wife third. That would have been too much for my vanity. So I knew, early on, that no romance could blossom between us.

Dogged Lloyd, however, made heavy weather of it and would send letters, telephone, or show up on the doorstep with regularity to attempt to persuade me. I told him no at least twenty times."

"Was that a no to romance or sailing?"

"Both. I get sea-sick. A big cruise ship would be fine for me. Lounging on a yacht in a harbour would be acceptable. Sailing halfway around the world in something only a little larger than a canoe with a sail was out of the question. I told him, I would never make a sailor. He always said, I would get over the sea-sickness and should try because he was convinced I would come to love it as much as he did."

"Is this tiring you?" asked Brent. "We can put it off, if you like."

Evelyn had grimaced as she felt some pain.

"No, I'm fine. I feel uncomfortable all the time. Dr Rinalada says the side effects will lessen eventually. Where was I? Yes... That lasted nearly a year. He was very nice in other ways and I valued him as a friend. He always spoke the truth in his funny, clipped way and he was intensely loyal and upright. Still is. Eventually, he saw that I could not be persuaded. By that time, Lloyd had become such a familiar fixture at our house that my mother would always set an extra place for dinner every Wednesday and Sunday without ever asking if he was coming or not." Evelyn paused.

"Then his habit continued after you were married to George?" asked Brent.

"Yes, it did, although his visits were less frequent. George never minded and came to trust Lloyd implicitly. He always said that Lloyd was the most scrupulously honest man he had ever met."

"There was no jealousy, then?"

"Oh, no. Not at all. You see, Lloyd married shortly after I did. He met someone with a similar passion for sailing. Betty was probably as obsessed about it as Lloyd was. They used to disappear for weeks - sometimes months - at a time."

"Yachting does require quite a lot of money, doesn't it?" asked Brent. "How did Lloyd and Betty finance their lifestyle?"

"Betty had some money of her own. Lloyd had some through his family but he's also one of those people who instinctively knows when the top or bottom of a market has been reached. He mainly invested in real estate and stocks.

He was always saying that passive income was the best way to free up one's life to do what one really loves."

"It's almost as though he constructed his whole life around sailing. That's quite impressive."

"Then you can see how a landlubber like me would never have fitted into such an arrangement. Lloyd realized it, too."

"Did he ever talk to you about his second voyage around Cape Horn?"

"Not at first, he didn't. He suffered badly when Betty died. He was quite in despair about losing her. In bits and pieces, it came out... It was obvious that he had thought strongly about suicide." She paused for a moment. "That's when he began to talk quite glibly about suicide, as though it were a cure for depression."

"In what way?"

"He talked about it as though it were an established fact... As though it were a normal, commonplace attitude everyone should have. If a person feels a little down then it might be time to die before it gets any worse."

"Was it like a filter had been removed?" asked Brent. "You see, I can easily visualize Lloyd saying to someone, "Feeling a bit miserable, are you? Just kill yourself and you'll feel much better.'"

"That is it exactly. I always thought it was as though Lloyd had placed suicide on a list of things to do... as a viable, practical, and acceptable possibility in case of emergency.... As though there were no emotion or heart-rending decision to be made about it."

"You do realize that, if Lloyd had been thinking rationally when you showed him the bottle of poison you had, he would have taken it away from you and got rid of it."

"That's right. I had never thought about that aspect of it before. I showed it to him because I knew that he would not mind in any way or create a fuss. Oh, it is so difficult to believe how I accepted and glossed over his attitude towards suicide. Now, it seems so utterly fantastic and foolish."

"I hold him indirectly responsible for your having nearly died. No sane person would have acted as he did and left you, a very depressed woman at the time, with the means to kill herself at hand."

"Do you think him mad?"

"Let us just say, he no longer thinks clearly because of the experience he had in losing his wife. Following on from that, how do you feel about Lloyd talking to Franklin about suicide and then offering him the poison with which to do it?"

"I should have known it was that. I thought it was murder at first, although I hadn't a clue who could have done it. After much rumination, I began to suspect Chloe… my dear, dear Chloe… how could I have thought such a thing? But now I can see it is so thoroughly Lloyd - to be there on hand, talking Franklin into committing suicide. In light of what you have just been saying, Lloyd seems never to have considered the consequences of what he says." Evelyn was quiet for some time. A nurse arrived to see how she was doing.

Chapter 33

Sunday continued

When the cheerful nurse had finished her duties in the room, Evelyn and Brent resumed their conversation where they had left off.

"I don't know what to think about Franklin," said Evelyn. She lay her turbaned head back on the almost upright pillow. "He's gone and I don't seem to feel any emptier than I did while he was alive. If anything, I'm numb about his death… What did you think of Franklin?"

"I see him as two distinct characters belonging to two different eras," said Brent. "Franklin the good and Franklin the bad. There's a transition phase between the two characters but once he had started to change, progressing from one to the other, he had, essentially, changed already. The seed had been planted and watered. The plant must grow and bear fruit."

"Yes, yes. For me, I think of him as though he went away over the hills. I saw him on each successive hilltop as he travelled, always becoming smaller and less distinct until I couldn't see him because of the distance."

Brent nodded and shifted in his chair. "Now, a big question. I believe I know the answer but I would like to hear it from your own lips. What prompted *you* to attempt suicide?"

Evelyn looked directly into his eyes as she answered. "It's uncanny how you seem to know everything… How you found out eludes me. As you know, Chloe was acting as a hostess - waitress - for the night of my homecoming from the hospital… Look at me now. I'm back here again. But that's my own stupid fault.

Chloe told me about her scheme to swap places and she found it immensely comical to fool everyone at the dinner table. I must say, she did do it awfully well. I barely recognized her and she kept a straight face the whole time. Jimmy stared right at her and didn't notice it was her. As for her mother and father, I don't know what to say. Sophia couldn't have looked at her properly. Mr Umber, surely a mother would recognize her own daughter?"

"You would think so under normal circumstances. Perhaps, she did think that the Rachel substitute she saw looked similar to her daughter but when the straight-faced Chloe gave no sign of recognition… Sophia dismissed it from her mind."

"I'll ask her if that's what she did," said Evelyn. "I haven't seen her on her own yet. Although, while a group of them were here and we were all marvelling at how you came to find me in time to save me, she did manage to mention that you had been told of Gillian's sad story."

"Yes, she told me everything. I wish there was something I could say or do."

"Far too late for that. Decades too late… I was so disappointed and hurt to hear that my boy did that to a guest in my house. And then afterwards, to compound the offence with his vile behaviour… I had hoped… For a long time, I had hoped he would see reason… and just change." She sighed deeply. "Gillian went her own way and there was nothing any of us could do… Such a shame." Her voice trailed away.

"I agree," said Brent quietly. "So, we have Chloe play-acting and doing it very well, too."

"Yes, Chloe. It was after Franklin died and the house was under that awful cloud. I never thought of suicide. Franklin always seemed too full of his own importance to be likely to have considered it as an option. So, I couldn't help myself, I kept thinking and thinking, 'Who could have killed him?' Then, when Chloe said she wouldn't, under any circumstances, get her friend Rachel into trouble… I foolishly went along with her suggestion. I should not have allowed it. It was because I didn't want Chloe or her friend to get into trouble with the police. After that, I began to think about everyone and I could do nothing to stop my thoughts. I began to suspect that Chloe had something to do with Franklin's death." Evelyn paused for some moments.

"It is very difficult," said Brent, "to rid oneself of a suspicious thought once it has occurred. It's a tenacious class of thought. It's only when something else can definitively disprove the original thought that it can be dismissed. Even then, there's a stickiness to a suspicion."

"That was certainly my state of mind. I could think of nothing else. When I found my jewellery missing, I thought Chloe had taken it. She had seen and admired it often enough. I began to connect the two events. There was no one I could confide in without betraying Chloe and I so wanted to be proved wrong. I would have given anything to be shown that what at first I thought and then subsequently believed was false."

"You thought that Chloe had stolen the jewels and then poisoned Franklin, who had somehow discovered the theft?"

"Yes. I couldn't see what else could have happened."

"How did you discover your jewels were missing?"

"That was because of Lloyd. On the night, before I went to bed, he said he was going to talk to Franklin and tell him he needed to resign from the company. He said, 'Franklin will take it hard. He might commit suicide, you know.' Those may not be his exact words but that is what I understood him to say. I obviously had no idea that he was intending to urge Franklin to kill himself. I never, never would have let him do that. It is all so absurd and nightmarish. The mad thing is that even though I knew of that conversation, I forgot it in my fear over Chloe's involvement. Nightmarish, that's the only word for it. I've been so mixed up."

"Yes, it has been nightmarish but it's over now. What you've told me is in keeping with Lloyd's character. He comes across as eminently reasonable while being obstinate and forthright. Armed, as he was, with the idea that suicide is a normal process - or, at least, a process normalized by his own reckoning - he was doing what he thought was right."

"How could he fall so far away from decent behaviour? You talk people *out of* committing suicide not talk them *into* it. It seems so alien… Like Socrates and the hemlock."

"That has crossed my mind," said Brent.

"Well, coming back to the night of Franklin's death, after the dinner party broke up, I returned my jewellery to the box. For the first time in years, I thought to look into the secret drawer it has. You'll laugh at this. I used to smoke, not very heavily, but it was a habit. While I was trying to stop smoking, I had great difficulties in lasting anything more than two days. It was awful. I would panic if I thought I had no cigarettes. That nervousness only made me think more about smoking all the time. Then I thought to keep a pack in my jewel box so that I knew I had them if I needed them. It worked. It stopped me from being anxious and I gave up the habit in a matter of days.

When George died I felt like killing myself, I did really. I didn't want to feel like that but there seemed no point in anything anymore and I couldn't stop myself. I decided to keep the means of killing myself to hand so that I would stop thinking about wanting death, in the same way I had been able to stop thinking about cigarettes and smoking. I got the poison from the company's store and it did help me tremendously, having it on hand."

"What made you choose thallium?" asked Brent.

"George had told me of its properties once. He had said it is the poisoner's poison because it was so difficult to trace. Now, here's what I don't understand. He said it was tasteless, colourless, and painless but it isn't true, is it?"

"Yes and no. What is usually said is that thallium is tasteless, colourless, and odourless. Yes, it is true in the sense that, with a large enough dose, symptoms do not manifest and the person dies quickly in a coma. If it is taken in a lower dose, the symptoms, such as you are experiencing now, become apparent, but there's very much more besides and it is very nasty and painful - or so I have read and as I'm hearing from you."

"Ah, that makes sense to me. Where was I?"

"Thallium in your jewel box."

"Yes. Having seen it was there, although now I understand that Lloyd had already tampered with the thallium - of which fact I was not aware, I went to bed. I'm rather vague about the time because it all became one big blur but at some point in the night I heard that Franklin had been poisoned. The tube of Thallium I had didn't even cross my mind. You see, when I had looked at the tube it was full. Then Chloe came to me the next day and I agreed to give her an alibi. I think that's the right term. So, as far as I knew at the time, Franklin was not killed with the poison from my bottle.

It was after that, Monday I think, I thought I would see what jewellery I should wear to the funeral. I think I was only keeping myself busy because I rarely wear any of the valuable items. I opened the box and the jewellery had gone. Imagine how shocked I was. They were gone and, as I explained, the first person I thought of who would take them was Chloe. And once I had that idea in my head, it didn't take long for another to join it - that Chloe was also responsible for Franklin's death.

From then on, I was in a terrible state. All I could think of was that Chloe had gone all wrong. Yet I still wanted to protect her. I seriously considered that there must be some sort of Brewster curse breaking out. I couldn't stand to see another person I loved turn wicked. I thought, if I kill myself, they will think I killed Franklin. That's why I left the note. I came to my decision during the service. I thought I could give Chloe a second chance. Do you know I could barely look at her once I had got to that point and I had already been avoiding her for some time." Tears came to her eyes and she brushed them away.

"I got through the funeral. I felt so hollow and scared. That dear Marjorie, she's been so anxious about me but I couldn't tell her anything, could I? Finally, I got to bed and Marjorie went to her room. As soon as I knew she had gone, I got up again and went to my sitting room. It took a while for me to get up the courage. I got out the thallium and mixed it in a glass of water and drank it.

It was an odd feeling, sitting there, knowing my end was coming in a matter of hours. It scared me, so I left a lamp on in my sitting room for some comfort and went back to bed. I lay there and thought I would never sleep. All sorts of thoughts crowded my mind… some of them were pleasant… but then I felt very lonely. After that, I fell asleep. I hadn't thought I would but I did."

"What happened while you slept? Did you dream? Were you conscious of anything?"

"Only patches of fractured thoughts. It was like a picture had been smashed and I saw bits of it that came and went but they made no sense. Mostly there was nothing - until here, in the hospital, when the sedative began wearing off. Then I began to feel pain. I heard voices. Sophia I remember, and Marjorie... Oh, and then you. That's right! You said Chloe was innocent. I remember that now.... What a nice man you are.... How can I ever repay you?"

"By getting well again," said Brent.

Evelyn smiled. It was evident she had finished her narrative.

"Thank you for telling me all those difficult things," said Brent. "It's time for me to tell you something you do not know. Your jewellery has been returned intact to your jewellery case."

Evelyn registered great surprise and then a thoughtful look settled on her face. She patiently took to smoothing out the turned back section of the top sheet on her bed. When she had finished, she looked up and said,

"I guess it was you who put the jewellery back. That is the only thing that makes any sense to me. Mr Umber, who took it in the first place? I know it wasn't Chloe."

"I am not at liberty to say who took the jewellery or who returned it," said Brent.

"That is grossly unfair of you," said Evelyn in a slightly irritated tone. "I have told you everything and you have told me nothing.... Well, that's not true but you know what I mean."

"I'm certain it seems that I arbitrarily keep things back. By the same standard that keeps me silent about your jewellery, I will also be silent about Chloe being present at the dinner. I have not told Lieutenant Darrow about either incident. They are not mentioned in my report. He will question me about them sooner or later and I will not tell him."

"I see. It seems I must accept things the way they are. Mr Umber, I can guess as well as you can. I believe I know who it was."

"Even if you guess correctly I will not tell you. Appearances can be deceptive, though."

"Do you expect me to puzzle that out on my own?"

"I do. It's better mental stimulation than doing a crossword puzzle."

"So, do you mean it isn't who I think it is?"

"Who do you think it is?"

"I am not going to tell you anything ever again."

"Then you won't marry me?"

"You are so silly sometimes. Everyone says you have a peculiar sense of humour." But Evelyn laughed quite heartily after she had spoken.

Chapter 34

Monday

*O*n Monday, Brent went to see Greg Darrow in his office in the Homicide Department.

"Where's Lloyd at present?" asked Brent.

"He's in a cell downstairs under a suicide watch," said Greg. "Probably the safest place for him."

"Do you believe you can get a murder conviction?"

"I doubt it. Still, that's not my decision to make. I think he'll be prosecuted on the lesser charge of possessing a controlled substance and administering it. He'll probably get a couple of years."

"Do you consider it to have been murder…? that he *murdered* Franklin?"

"I think he did," replied Greg. "He prepared everything in advance. He anticipated the deceased's reaction to his suggestion. He went to him and, I wouldn't say he twisted his arm, but he left his victim with no psychological alternative but to take the poison being offered and end his life."

"That's all too true. He had also mounted a justified campaign to remove Franklin from the company and that means that what happened on the night of the dinner was only a matter of closing the deal for him, resolving the issue. Why do you think he wouldn't be convicted of murder?"

"There's only his own statement as evidence. That would allow the defence to have a field day. They would say he was coerced into signing his statement by you and me, de Sainte Croix was mentally unbalanced at the time, and they could also come up with all kinds of other imaginative stuff to convince the jury. You do realize there's a chance he might walk away from all and any charges we might lay against him?"

"If he did walk away from them, Lloyd would choose the honourable way out - honourable, that is, according to his own lights."

"Do *you* think he's a murderer?" asked Greg.

"In a legal sense, yes. From his perspective, I can understand why he did what he did. From my perspective, it seems a pretty despicable thing. Bad as Franklin was, it was like kicking him when he was down. Lloyd manipulated an unbalanced mind with the objective that Franklin should die. Lloyd's actions produced an outcome that was irreversible and irreparable. My opinion…? I don't know that I really have one at the moment. I think, if anything, perhaps it would be best all round if Lloyd boarded his sloop and went sailing. He almost certainly wouldn't come back this time."

"Yes, I'm sure he'd like that." Greg paused for some seconds before saying, "Your report's a bit of a joke, isn't it?"

"Joke? Huh, I thought it was a respectable piece of prose that explained matters succinctly."

"As far as it went, it wasn't bad. I'm not being your English teacher here. I'm talking about the things you left out."

"Left out something, did I? Such as?"

"At least three people accessed the jewellery box - Mrs Brewster, de Sainte Croix, and you - although you omitted that last fact. Care to explain it?"

"Er… No, I don't want to. I may have looked in the box and noticed something. Are you recording this conversation?"

"I should, shouldn't I? There's obviously something at the back of this. Somebody stole the jewels and I'd say it was Fortier and Brewster who worked it. That's the only plausible explanation for all their running about in the garden, hiding something. What I wonder is, how did the jewellery get returned?"

"Do you wonder about that? I do, too. We must live in an age where miracles still happen."

"Ignoring your flippancy for the moment, Brent, I can read you like a book that only has a few pages stuck together. I know where the story goes and how it ends - I don't know some of the details. I believe you understand me."

"Yes, sir."

"Now, who was the mystery person you mentioned earlier but who didn't appear in your report?"

"I'd forgotten about that. One person was putting on an act. I counted the extra persona as another person - the mystery person. It didn't come to anything. The person was not involved to the slightest degree."

"Huh, what am I going to do with you? You're always making it complicated. Also, and I can't quite get this one but there was something else that happened and it definitely upset Mrs Brewster. If I had to guess, I would say it was something to do with Chloe Halliday. I've half a mind to bring that girl in for questioning and find out what she knows."

"Why not Evelyn? She's at your mercy, lying in a hospital bed as she is."

"You're not going to tell me?"

"Evelyn and Chloe have a special bond of love. They had serious misunderstandings about each other and, based upon those misunderstandings, they both acted foolishly one way or another. However, nothing they did has any bearing on Lloyd's impending case. Now they are reunited once more. I'm sure you wouldn't want to spoil that."

"I probably won't. You know, Brent, if you were in the department here, you'd be the kind of detective who either gets rapidly promoted or promptly fired. Eventually, you would be fired, anyway….

Just remembered something. Brewster's son goes by the name of Adam Smith."

"You found him! That was quick."

"Brewster's lawyer had the information," said Greg.

"Okay…. Does he inherit? And what does he inherit?"

"It looks like he was adopted which means he no longer has any rights to Brewster's estate. It means he's not a legal heir and he's out of the trust. However, he was specified in Brewster's will. Guess how much."

"I don't know… Ten per cent? Twenty?"

"The lot. That's about eleven million in all."

"How about that… I never would have guessed… When was the will drawn up?"

"Five weeks ago. It was his first will as far as his lawyer knows."

"Think Franklin was planning for something?" asked Brent.

"It certainly looks like it but it's not proof. It's likely to be just one of those weird coincidences."

"You're probably right." Brent went quiet as his thoughts turned to Gillian and how simple it would have been for Franklin to have helped her all those years ago.

"What are you doing next?" asked Greg

"Oh, ah, not much at present. Do a few chores around the house and see a few people - that type of thing. What I'd really like is more work from you.... Not that I want a crime wave to break out or anything like that; in fact, the absolute reverse is true."

"There's plenty to do as it is. Unfortunately, there's nothing I have that's suitable for you. I'll call you as soon as a promising case comes in."

"Thanks, Greg. All joking aside, I like working with you. You're quite a sensitive soul beneath that gruff exterior of yours."

"Oh, go on, Brent. Get out of here, I have work to do."

"Why, Brent. It's nice to see you. Come on in." Eric, Brent's gardener, a tall, gaunt man in his seventies, stood back from his front door to admit his visitor.

"I tried calling you numerous times but it just rang and rang every time. Is your phone out of order?"

"Telemarketers. I can't stand them. I unplugged the phone. That's the only way to deal with them. Go into the front room."

"But people can't reach you."

"If it's bad news, it can wait. So, what brings you here? Want a coffee or tea or something?"

"No, thanks. I've come to discuss gardening."

"Oh, good. Let's have a beer, then. There are a few things I have in mind to say."

Brent waited while Eric disappeared into the kitchen of his small house to fetch some bottles of his own powerful and pleasant-tasting home-brew.

To visit with someone, as he was doing now, was a way for Brent to kind of decompress after the case. He felt drained after the excitement of what he had been through and he had decided to take steps this time against the mild depression that always threatened immediately after his involvement in a case came to an end.

Eric returned and set down four bottles and two glasses. With quick, decisive movements, his huge, gnarled hands had the cap off a bottle and the amber liquid was soon streaming into each glass.

"There you go, Brent." Eric handed him a glass. "Your good health."

"And the same to you," said Brent. He tasted the beer and it was good.

"Now, then, what's on your mind?"

"I was on a case that's just finished. It was at a house that had an Italian garden which will be absolutely glorious in the summer. It was very well laid out. There was a gorgeous conservatory there... a huge one. It was so pleasant to sit in it and see the snow outside and yet be surrounded by flowers. If you like, I think we can go up there and you can see it for yourself."

"That good, was it?"

"Oh, yes. While I was in the conservatory, I thought, why don't *we* put one in. Just a small affair of course... about twenty by twenty. It would give us something to do in the winter... potter about in the cold months, tending to plants."

"Conservatory, eh? Where'd it go?"

"Back of the house on the west side. We could move the beds and compost bins beyond the shed and it would fit in nicely."

"But that's where the runner beans will be. It's perfect for them there."

"I know. We could put those in further along the fence."

"Hmm. Them runners will be tender and have a crispness you can't find anywhere. Still, they'll have to be rotated eventually. A conservatory, eh? That's a lot of work and expense."

"It would be, I agree. We'll get it done professionally. Somebody gave me the name of Randall's."

"They're good, they are…. Hmm, I don't reckon it. There's a lot of perennials that would have to be shifted and we only just put them in."

"We can do it. You can have a free hand deciding where everything goes."

"Why'd you want one, anyway?"

"Like I said, flowers and lush growth in the winter. Also, I saw a beautiful lemon tree there. It was so heavy with perfect fruit. I was amazed."

"I've nothing against citrus. Why don't you just buy the lemons at the market?"

"It's not the same, Eric. You know that. I thought you would jump at the chance."

"Who me? No. I think it would cramp the look of the garden. We only have so much space and we don't want it looking congested."

"It won't if we make just a couple of changes."

"No. I don't see it."

"I'll let you have the Rozanne and I'll give up the Cosmos."

"That's very nice of you, thank you. I thought you'd come round to my way of thinking. But I'm against a conservatory going in."

Brent sipped his beer to hide his disappointment. Then he said, "What is it *you* wanted to discuss?"

"New seed catalogues are starting to come out. I've already got one and we have to decide about the cold frames. We'll need them soon enough and you've been putting off building them."

"I haven't been putting it off."

"Sure you have. I asked you twice about them before and both times you said, 'We've got plenty of time.' Well, now we don't. If we don't get them done now and then we have a lot of snow over the winter, we won't get to them until early March. I don't want to be building cold frames in March as there's plenty for us to do then, anyway."

"Very well. Do you have any drawings?" Brent knew there would be drawings.

"Course, I do." Eric took a large pad of graph paper from a drawer in his sideboard and laid it out for Brent to inspect. The clear drawings were simple and effective. Brent liked looking at Eric's garden sketches and layout plans.

"You know, Eric, if one of those was a bit larger we could make a conservatory out of it."

"Huh-uh, you're funny sometimes. I like conservatories but I don't see it in your garden except it were a small one and then the expense would be too high for what you would be getting… I'll tell you what, though, why don't we go up to that place you know so I can see what it is you're talking about?"

"We can do that. It's a big house called Hill Hall."

"I know it! The Brewster place. That's right, that's where the fella died. I've done lots of work there off and on over the years. Put in some cypresses. The lady fussed over their position like you wouldn't believe. In the end, put 'em right where I said straight off but it took her an hour to make up her mind."

"I don't believe it. Would that have been Evelyn Brewster?"

"I suppose so. She had very pretty copper-coloured hair and I remember she wore a long string of pearls but it were a while back. I recall the conservatory though - big long affair jutting out into the garden."

"That's it. What a small world it is."

"Let's go up there, Brent. I'd love to see the place again. There was a big Victorian greenhouse that I particularly liked. Used to be a couple of lovely old maples nearby it but we had to take them down because they had Heart Rot."

"That's sad about the trees…. Evelyn has white hair now."

"Does she…? Yes, I suppose she would." Eric looked very thoughtful for a while. "My hair used to be the colour of wheat back then but you wouldn't know it now except I told you.

Anyway, enough of the old days. You got that murder sorted out, did you?"

"I did. I'd rather we stuck to gardening tonight. I can tell you all about the case on our way over to Hill Hall."

"That's fine by me…. I reckon we need at least three of these cold frames and four would be better on account of Maria's vegetables. Want some more beer there, Brent?"

"A half glass and no more. I have to drive home."

"Right you are." Eric carefully poured out the beer…. There you go. I've got a new batch that's almost ready."

"You and your beer. It's very good, though. What would you do if you ran out?"

"I did once and I got so annoyed with myself that I vowed I'd never let it happen again."

"So let's build four of them," said Brent, smiling. "We could put them against the eastern fence."

"Funny you should suggest right there. I thought of the exact same place. If we're agreed, then we should look through the seed catalogue tonight and start our orders early.

Also, I've been thinking about what you said just now. We've probably got enough space so we could put in Rozanne *and* some Cosmos. What do you think? I can draw it out for you."

A little after ten that night, Brent was at home and logged in to his Hearts Entwined account. He was trying out a new online dating and psychological profile-matching website.

"Monty, you might be interested in this one. It's a message from FluffyCat123. Here goes."

The message opened and photos appeared.

"I suppose that's her behind the white, furry monster. No, no. Too much of the cat in everything. Are you interested, Monty? You should be... What are you doing? Pull yourself together and look at the screen... No, I don't think she and I would be compatible. I'll reply to her later, though, as she did take the time to contact me.

Here's another message and it's from... TheSavageVixen... Oh, dear, no. Definitely not. What on earth did I put in my profile? Only two responses and both with animal themes.... Well, these are early days."

Epilogue

*O*ver time, all of Brent's connections with Hill Hall began to dissolve until only a few remained. Evelyn kept up a correspondence by email which Brent suspected had to be typed by Marjorie. After the initial expressions of Evelyn's gratefulness had subsided, the brief, intermittent exchanges between them took on the character of an elderly aunt corresponding with a young nephew.

This correspondence was punctuated by the arrival at Hill Hall of both Brent and Eric in the middle of January when a foot of snow covered everything. Evelyn, fully recovered from her hip surgery and wearing a wig similar to her usual hairstyle, was thrilled to see Eric again after so many years. She fussed over him greatly to the old gardener's amusement and slight embarrassment. The talk of gardens ranged far and wide. Evelyn found it quite remarkable that Brent knew Eric and said many times how delighted she was to see them both.

To Brent's amazement, a photograph album was produced. In it was a happy group shot, colour photograph from the mid-seventies. In it, standing on a broad, summer lawn, was a forty-year-old, dark auburn-haired Evelyn dressed in a beautiful long green paisley-patterned dress, accented by a chunky amber bead necklace. Standing next to her in a line were three gardeners. The nearest and by far the tallest of them was a straw-haired Eric whom Brent would not have recognized as the man sitting across from him in the lounge of Hill Hall.

After a while, Eric excused himself from the meeting, saying he wanted to look over the greenhouse once more. While he was gone, Brent and Evelyn began to talk.

"How are you?" asked Brent. He was asking the inner Evelyn the question.

"I'm doing very well. Everything is behind me now and I can consider things more rationally... Lloyd's health is failing."

"I'm sorry to hear that. Is it something serious? You look very concerned."

"I am.... It's nothing specific; he's given up on living... I don't think he will make it to the trial."

"I see. And do you feel conflicted about that?"

"Very much so.... The part that stings is that, when he's gone, there won't be anyone left from the old days... It has to happen, I know, but there it is... At least I have lots of family members who I see often. The trouble there is they look up to me and it's not the same as talking to a friend, an equal... Seeing Eric again is something I can treasure.

I have to tell you something, Brent. Promise me you won't mention this to him... He used to be so rude to me. He was positively the rudest man I had ever met... I liked him for it because he would not let me ruin the garden with fanciful things. He came to work with the desire to make the garden as beautiful as it could be - he didn't come to kowtow to or to please me - so we often clashed. George said I should fire him but I didn't."

Brent slowly smiled. "I'll tell you something then... He hasn't changed that much. It's the beauty of the garden first and I might as well be his apprentice who's only just started."

"Isn't that extraordinary? That's exactly how I felt. It was why I didn't want to fire Eric -because the blasted man was always right." Evelyn laughed freely.

They talked of a few other things - Brewster family events for the most part - until Eric returned. The three of them went to the conservatory.

"See, Evelyn, Brent here was enamoured with your conservatory, and rightly so because it's looking well-kept. He wanted one of his own. But I said to him we haven't the room at his place to put one in and have it look as nice as it should."

Evelyn managed to control herself better than Brent did.

"Well, both of you are welcome to visit this one any time you care to come," she replied with a straight face.

Brent, struggling with a smile that threatened to turn into a laugh, said,

"You're quite right, of course, Eric. I think I was enchanted with this particular conservatory and a lot of that was due to its size and setting."

"Ah," said Eric. "There you go. And thank you for the invitation," said Eric to Evelyn. "If you don't mind, I'll poke about for a bit." He walked away further into the conservatory and began to examine individual plants until he was so engrossed he was in a world of his own.

Evelyn looked at Brent. Then her smile broke out.

Lloyd died a month later. Evelyn died a year and a month later from a heart attack. Brent went to both funerals. Lloyd's funeral was very sparsely attended, although Evelyn, Marjorie, Mrs Vance and Henry Jackson were all present. The butler, as formal as he ever was, seemed pleased to meet Brent again. Mrs Vance, a person prone to tears at funerals, was nevertheless delighted to talk to Brent once more and seized upon the opportunity to the extent that Brent thought he might never get away - not that he minded. It was only Jackson's reminder that the last car back to Hill Hall was about to leave that compelled Mrs Vance to tear herself away.

When Evelyn died Brent felt her loss like a heavy blow. He realized that even *his* trajectory had been deflected a little more than he had realized and although he had not been persuaded into her orbit, Evelyn had innately changed his direction but without him knowing where it was sending him.

About a week after Evelyn's well-attended funeral, Brent received a letter from a lawyer he did not know requesting he come to his law office concerning Evelyn Brewster's will.

Brent went. Evelyn's bequest to him amounted to four and a half million dollars and one Delft vase with an old crack in it. There was also a private letter delivered to him from her that restated her profuse thanks for what he had done for her and her family. He later learned that she had left Eric a hundred thousand dollars and Marjorie, her companion, three million. Perhaps Marjorie would buy her idyllic farm now.

He was deeply moved at being remembered by Evelyn. Money aside, he found her thoughtfulness quite overwhelming. He doubly appreciated her remembrance of Eric in such a significant way.

As to the others of the Brewster clan, he received pleasant emails from both Laura and Sophia soon after the case ended but these contacts ceased over time. One item of news he was pleased to receive concerned the forthcoming marriage of Jimmy Brewster and Merrell Fortier which was planned for later in the year. He was not invited to the event and he would not have gone anyway - it being likely to prove a little too awkward for him.

In March, Brent's hunch was proved to be correct - Karen's romance had ended almost without a murmur sometime in January. Karen guessed what Brent's hunch had been but was polite enough to be impressed when Brent produced the card she had signed. The three teenage girls and the private detective, age thirty-two - who felt much older while he dined with them - did have an amazing, like, awesomely cool time in the expensive restaurant, the girls listening to Brent's, like, weird, gnarly stories. Brent, however, was glad to have conducted the experiment and learned quite a lot through his observations but he realized he need never repeat the study because, as he freely admitted, it would always be impossible for him to understand young, teenage girls.

Epi-Prologue

Since being closely associated with the Newhampton police, Brent had investigated three murder cases in quick succession. And, despite the emotional toll it took upon him, he was ready for the next investigation within a week of the conclusion of the Hill Hall affair. He fully expected that, any day, Greg Darrow would call him, asking for his assistance. They spoke regularly but no new case presented itself with the right set of conditions for Brent's skill-set to be suitably employed.

Since he had just worked three cases in less than two months, the result of a simple mathematical equation revealed to Brent that he should, on average, be called in every three weeks or so. Four weeks passed by and his equation was blown out of the water. He resigned himself to being patient - which saw him through almost the entire fifth week. At six weeks he convinced himself that the next case would be more intensely challenging than anything he had ever known before. After two months, he went on vacation.

Making a snap decision and acting on it, Brent was completely unaware that, while airborne, heading for a winter getaway and a chance to go skiing, he was actually also heading towards his next case - a case that would prove to be both dangerous and challenging as well as one that would be further complicated because he would be without his usual network of support.

If he had known what lay ahead of him, he might never have got on the plane and, if he had thought about it carefully, he might never have become involved. But who are we kidding? Of course he would go and of course he would put himself right in the thick of things - no matter what the cost!

OTHER TITLES IN THE BRENT UMBER SERIES

Death among the Vines
Death in a Restaurant,
Death of a Detective,
Death on the Slopes
+ Two more Brent Umber stories!
Coming soon - by the end of 2021.

NEWSLETTER + FREE STORY CYCLE

If you liked this story, a great choice is to sign up for the **monthly newsletter** and be automatically included in the **Free Story Cycle**.

The current cycle of novella length stories is entitled:

The Village of the Sevenfold Curse
- Murder Mystery through the ages

This new series of seven unpublished stories are free - exclusive only to newsletter subscribers. But it doesn't stop there. When one **Story Cycle** ends... another begins.

https://gjbellamy.com

Printed in Great Britain
by Amazon

42171515R00179